# FOLLOW THE MASTER

GRAHAM DONNELLY

The Book Guild Ltd

First published in Great Britain in 2023 by
The Book Guild
Unit E2, Airfield Business Park
Harrison Road
Market Harborough
Leicsestershire, LE16 7UL
Freephone: 0800 999 2982
www.bookguild.co.uk
Email: info@bookguild.co.uk
Twitter: @bookguild



Typeset in 12pt Adobe Jenson Pro

Printed and bound by CPI Group (UK) Ltd, Croydon, CR0 4YY

ISBN 978 1915853 028

British Library Cataloguing in Publication Data.
A catalogue record for this book is available from the British Library.

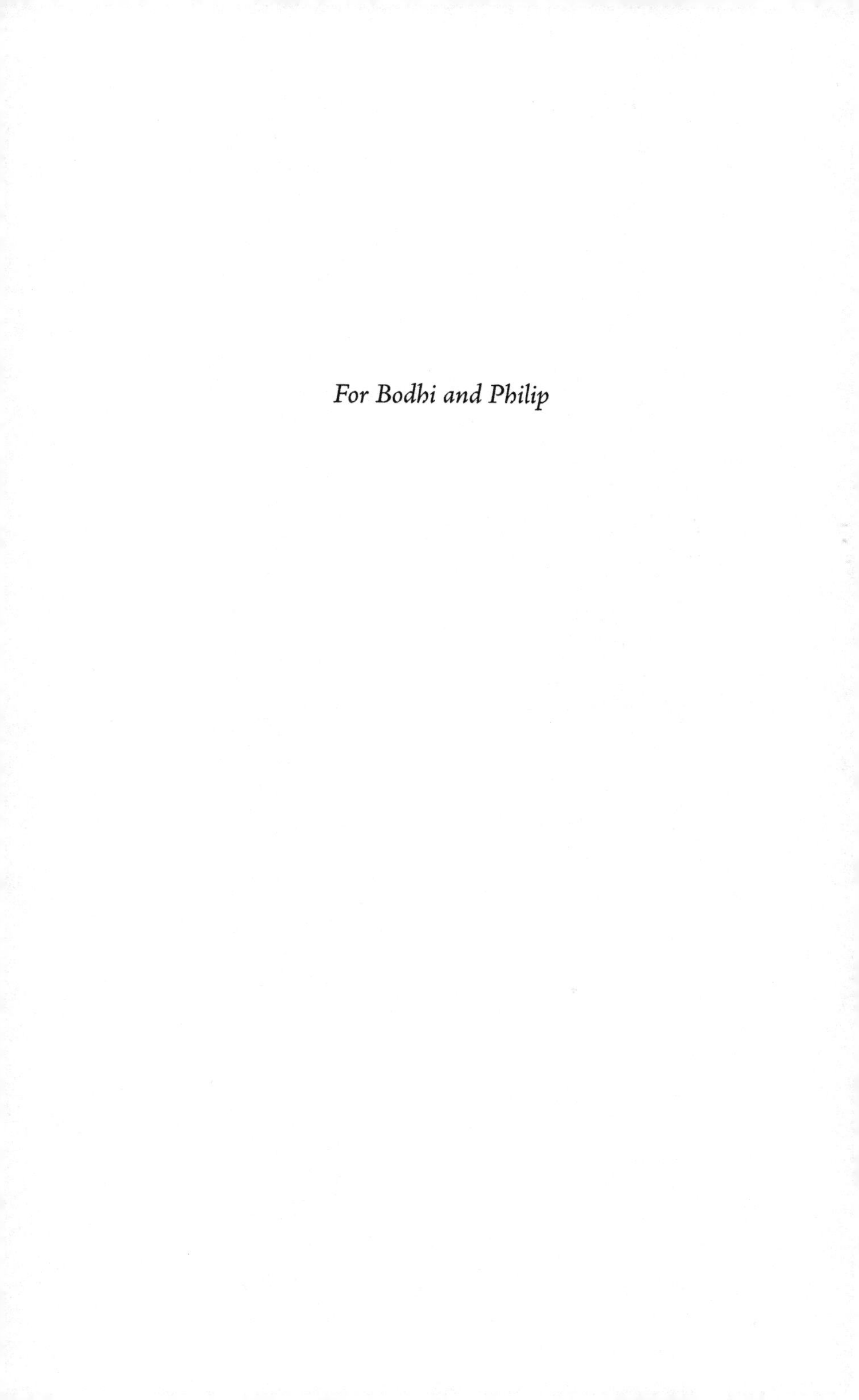

*For Bodhi and Philip*

# PART I

# *THE MASTER*

# *MOUNT OLYMPUS*

IT WAS THE END OF JANUARY, A FEROCIOUS JANUARY which had deterred all but the most resilient from straying out too often in the evenings. Finally, tired of listening to the radio and bored by the wallpaper, I dragged my wife Lina out to the cinema in Maidenhead, despite her reluctance to venture out into the freezing cold and the blanket of gloom which accompanied the remaining blackout restrictions. At least we didn't have to worry about the V2 rockets whose range didn't stretch to this part of the Thames. Setting out on this minor excursion, I could not know then that my trip to the cinema would be the starting point of a sequence of events into which I was reluctantly pulled, and which would have a profound effect on the rest of my life.

We enjoyed the film very much: Laurence Olivier's *Henry V*, adapted from Shakespeare's play. It was bound to strike a note with the British audiences at this time, a stirring victory against all the odds over a powerful enemy. After the end of the film, we stayed in our seats to watch the Pathé News roundup. The first two stories covered the progress of the war in Europe and the impact of a V2 rocket which had killed sixteen people a couple of days earlier in the East End. These were undoubtedly important, and the second one tragic for those involved, but it was the third item which made me sit up in my seat. The narrator referred to a conference on the post-war financial settlement and an aeroplane was shown landing at an RAF base not far from London. From the plane emerged a waving Lord Keynes, the leader of the British delegation, referred to by the narrator as the 'Master Economist', such was his reputation in this field. What made this item of particular interest to me was that I had known John Maynard Keynes for over forty years, and he was someone I counted as a friend. As I watched the screen avidly, Lina smiled and squeezed my hand; she knew how pleased I was to see him and share, from a distance, his success. While my working life had rarely been worthy of note, Keynes had built a great career in academia and government that had made him one of the most important men in the country, though little known by most of his fellow citizens. For a few moments I bathed in the reflected glory of the man illuminated on the screen, a man I could claim to know well. I was often asked what he was really like by those who envied me.

As the news bulletin moved on, my attention shifted to my relationship with Maynard and how long it was since I had seen him. I felt a twinge of concern that circumstances were conspiring to drift us apart, a fact I regretted, and I made a vague resolution to prevent that happening by contacting Maynard as soon as I had a free moment.

As we walked to our car, Lina slipped her arm in mine. "These dreadful rocket attacks," she said. "They can't win the war now. What's the point?"

The war was moving to its inevitable end and we both knew it. Yet though the pragmatic Italians had ditched their deluded popinjay, Mussolini, and switched sides eighteen months before, the Germans still showed less appetite either for throwing in the towel or even getting rid of the architect of their impending defeat. "Yes, what is the point?" I replied. "I suppose they carry on fighting because until they surrender, they won't have to face reality."

"The reality that they have truly lost?"

"Yes that, and also that they were taken in by Hitler and his gang. They closed their eyes to all the evil that was done in their name and now they will pay for it. In the meantime, their rockets kill people to no purpose and soldiers and sailors and airmen have to die on both sides without it changing anything as to the final outcome."

Lina knew what I was thinking. Our only son, Charles, was fighting in Germany and we both feared, like all the other parents with children in the armed forces, that our son might be one of the unlucky ones who don't live to see the end of the war. I thought again of those poor devils who died in Boleyn Road and the surrounding streets through that V2 rocket a few days before. What fate can be worse than being the last casualty of any conflict? I thought back to the last war.

"You know, in 1918 when we were notified the armistice would come into force at eleven o'clock, our troop stopped actions straight away, other than keeping watch. We couldn't relax though as a German machine-gun company kept up firing at regular intervals until eleven o'clock precisely. There was a young Canadian, a chap named Price, who was killed at two minutes to eleven. His captain was bitterly upset about it, I remember him telling me later."

"How awful. His poor mother," said Lina.

We drove in silence for a few minutes, each with our own fears and hopes, till I changed the subject.

"Seeing Maynard in the newsreel reminds me I haven't seen him for ages. Now that he's back in circulation I must try and have lunch or something with him."

I spoke casually about Maynard, but Lina knew how much I admired his work in rebuilding Britain's ruined finances and striving to establish a new international monetary system. For Churchill and the military leaders, the work of winning the war was nearly done. The future belonged to Keynes and others like him who would have to restore Britain's economy and win the peace and I always experienced a twinge of pride when someone said to me, "You are a friend of Maynard Keynes, I believe."

When we arrived home, Lina made some coffee for us and we sat in the drawing room, me with a brandy, discussing the film, the news, Maynard, this and that. We had been married now for over twenty-five years and had yet to encounter the curse that had befallen some couples of my own acquaintance: that moment when, without necessity, they find they have nothing to say to each other.

"I've been thinking about retirement," I said.

She smiled. "You often say that," she replied. "But have you come to a view?"

I nodded and returned the smile, knowing that for Lina my prevarication on the subject had reached legendary proportions. "I know, but this time I have. I'm going to pack it in before my next birthday. I'll see the war out and then make arrangements for a smooth exit. I'll tell the partners at our next meeting."

"What helped you make up your mind?"

I stared at her for a moment or two and thought how beautiful she still was, especially when she smiled in that way. The blonde hair of her youth still fair, the sparkle of her grey-green eyes undiminished, her figure inevitably filled out but all the better for it. I wanted to say that I would like to spend more time with her but, true though this was, I thought it might sound glib or facetious, so I gave my equally true but more mundane reason. "I have had a relatively successful career and gone as far as I can in my profession. I have finally come to the conclusion that I don't relish the working day anymore. Tedium has begun to set in and I want to see what else there is in life before I'm too old to enjoy it. Anyway, I don't need to work and I'm already older than my father was when he retired."

Lina looked at me a little sceptically. "I would be very happy to see more of you at home but are you really ready to have a lot more time on your hands? You have always been so involved with work and sometimes when you have to resolve a problem at the office or there has been a crisis in the market and you look all-in when you get home, I can tell you are loving every minute of it."

I laughed but I knew there was truth in what she said. "I'm not giving it all up. I'll still act on my own account, but I won't have to spend hours convincing people of the right course of action only to see them do something completely different. Then there will be time for more sport, more time for interests, hopefully grandchildren one day and, above all, more time for us to do things together."

She nodded. "Perhaps you could phase your retirement in, say four days a week, then three and so on."

"Good idea. Or I could go in most days and have longer lunch hours and come home earlier."

She laughed. "That sounds more like you."

Yet, if I were honest with myself, there was something else underlying my resolve to retire which had raised its ugly truth when I saw Maynard Keynes on the newsreel. It was a sense of failure or, more accurately, an acceptance that in my career, I had not made a difference, unlike Maynard who had and was now, bringing about changes which would benefit the world. It was not for a lack of trying. In my forty years in the Square Mile, I had endeavoured to give good advice to clients and help them to negotiate the peaks and troughs of stock market investment. But I had failed to make a difference. I had too often been through the same cycles of market boom and bust, witnessed regularly the over-reactions to market forces of those two imposters, certitude and fear, and witnessed each new generation of clients act exactly as the ones before. I had learned that we can't control the stock market cycles, we can't change the behaviour of clients and basically we can't change anything and I was tired of the helter-skelter of it all. Much as I admired Maynard Keynes, I sometimes doubted whether even he would be able to change human nature enough to bring about an end to the inevitable economic cycles which had plagued mankind throughout its history. But I hoped he was successful in what he was trying to achieve. After all, my one real achievement was that Maynard was my friend and he had sometimes sought my advice.

At a partners' meeting at the end of the week I indicated my intention to gradually reduce my commitment to the firm, from senior partner to eminence grise, then to partner emeritus and finally to disappear altogether. As I was the senior partner nobody opposed my plan and I could sense that my colleagues, despite their cordial expressions of sadness at my leaving, could see nothing but potential advancement for their own careers in my decision.

In line with my new working pattern, I began arranging more lunch engagements with old friends and the following Tuesday, on the way to work, called in at Maynard's office at the Treasury to see if he could find the time for me to take him out to lunch. Not being a Treasury official, he had engaged his own private secretary, a young man named Alec Harborough, who maintained his complex diary, opened and responded to much of the copious mail he received every day, occasionally represented Maynard at conferences and sometimes accompanied him on his overseas trips. I didn't know much about Alec's background, only that he had read economics at Cambridge and had worked in research of some sort before being recruited by Maynard to be his assistant. I had met him a couple of times before, once when Maynard was delayed for an appointment with me and the other time at an event at the Royal Opera House. On the latter occasion we had discussed Maynard's crucial role in trying to establish a future world economic and financial order and Alec had waxed lyrical about Maynard, telling me what a great man he was and of Alec's own admiration for and loyalty to him.

The grand building, built as part of the redevelopment of the imperial capital in the Edwardian era, had only been occupied by the Treasury since 1940 when the William Kent building was damaged in the blitz and Maynard had acquired his own office suite, looking out on the central courtyard. When I arrived, Alec was standing up, opening the pile of mail on his desk in the small outer office. He had endeavoured to brighten up his personal space with a couple of Aubrey Beardsley's less lascivious prints and some house plants, including the once ubiquitous aspidistra. He asked me to take a seat as Maynard was expected within half an hour. I sat down in the small leather armchair, took the newspaper Alec offered me and occasionally looked over at him while he ploughed through the heap of mail on his desk, his dark hair falling over his forehead as he examined each letter and applied them to different piles.

"Is that *one* morning's post?" I asked.

Alec smiled, "Huge, isn't it? It's like this most days and grows all the time. He tries to have all his post delivered here, except for personal letters from those who are on his 'home list' as he calls it, like you for example."

"I suppose he's famous and important enough to get fan mail now."

"Some of it you could call that. He is such a high-profile figure now that he receives so many official and professional papers. Then there are people asking for advice or inviting him to join a committee or write a paper or give a speech. Others are from people who don't agree with him and are pointing out to him where he's wrong. But yes, there are letters of admiration and encouragement too; not that he needs them particularly."

"Do you reply to all of them?"

"If they need a reply, yes, except for the obvious cranks, most of whom have a penchant for using purple or green ink. I divide them up into various categories and we have several standard replies so it's not too onerous."

I sat back in the chair and read the newspaper while Alec went about his business methodically, occasionally drawing my attention to something amusing or outrageous. Then, while I was watching him, he opened a letter and his jovial expression changed. He stood staring at the paper in his hand for some time, then examined the envelope at least twice before putting the letter and the envelope in his jacket inside pocket. He was suddenly aware that I was staring at him.

"Just a crank and rather nasty; I don't think Maynard need be bothered with it," he said, before continuing, more slowly now, to sift through the letters. I could tell there was something on his mind but thought it none of my business.

Then he stopped and turned to me. "Lewis, there is a problem, and it has to be handled carefully as there could be serious ramifications for Maynard. I know you have a great regard for him so I can trust you in what is a very delicate situation. The fact is I would appreciate your help and advice. Would it be possible for us to have a conversation later? It is very important that we don't speak of it in front of Maynard."

I found this suggestion rather troubling. "I would be pleased to help in any way I can but don't feel comfortable going behind Maynard's back," I said.

"You will understand when I tell you what this is about. I wouldn't ask were it not deadly serious."

"Very well, but I must reserve the option to raise the matter with Maynard if I think it right to do so."

He nodded. "Could you come round to my flat at about half past five?" He scribbled an address off Portman Square and added a telephone number, "In case you get held up."

I took the piece of paper. "Couldn't you give me some idea what this is about?"

"Not here. He might come in at any minute."

As if on cue, the door opened and in walked Maynard.

"Lewis, what a pleasant surprise. How are you?" he said, taking off his Homburg hat and hanging it on a hatstand and revealing his now almost-white hair.

"Very well thanks, Maynard. What about you?"

"Not bad, a bit tired. All the running about, I'm afraid. You know how it is. I hope you've not been waiting long?"

Despite his reassuring comment about his health, I thought he looked quite ill: a poor skin colour, apart from flushed cheeks, and haggard around the eyes. I let it go; to say anything would probably make him feel worse. "No, just a few minutes," I said. "I saw an item about you on Pathé news. How are the talks going?"

He smiled. "So-so. The Americans like my proposals for the international monetary system but they are driving a hard bargain with regard to our financial situation. I'm afraid they have us over a barrel, and they know it. It's quite obvious their ambition is to replace London with New York as the world's main financial centre and that would strengthen their position in world trade. So, it's a bit of an uphill slog."

"They say you should never borrow from a friend," said Alec.

"Surely Roosevelt is more sympathetic to our situation," I said.

"Possibly, but he doesn't get involved in these discussions very much. He has the post-war political situation to deal with and he's tied up with the Yalta conference at the moment." Maynard gestured as if waving the problem away. "Anyway, to what do we owe the pleasure, Lewis?"

"I wondered if you were free for lunch today?"

He smiled but shook his head. "I'd love to, but I've got such a lot on. Another time?"

"Yes, I'll give you a ring."

"Splendid, but not this week." He smiled and opened his briefcase and I took that as my cue to make my departure. I said goodbye to them both and nodded to Alec while Maynard was removing some papers from his case.

I arrived at Alec's flat just after half past five and he responded to the ring on the bell almost immediately. He welcomed me straight into his fairly small living room. The decor was very modern, almost brutal, with dark colours and hard furniture. Cubist pictures and a copy of Salvador Dali's *The Persistence of Memory* decorated the walls.

"Would you like a drink?" he asked, walking over to a well-stocked drinks tray.

"I think I'm going to need one; brandy, please."

"Soda?"

"No thanks."

He brought me a large brandy, poured himself a gin and tonic, and invited me to sit down.

He sat opposite me. He had taken off his jacket and tie and appeared quite relaxed as he raised his glass and said, "Cheers."

"So, what's this about?" I asked, slightly impatient that he seemed in no hurry to get to the point.

His smile faded and he took a large mouthful of his drink. "To put it bluntly, someone is trying to blackmail Maynard."

I snorted in disbelief. "I'd like to see somebody try. Maynard is a man of the utmost integrity. Any minor failings in his character or petty misdemeanours would be dismissed as a trifle against the great services he has done this country and the world." I realised I sounded rather pompous and took a sip of the brandy: it was quite good.

"We may wish that it were so, but these are serious allegations and likely to be at least a major distraction while Maynard is undertaking these very difficult negotiations with the Americans. Maynard must be completely at his best and focussed on the job if we are to have any hope of achieving better terms, so dealing with blackmail allegations would be impossible. Apart from that, he is not a well man and cannot under any circumstances be placed under further pressure."

"Well, what does he make of the accusations?"

"He doesn't know of them. I didn't think it right to trouble him."

"For God's sake, he must have the opportunity to challenge their veracity. He might dismiss them as a pack of lies."

"They are true, I can attest to that."

I finished my drink and accepted Alec's offer of a refresher. "How can you be sure, without checking the facts with Maynard?"

"I have my sources."

My mild irritation had now developed into a sense of peevishness that this young man seemed to know so much about Maynard's life that was closed to me and further, he appeared to have taken charge of the situation, excluding even Maynard from having a say in his own potential downfall.

"May I ask what gives you the right, a young assistant of what, twenty-six or so, to take on the management of what you consider a crisis from the man whose career is at stake?"

"Twenty-eight actually. I told you; I don't believe he has the strength to deal with it when there is so much else depending on him."

"Yes, but why you? With all due respect, there must be others in a more appropriate, more influential, position to help Maynard."

"There is nobody else."

"His friends and colleagues, surely."

"His colleagues would be placed in a compromising position if they were involved, and some might be tempted to use the knowledge against his best interests."

"Surely not."

Alec smiled. "Ambitious people see the fall of another as a potential opportunity for themselves."

"Friends then, he must have so many."

Alec laughed. "Oh, he has or so I thought, but most of his closest friends are members of what's left of the old Bloomsbury Group. Duncan Grant can't be trusted to fix a price for his paintings and most of the others couldn't be trusted with anything. As for the rest of those people who call themselves his friends, when you ask for help there are sudden excuses: some are suddenly merely acquaintances, some are afraid of guilt by association, some are afraid to get involved and others are too old."

"I'm over sixty myself, dammit."

"I realise that. I hoped you might be willing to help me but I understand if you would prefer not to get involved."

"But why me?" I asked, "I have never been privy to Maynard's secrets, nor has he sought my counsel on anything that might have led to him being blackmailed. I can hardly be expected to know his mind, let alone venture an opinion on what is to be done."

Alec was silent for a few moments. "I am asking for your help because I believe you are a man of sound judgement and can be trusted, but to be brutally honest, there aren't too many options."

"Perhaps you ought to tell me exactly what the allegations are." I said, rather testily.

"Not yet. I think the fewer people who know the details of this the better. I have to decide what to do and I should welcome your advice once I know you are prepared to help, without reservation."

I admired Alec's calm. Despite his youth, he was showing great maturity in neither acting hastily nor blurting out the details to just anyone.

"When you say you are asking for my advice, is that all or might you expect me to get involved in dealing with the blackmailer?"

"I'm not sure. I will try to do it all but I may need some help."

"You are asking me to sign a blank cheque without knowing what I am buying. Can you not at least tell me the nature of this blackmail?"

Alec shook his head. "I will not divulge this to anyone who will not give their total commitment to help save Maynard, whatever the reason for his being blackmailed, otherwise that person will himself have a hold over Maynard."

"So, you don't fully trust me?"

"You will still be free to walk away at any time. I have no control over your actions."

"I understand. Will you at least let me sleep on it before I make my decision?"

"Yes, of course."

I finished my drink and, with nothing else either of us wanted to say, I departed for the drive home. As Alec saw me out, he thanked me for listening to his dilemma and assured me that he would understand if I chose not to help but wished earnestly that I would want to assist an old friend.

In the car I tried to imagine what Maynard might have done to lay him open to blackmail, a distraction I could have done without while driving through the murky London streets at night while blackout regulations were still in force and car lights were partially restricted. I received an accusatory glance from a policeman directing the traffic when, my mind elsewhere, I pulled up behind him a little too close for comfort. Despite my intention to concentrate on the road, my mind soon reverted to blackmail and Maynard's possible misdemeanour or crime.

While I supposed a sexual peccadillo possible, I thought it unlikely and, in any case, it would not prevent my helping him. Treason or espionage I dismissed as inconceivable, as I did murder or other crimes of violence. I thought the most likely would be some kind of financial impropriety, though I couldn't imagine Maynard being involved in a swindle. But then the thought crossed my mind that perhaps it was something despicable that Maynard had done and that was why Alec wouldn't tell me until I had undertaken to help him. But when I thought of the most evil crimes like murder, rape, molesting a child or grievous bodily harm, I couldn't imagine Keynes doing any of those things. I came to the conclusion it must be an act of impropriety rather than a crime but was stumped for an answer.

When I arrived home, Lina asked why I was late and I was a little cagey in my answer, referring to a meeting with a colleague of Maynard's and hinting it was on a confidential matter. I told her that I had some work to do after dinner and I went to my study and spent the evening and well into the night wracking my brains for events in Maynard's life, as I knew them, all the way back to our time at Cambridge, that could have led to his being blackmailed. Of course, I could imagine many things but found none of them credible. I started again from the beginning and put his life, as I knew it, in some sort of chronological order and my mind inevitably turned back to my first days at Cambridge and my own early life.

# CAMBRIDGE

John Maynard Keynes and I had been at Cambridge together, or more accurately we had been at Cambridge at the same time. We moved in very different circles and though I knew of him and his role at the centre of university life, our paths rarely crossed and we exchanged barely a few words during this period.

Keynes had gone up a year before me and read Mathematics. He had been a King's Scholar at Eton and won major prizes across a range of subjects, followed by another scholarship to King's College where his reputation as a brilliant student had preceded his arrival. Such was his reputation that Alfred Marshall, the renowned Professor of Political Economy, practically beseeched him to read Economics. However, he insisted on staying with his first preference of Mathematics. Inevitably, he was soon courted by the prestigious societies and clubs at Cambridge and became one of those illustrious members of any class or profession whose name trips easily off everyone's tongue and he was quickly recruited to the exclusive private members' Pitt Club. He was one of those who excelled at most things. In addition to being a brilliant student he was also amusing company socially and competitive at sports, especially rowing. Feted and celebrated across the colleges, many admired him, most envied him and a few begrudged him. I was enthralled by him.

Tired of study and examination, I had hoped to finish my education with my last day at school and make my way in the world. But my father had insisted that I go to university since, in his words, I would learn to hold my drink, be reassured that there were people far more stupid than me in the upper classes, and could make a fool of myself as often as I wanted without doing any damage in the real world. So, reluctantly I went up to Gonville and Caius College in 1903. My interview was conducted by one old don who read me a series of questions without once looking up at me from his paper. Judging by the questions he put to me, I think it was my reasonable prowess in team sports which secured my place, rather than my fairly mediocre academic career at a fairly mediocre minor public school. At this time Oxford and Cambridge universities were regarded as elite institutions in English sport, much of which was dominated by amateurs. This was manifested not only in the annual boat race on the Thames and their status in first-class cricket but also other major sports such as athletics, rugby union and football. Oxford University had won the FA Cup in 1874 and the annual varsity matches in soccer and rugby continued to be national events at this time. I was not surprised, therefore, that my interview concentrated on my sporting interests, and it accorded with my own assumption that on the sports field lay my only realistic expectation of achievement.

Lacking the natural talent necessary to learn effortlessly and unwilling to work hard and thereby earn the unwanted sobriquet of a swat, I was faced with the thorny question of what I would read. I had vaguely indicated a preference for history at my interview but now I gave the matter serious thought. University reform had only latterly jolted Cambridge out of its isolationist mentality and resistance to join the modern world and, as is often the way in England, modernisation had endeavoured to leave as much as possible looking and feeling exactly as it had before. Certainly, the majority of the available courses of study did not immediately appeal to me: I thought the Classics too daunting, the Sciences and Mathematics too definitive and the Humanities too dry.

After some research and reflection, I alighted on what seemed the perfect choice: Economics. As an academic subject it was relatively modern yet had a Greek word as its title to add a hint of Classicism. It had claims to be regarded as a science yet was released by its connections with human behaviour of the need for scientific certitude. Best of all, the few theories I had come across, like the Law of Diminishing Returns and the Pareto Principle, though couched in scientific terminology, seemed relatively easy to grasp and contained an element of common sense. I was fortunate to arrive in Cambridge at the same time as a separate Economic Tripos was established outside of the Moral Sciences Tripos. This was due to the efforts of Alfred Marshall, supported by John Neville Keynes, economist and secretary of the Examinations and Lectures Syndicate and father of John Maynard Keynes.

However much Cambridge opened my mind to new ideas, it did little to broaden my social connections as, apart from some scholarship students, almost all my contemporaries had similar educational and social backgrounds to myself. Such differences that did exist were merely of degree within the upper and upper middle classes, so the choice of circles within which we moved was determined primarily by matters such as interests, views and attitudes. Some embraced Cambridge as a seat of learning, throwing themselves fully and devotedly into their subject and into life at college. Those who did not develop a superiority complex nor seek to impress others with their knowledge were undoubtedly admirable. There were others who were more interested in enjoying specific aspects of university life such as sporting excellence or the social amenities that were on offer. Then there were some for whom Cambridge was a finishing school for the last years of youth with an emphasis on pleasure and tomfoolery. As few required a degree of any sort for their future career, many did not complete their course of study but went down when they wished. As long as one wasn't *sent* down, the early termination of one's studies reflected little on the future success in life of most. A few excelled as students, sportsmen, bon viveurs and excellent company and one's temperament determined whether one looked up to them, viewed them from a state of equanimity or regarded them with envy or loathing. Of course, all these different types overlapped and most of us mixed in a range of interests and groupings. Underpinning the whole edifice of university life were the rituals and traditions of an ancient institution which some embraced with enthusiasm, others grew into accepting, a few bridled at and others, including myself, went along with while retaining a sardonic eye or ear for the absurd.

I knew two of my fellow students from my old school, one in the same year as me though at a different college, and they were my early contacts until I found my way around. As my only claim to proficiency lay in sporting activities, I was naturally attracted to join the university sports clubs. My primary ambition at Cambridge was to be awarded a blue in cricket and possibly in football too. Having been, in sporting terms, a fairly large fish in a small pond at school, captain of the cricket first eleven and a regular member of the football first eleven, I was fairly confident that I would be able to achieve my aims. However, I soon discovered that I was now merely a sprat in a very large sea and my hopes would not be so easily realised. But I trained hard and practised regularly and did make the grade in both sports, on the left wing at football and as a moderately successful left arm off-spinner and lower-order batsman at cricket, without being a particularly luminous star in either sport. Many of my new friendships were made either in the sports clubs or with others who didn't take themselves or anybody else too seriously. Particular among them was Lyndon Ashley who, like me, played in the first eleven in both football and cricket and Ralph Talbot, a fellow economics student, who was my bridge to the more intellectual pursuits of the university, always able to give me a précised version of most philosophical or artistic subjects so I could usually hold up my end in most conversations with young ladies I wished to impress.

I was also able to indulge my two other talents: one useful, the other merely a source of amusement for my friends. The first was a gaming instinct and a certain flair for it, developed at school in after-hours backgammon sessions and card schools, then played for pennies whereas now it was for shillings. My father gave me a comfortable allowance and my repeated success at the card tables and on the backgammon board ensured I did not need to ask him for further support to indulge my various social activities. I also developed into a pretty decent bridge player through the Bridge Club and soon found myself occasionally being asked to partner elderly college fellows or their wives at bridge parties, playing for small stakes and enjoying generous hospitality.

The other talent was a gift for mimicry. I had first been aware of it at school where, before my voice broke, I could do a very passable impression of matron's voice and other boys frequently responded to her call only to find that she hadn't shouted down the corridor to them at all. Later, I was able to imitate some of the masters, in particular the headmaster, and this provided some moments of humour to speed the day. My favourite one was when, our form-master having not yet arrived, I gave a brief talk on good behaviour in the voice of the headmaster. A few minutes later our form-master knocked on the door and began an apology for interrupting the headmaster until he noticed that the only person on the teacher's platform was me, now pretending to clean the blackboard. Within a few weeks at Cambridge, I had mastered the voices of several of the dons, including Alfred Marshall, and I would occasionally oblige my fellow students' calls for an impersonation or two at parties.

Thus, by the end of my first term at Cambridge I had established a persona with which I was comfortable and had no wish to alter. I had yet to appreciate that if one is still alive, one will inevitably change, though always remain somebody described as 'oneself'.

Despite my prosaic reasons for choosing to read Economics, I soon found I actually enjoyed the subject and surprised myself by taking my studies seriously, much to the consternation of those of my friends who were more relaxed in their application to study. It was impossible for me not to find in the long-haired and walrus-moustachioed, slightly eccentric looking, Alfred Marshall a man of genius. In his book and our main text, *Principles of Economics,* he had expounded for the first time many of the key theories of Economics which would dominate the subject for over forty years. I also found him an excellent teacher, forsaking dry lectures and mere description for opening up the possibilities that economic theory generated and engaging his students in the development of ideas. Of course, his style was better suited to smaller groups of about twenty rather than the mass gatherings of a large lecture theatre and it was sometimes difficult to take notes, to the regret of some students. But I loved his lectures and how can one fault the style of a teacher who inspired rapture for a subject in the least enthusiastic of students? I also liked him for his modesty as he often pointed out that the more he studied economic science the more conscious he was of his ignorance of it, a quality I for once felt able to match.

Although applying myself more to my chosen subject, I did not neglect either my sporting activities or my social pleasures, merely using my time more wisely when the occasion demanded. One Saturday evening during my second year, I attended one of my regular bridge parties at the home of a senior don who was well-known for his generous hospitality. I was dummy in one particular hand and, my partner being rather slow to play the hand, I helped myself to a drink and lit a cigarette. I sat down in a chair opposite Saxon Sydney-Turner, somebody I knew by sight but had never spoken to. He was crouched over a notebook and writing letters in columns, his mind elsewhere. His preoccupation permitted me to observe him without embarrassment. He was aged about twenty-five and quite good-looking and had a passive expression which betokened intelligence and seriousness. Suddenly, he looked up and smiled.

"Good evening."

"Good evening. Mr Sydney-Turner, isn't it?"

"Yes. Sorry, I don't..."

"Lewis Durrington, Caius." We shook hands.

"Ah yes, you have a fine organist in Charles Wood."

"I didn't realise you played bridge."

"I don't much. I was asked to step in at short notice as a favour to make up the numbers. I'm sitting out the present hand as dummy; a role my friends say I perform very well."

I smiled. "I am in the same position; my partner likes to

take her time. May I ask what you are doing there?" I pointed to his writing.

"Just a Greek acrostic I am working on. Do you like puzzles?"

I shrugged. "Sometimes; remind me what an acrostic is again."

"It's a poem in which the first letter of each line or some other pattern contains a word; Lewis Carroll was very fond of them and so am I."

I later learned that he had gained his place at Trinity through being the only candidate who could solve a particular Greek acrostic. "I take it you do like puzzles?" I asked.

"Very much so. I believe puzzle-solving to be one of the principal attributes of human consciousness. When we are not doing it by necessity, we do it as a recreation, as in bridge, for example. Or do you play only for money?"

"I do like gambling, but only when there is some skill involved. Bridge provides that."

He nodded. "Gambling without skill is no more amusing than buying a raffle ticket. I like the occasional flutter myself. Ah, I see I am being summoned for the next hand. I should have liked to continue our conversation on gambling, but I shall bump into you again no doubt." He smiled and went back to his table.

For some reason, Saxe took a shine to me after that brief conversation and when our paths crossed a few weeks later he invited me to join him for a drink. I thought his conversation might be rather serious but he began by asking me about my forays at the card and backgammon tables.

"I win more often than I lose, so that's enough for me," I said.

"The thrill of the chase does not come into it?"

"Of course."

He smiled. "Does the greater excitement arise from winning or the possibility that you might lose?"

I thought about the question for perhaps a minute while he waited patiently. "D'you know, I really can't answer that other than by saying, 'It depends'. You must have considered the question before, so do you have a view?"

He puffed on his pipe for a moment, "Probably for me it is the latter."

A little unsettled by his answer, I changed the subject, but I had cause to ponder that remark many times in my future career when I attempted to understand how the minds of gamblers and risk takers work.

"I take it you are here for the Apostles' meeting?"

"Yes."

The Apostles Club had begun as a discussion forum on ethical and moral questions for a group of Christian evangelical students in 1820. As there were twelve of them, they soon gained the nickname, 'The Apostles'. Now, the Apostles Club had become an exclusive club, membership by invitation only, at which discussion papers on ethical and moral questions were presented by members, often inspired by the classic philosophers, particularly Plato. Membership was a recognition of that person's intellectual qualities and was retained after the person graduated. Saxon had graduated with a double first in Classics in 1902 and had continued to attend meetings regularly.

"You still enjoy the meetings as much?"

"Yes, I have several good friends in the club and though the subject matter has changed over time to include the arts and so on, it's still concerned with what one might call the great questions of life, especially what it means to be a good human being. The meetings are very convivial and thought provoking."

After that we occasionally had a drink and a brief chat when we were both around and it was through these chance encounters that I met Leonard Woolf and two or three other Apostles, though not Maynard Keynes, much to my disappointment. As I came to know Saxe better, I found him a friendly but taciturn man. He would be quick to buy a round but then took little part in the conversation that flowed, usually unwilling to express a view, despite his well-known erudition when he did contribute to any discussion. His friends often teased him about his tendency to silence in debates, perhaps because they missed his wisdom or because they thought his silence a sign of aloofness.

Once, when we were left alone, I asked him why he had a reputation for rarely participating in the Apostles' discussions at the bar. "I say nothing because a lot of what they say goes over my head, but your insights would be useful, surely?"

He smiled. "Usually, people are irritated when somebody else talks too much and deprives them of their chance to hold forth. How strange they should find my willingness to let others speak such an inconvenience."

"I suppose they would like to hear your point of view."

"I like to listen because I may hear something which educates and refines my own view of the matter. I find the more I listen, the more I understand and the less I can add to the subject in question. How boring it is when one has to listen to the same arguments or their rebuttals over and over again."

"But if they ask your opinion?"

"When people ask for another's opinion, they usually hope to gain support for their own position. If they don't receive that support, they tend to ignore what is said, so there was little point asking in the first place and no point whatever in responding."

I laughed. "I must try to keep my mouth closed more often."

My fellow economics student, Ralph Talbot, was invited to an Apostles meeting as a guest, often the precursor to the offer of membership, and I was interested to hear his reflections on the evening because of my friendship with Saxe.

"So, how did it go?"

Ralph shook his head. "An odd experience. Ostensibly, it's a debating society of sorts and philosophical papers are presented and discussed. From that point of view it's worth going but it's also beset by silly rituals."

"Rituals? Such as?"

"The meeting takes place in the room of the person delivering the paper and he has to stand on a hearth rug to give his talk. Afterwards everybody eats sardines on toast; all rather puerile."

I laughed. "Most groups of this type have peculiar customs. They think it adds charm."

"True. What disappointed me is that the emphasis is tending to shift away from philosophy towards aesthetics and there is a certain amount of self-satisfaction or even narcissism."

Ralph did not become a member.

Though Keynes graduated in 1904, he stayed at Cambridge for the next two years to continue his studies in Philosophy. He rarely missed a meeting of the Apostles and I often saw him on a Saturday in term time with a group of club members with whom he shared common interests: the Strachey brothers, Roger Fry, Arthur Hobhouse, and a few others. But though our paths crossed we had at that time barely a passing acquaintance. I told myself it was not that important: I had developed a wide range of interests and several good friendships that I would take with me into later life. Although my studies became more important to me as each term passed, my happiest days were spent in the summer when, studies over, I played cricket at Fenners, the Cambridge cricket ground originally leased from my own college, or travelled round the country playing the county sides and meeting some of my cricketing heroes. In June 1905 we played the Australians at Fenners and although we lost by 169 runs, I was in rapture at the experience, and so pleased for Guy Napier who took ten Australian wickets in the match. I loved playing cricket: is there any other sport like it for the participant? Though like most sports there are periods of intense concentration and tension, there are also times to relax even during the game. In the dressing room, waiting to bat, one can watch as a spectator, read a book or chat to other members of the team. Then, on a warm summer's day, what can be better than fielding at cover when the batsman is working everything to the legside, feeling the gentle breeze, enjoying the sweet smells of the summer and letting the mind wander who knows where, without a care in the world?

Towards the latter part of my final academic year, in 1906, Keynes obliged Marshall by attending some of his lectures as a graduate student. At last, I came to know a little more of the man behind the image. Keynes was a dominating physical presence, at well over six feet much taller than most of those at the lectures, including myself. He had dark straight hair, parted just off centre and a modest moustache, an appearance he would maintain for the rest of his life, the moustache growing thicker and longer and the hair thinner and greyer as the years passed. Introduced and welcomed by Marshall as the son of John Neville Keynes and a postgraduate student, he made no attempt to stand out from his fellows, choosing neither to impress us with his knowledge nor to sit in aloof silence. He listened intently, occasionally asking a question or making an observation. Though seeming serious, perhaps a little morose, in repose, he joined the other students in appreciating moments of humour with a broad grin. He was not particularly good-looking, having large features, but he had a natural charm and whether it was this or because of his reputation, the rest of the group were drawn to him and treated him as a special guest rather than a fellow student.

Keynes sat next to me at one session and, to my surprise, turned to me after the lecture and held out his hand. "You're Lewis Durrington, aren't you?" he said, with a smile. "I've seen you around, obviously, but I don't think we've ever had a proper conversation. We have a mutual friend in Saxe Sydney-Turner. I gather you get more out of Saxe in conversation than all the Apostles put together."

I laughed. "I wouldn't say that. We have one or two common interests, I suppose. Are you enjoying Marshall's lectures?"

"Very much. How about you? You must have attended many more of them than me."

"Yes. It's because of Marshall that I have a real interest in the subject. I had originally chosen to read it because I thought it might be an easy option."

Keynes raised his eyebrows. "I'm sure he set you straight on that particular view."

I laughed. "Oh yes."

"His *Principles of Economics* is one of the great books of economic theory: we owe him a good deal for his development of the subject."

"As we do your father; I have read *The Scope and Method of Political Economy*."

Keynes smiled. "You have? Very good. You found it useful?"

"Most certainly."

"Well, it's kind of you to say so. My father is inclined to underrate himself so I will pass on your compliments."

We talked briefly about our plans for the future, him going into the civil service and me into finance of some sort. Then he looked at his watch and said, "Well, I have to go. It's been a pleasure, Lewis. We must keep in touch." Then he was gone.

That was the last time I saw Maynard for nearly twenty years but on that one conversation I based my oft-repeated claim to friends and colleagues alike that I knew Maynard Keynes personally and had studied Economics with him at Cambridge. I exchanged addresses with Saxe Sydney-Turner, however, and I did maintain contact with him after my Cambridge days were over.

I was rather pleased when I graduated with a Second and my father rewarded me by financing a long holiday on the Continent before I settled down to my professional life. My academic studies complete, I played out the rest of the cricket season with the university. In June there were two matches against a WG Grace XI, the first at Fenners and the return match at Crystal Palace. I was nursing an injury and was not able to play at Fenners and was not selected for the return match but acted as twelfth man and did at least get to field. I remember watching from the pavilion as the great WG, now aged fifty-eight, trudged out to open the batting, his great long beard heavily flecked with grey. He autographed a young boy's bat on his way from the pavilion and was clapped all the way to the wicket. Unfortunately, he was soon out for a duck and scored only one in the second innings. But if he was frustrated, he didn't show it, and he bowled nine overs when we batted, taking the wicket of one of our openers and receiving a tumultuous cheer from the crowd. We won the match by an innings.

It was the end of my life at Cambridge and it was also the end of my career in first class cricket, though I continued to play in a local club side and turned out for Berkshire on occasion. Many of my cricket teammates went on to play first class county cricket and one, Dick Young, played as wicket keeper in two Tests against Australia. Looking back, that team spirit and camaraderie I enjoyed then were probably the greatest pleasures for me of the time I spent at Cambridge.

# THE CONTINENT

ON THE DAY BEFORE I SET OFF FOR THE CONTINENT, my father called me into his study and gave me a generous sum of money for out-of-pocket expenses on my trip, the main costs having already been paid through bookings with Thomas Cook.

Having poured us both a glass of dry sherry, he stood with his back to the empty fireplace and smiled at me. I noticed for the first time that his hair, neatly parted in the middle, was showing signs of grey but he still had that twinkle in his eye that was always for me his dominant characteristic.

"Well, my boy, you have earned this trip through your endeavours at Cambridge. I am proud of what you have achieved." He raised his glass to me and I reciprocated the gesture.

He continued, "How you spend that money and how you pass the time on your vacation I leave entirely up to you. But if I may give you a few words of advice?"

"Of course," I said.

"Well, first, don't wire me for any further money. There is enough there for the most prodigal of sons to satisfy their every need and desire. If things get tight it will be due to either stupidity or recklessness on your part and it will give you good practice in managing a budget. If you find yourself destitute, it will give you the opportunity to develop the skills necessary to return home by your wits and imagination alone."

"But I always managed my money well at Cambridge, Father," I said, slightly miffed.

"Quite so, but the English have a weakness for losing their self-control when venturing abroad. It almost happened to me when I was your age, but that's another matter. That brings me to my second point. You will undoubtedly be charmed by the attractive qualities of the young women you meet, especially against the background of the intemperate climes and new cultures you will encounter. If you do happen to become infatuated by any of them, remember that any spell you fall under will rapidly dissipate as soon as you board the ship for home, so beware of making any promises you will regret later. Finally, always be aware that, however handsome and charming you may consider yourself to be, some of the people who take an instant attraction to you and can't have enough of your company, may be more interested in your wallet than any other merits you enjoy. Aside from all of that, I wish you a great adventure." He toasted me again and recharged my glass.

I spent the late summer around the Italian lakes, principally Lake Garda, and the Veneto, in the company of two Cambridge friends, Lyndon Ashley, my old football and cricket teammate, and Ralph Talbot, my guide to all things intellectual. They were excellent company and of contrasting characters: Lyndon, easy-going, devil may care and game for anything, but preferably nothing too serious, Ralph, witty but rather thoughtful, interested more in cultural sightseeing than pure leisure and acting as a brake on some of our more ludicrous flights of fancy. They presumably had their own assessments of me but I was not concerned; I was enjoying every moment of our sojourn in this captivating country.

We stayed in a villa not far from Verona and, apart from time spent on and by the lakes, we went on excursions to Vicenza, Verona, Padua and Mantua, leaving out Venice as being worthy of a longer trip on a separate occasion. For me, the dominant memory of this vacation was that of experiencing a vibrant culture where so much was new and vastly different to my everyday life: the drink, the food, the people, the language, the music, the customs, all these made the trip unforgettable. Ralph was rather more interested in art than either Lyndon or me and we traipsed behind him as he led us from one gallery to another, one church to another, one museum to another. We viewed series after series of paintings of biblical or classical scenes by old masters and their imitators which, despite their often lurid depictions of martyrdom, tragedy or disaster befalling scantily clad, relatively small-breasted large women, left me devoid of artistic appreciation. Yet, Philistine that I considered myself to be, I could not fail to be impressed by the architecture of the cities we visited like Verona with its great Roman amphitheatre and Padua's Cappella degli Scrovegni. In Palladio's city of Vicenza I was most impressed by his Teatro Olimpico, built in the sixteenth century and still in use. Finally, nothing prepared me for my first sight of Mantua as we approached it, surely the most beautiful cityscape I had seen at that time, perhaps ever. Inevitably for me, the happiest times involved socialising with a wide range of interesting people, pursuing, not always successfully, the pleasures of the flesh, acquiring a taste for the local cuisine and wines and sharing with my friends the triumphs and failures of our ventures and enjoying and laughing about them all.

In September we travelled to Florence and stayed once more in a villa in the surrounding hills. Each day we ventured into the city in a carriage driven by the quiet coachman from the villa, while the horses trotted enthusiastically along the narrow streets between high walls on a route they knew so well. Occasionally I held my breath as the walls seemed perilously close but there was never a mishap. Spending so much time together I suppose we all became more aware of each other's irritating foibles and mannerisms as well as the qualities which cemented our friendships, though we certainly didn't mention them. Despite my friendship for Ralph, it was in Florence that his tendency to impress us with his knowledge of the Italian Renaissance and its artistic treasures did wear a little thin. As we visited the Duomo, stared at the vacant plinth in the piazza which had once supported the statue of David by Michelangelo and went round the Uffizi, Lyndon and I were subjected to a running commentary of everything we looked at. The final straw was when we went to the Galleria dell'Accademia to see the statue of David in his new location. Lyndon and I mistook Michelangelo's unfinished statues of *I Prigioni*, 'the prisoners', for 'bits of old stone' without actually taking the time to look at them and realise they were the object of our search. Ralph found this very amusing and began a lecture on the meaning of the statues, which led to Lyndon huffing and walking out of the gallery with the remark, "I'm going for a drink. You'll find me in the first bar you come to if you turn left out of this place."

"Whatever's the matter with him?" asked Ralph.

"It's been a long day," I replied. "I could do with a drink too." I led Ralph out of the gallery before he could continue his lecture.

When we finished our stay in Florence, Ralph had other demands on his time and did not accompany Lyndon and me to our next venue: Rome. There, we had an enjoyable week with what we felt was the right balance of pleasure and cultural enhancement. We visited all the famous Roman sites but just as much enjoyed our time doing nothing in particular and frequently visiting Babington's, at the foot of the Spanish steps near poor old Keats's house, to enjoy the one thing we had occasionally missed on our travels: a decent cup of tea. Despite my father's warnings, I did get conned out of a meal once and bought more than my fair share of drinks on occasion, but I rarely carried too much money in my wallet. I managed my finances fairly well and, after Lyndon's funds ran out in Rapallo and he headed home, I travelled for a while on my own. On my slow journey back to England I spent ten days on the French Riviera, staying in Nice and Antibes and a couple of days in Monte Carlo. There I played the tables at the Casino, for the experience rather than with any hope of breaking the bank. I was not disappointed in the first ambition and not surprised by my lack of success in the latter.

I spent much of my time watching the behaviour of the players and one event taught me how irrational the behaviour of gamblers can be. A rather attractive lady placed 20 Francs on the number 18 at a roulette table and she won: 700 Francs. She left the entire sum of 720 Francs on the number 18 and on the next spin of the wheel she won again: 25,200 Francs, a return of 1,369 to one and worth over a thousand pounds. The lady then picked up her winnings and, after giving a large tip to the croupier, she went off to the bar with her companion. So far so good. Then the most extraordinary thing happened: as she walked away from the table, two, perhaps three, other players placed a bet on number 18. The probability of number 18 coming up three times in a row is over 50,000 to one but it did not dissuade some. I had learned how reckless some gamblers and their close relations, the speculators, can be.

I enjoyed the cosmopolitan atmosphere of the miniature country of Monaco with its mix of the wealthy, seeking safety and privilege in their own company, but open to the wiles and deceits of those who wish to take their place or their money. After I left Monte Carlo, the final stop on my way home was in Vichy so that I could convince my father that I had not had an entirely unhealthy sojourn on the Continent. There I sampled the famous water, which I thought tasted dreadful. I declined the baths, reasoning that if they were full of people with ailments, whereas I was fit and healthy, I was more likely to catch something unpleasant than improve my state of health. I loved the small but strikingly beautiful city with its fine buildings from the Second Empire and the Belle Epoch. Napoleon III had spent a great deal of time there and it was under his patronage that it was imbued with a style and grace to rival many a capital city. Naturally, there were great numbers of *curistes* who came to bathe or take the waters and I made the acquaintance of a very attractive young lady who was accompanying her mother, a lady who had an indeterminate ailment she was sure the baths would clear up. While her mother made full use of the spa's facilities, rested in her room, or ate little and often, or rather very often, I spent a very pleasant couple of days accompanying the young lady in walks round the city and enjoying the local cuisine. A particular delight was the Parc des Sources which had a metal boardwalk covered by an ornate metal canopy which permitted a perambulation of the park in all weathers. On my last night there I accompanied both ladies to the magnificent new opera house and the following morning left for home.

The holiday had acted as a watershed between my student life and the world of work but it had also cemented my friendships with Lyndon and Ralph, which would persist for the rest of our lives, one of which would be cruelly cut short.

# IV

# *THE CITY OF LONDON*

In quiet moments during my travels in Europe I reflected on my impending choice of career. There was no family business to enter. Such wealth as my immediate family did have was the result of the last couple of generations looking after their inherited wealth and receiving enough unearned income to enable whatever they earned through employment to ensure a very comfortable standard of living. My father had been a successful commodity broker and had recently retired at the age of fifty-eight to pursue his various interests, none of which represented a large drain on his capital. Of his five children I was the youngest and by the time I went down from Cambridge my three elder sisters were all married and my elder brother, the oldest of us all, was a director of one of the merchant banks operating in the City.

On my return from the Continent, I turned my attention to considering my career in earnest. In all honesty, at that time it wouldn't have been difficult for a person of my social standing to make a reasonable stab at anything. Those of my background who lived through the Edwardian era still remember it with great nostalgia as a golden age. The economy grew steadily without serious setbacks and prosperity increased for all, though especially for those in the wealthier classes. Health, hygiene, communications, education: all these areas were improving, and leisure activities and sport created amusements for even the most discerning. Of course, the class system was at its height and snobbery among the upper classes was self-indulgent to the point of decadence. The third and fourth generations of the men who had made fortunes in the industrial revolution and the commercial expansion which followed in the last century too often exhibited a distaste for trade if not the fortunes which had derived from it. Some might try their hand at one of the professions, the army, law, church or medicine, but for others it was only the arts or the classics which were worthy of their labours and for many nothing at all. I had mixed with plenty of all of these categories at Cambridge.

It was doubtful whether my family's wealth was sufficient to keep me in unearned luxury, but it was irrelevant as I wanted to work. Despite my respect for the protestant work ethic, this had no part in my decision. I had a need to test myself and do the best I could in a competitive environment, just as I did on the sports field or at the card table. Had we a family firm I would happily have joined it, but we did not, so I was pleased to go into the City to follow our family tradition. I discussed with my father and my brother the various options open to me and decided that broking was more to my liking than banking, if only because it appeared to promise a closer association with the functioning of a volatile and therefore unpredictable market place. By nature, I preferred the frisson of risk to the dead hand of certainty which at that time I associated with banking. On reflection this was probably partly because my brother was a solid, reliable chap who carried out his banking duties impeccably but had not a whiff of adventure about him. He had embraced middle age almost as soon as he began shaving and he now resembled a younger version of my father. It was only later that I discovered that his stolid behaviour was a reflection of his nature rather than his profession and that bankers were just as likely to indulge in speculative and dangerous behaviour as those in any other business. No wonder governments had been slow to grant their directors limited liability.

I chose stockbroking merely because, despite knowing virtually nothing about the profession, I considered I had a natural affinity with it. I fancied I took after my father whose broking activities seemed to me tinged with an element of excitement and the exotic. I had heard him since my childhood refer to trade in products from the Americas, Africa and the Orient without ever knowing exactly what they were. Accordingly, my father made a few enquiries of his contacts and I was invited to join a long-established firm of stockbrokers with which I began to learn my way around the City. Despite my academic qualifications I still started as a kind of apprentice and was happy to do so. Knowing the theory of supply and demand or the law of diminishing returns was hardly enough preparation for diving straight into the whirlpool of market forces.

As is so often the case, the translation from university to working life led to a slow but steady decline in the number of friendships I maintained from my days at Cambridge. I kept up with several from my sporting associations, especially Lyndon Ashley, as well as Ralph Talbot and a few others but, as always, many friendships had been of their place and time and shrivelled through neglect on both sides. I did, however, seek to maintain my friendship with Saxon Sydney-Turner and hoped, through him, to keep up my tenuous link with Maynard.

My career dominated my thoughts at this time and as a fledgling broker I was placed in the care of Norbert Dilhorne, one of the senior partners and referred to as Nobby by everyone, though not to his face by the junior staff. He was a man of about sixty with a thick mass of curly grey hair and a full beard which covered much of his reddish complexion, the consequence of frequenting Coates' wine bar in Old Broad Street for the odd glass or two. At first, I was trusted only with taking clients' instructions, updating them on movements in share prices and researching particular companies. This last function frequently took me to Companies House, banks, and other advisory services in the company of one of our senior clerks. To prepare myself for giving advice I maintained a dummy trading account in which purchases and sales of shares were logged but never actually executed. At first, I suffered heavy imaginary losses, which I put down to bad luck. Later, I began to make profits as well as losses as I learned to ride the waves of the market. My luck seemed to improve the more I understood the way the market worked.

My visits to the Stock Exchange were rarely dull and, though usually serious, often entertaining too. The two principal participants on the floor of the Exchange were brokers, buying and selling shares in companies on behalf of their clients, and jobbers who acted as market makers, matching the orders to buy and sell a share. Jobbers fixed the price in response to changes in the level of demand and supply of a particular share. When the market was very active, the business was hectic, even frenetic, and the buzz around the place as brokers sought to get the best prices for their clients and jobbers worked hard to make an efficient market was quite gripping. When trade was quiet in the market there would be opportunities, particularly after lunch, for pranksters to play the traditional practical jokes of the Exchange. Accordingly, one had to be careful not to read a newspaper while on the floor as someone might well set light to the bottom of it. A non-member who strayed onto the trading floor risked being called out as a 'stranger' and being debagged, though I never witnessed anyone having their trousers pulled down myself. Any member who dared wear a boater in the Exchange was liable to have his hat knocked off and trampled on. I believe that some members actually provoked it by wearing a straw hat when they knew the consequences. I thought these silly jokes very amusing when I was young. Later, I thought them rather benignly puerile, recognising they served their purpose as a way of letting off steam in what was often a febrile environment.

When I first went onto the trading floor, I naively thought it close to the 'perfect market' of economic theory I had been taught by Alfred Marshall. It seemed that all those wishing to buy or sell had access to all those trading and, having complete knowledge of what was on offer, were able to deal at the best price. But I soon realised that, as in all markets, knowledge was by no means perfect and market makers did not underbid each other as they all sought to maximise their profits. In addition, trading was always influenced by insider knowledge and rumours as well as the human proclivity to extremes of euphoria and panic, boom and bust, bubbles and bursts.

My first experience of a major bubble on the Stock Exchange came in 1910 with the so-called 'Rubber Frenzy' of that year. Since the turn of the century, the rapid growth of the cycling and motor car industries had increased the demand for rubber year on year and though production rose to meet the demand, it could not keep pace. The price of rubber soared and rubber companies on the Shanghai, New York and London stock exchanges saw their prices increase by as much as ten times. In response to the higher rubber prices, new exploration and development companies were launched in South America and Asia, particularly Malaya, and floated on the Stock Exchange. The public were swept up in the fever pitch of demand for shares in these new companies and many missed out in the ballot. In consequence, as soon as dealing in the new shares commenced, their price rocketed. There is nothing like a shortage of anything to convince people they must buy it and the pool of buyers was swollen by gamblers, speculators and inexperienced investors who believed that rising prices must go up forever. Inevitably, there was a long pause before these new companies could actually begin production and, as other sources of rubber became available, the bubble burst and there was a collapse in the share prices of these companies.

As a young broker I felt overwhelmed by the chaos in the market during this period. It was often impossible to deal and orders had to be left in writing for jobbers to execute when they could. Naturally the jobbers made large profits as they barely had time to relax from the constant demand for orders to be filled. Then, when the bubble burst, the brokers were frequently 'out to lunch' all day so that anxious clients were unable to stem their losses and their once highly priced shares were now virtually unsaleable. During normal times the trading floor was covered with hundreds of pieces of paper by the end of trading but during the mayhem of the rubber frenzy the floor was awash with thousands of pieces. The dust built up too and 'waiters' would walk round with large watering cans to dampen it down and keep the air clearer. Fortunately the atmosphere was not further worsened by smoking which was only permitted a few minutes before the end of trading.

Old hands in my office said they had seen it all before and took such convulsions in their stride, referring me to the South African gold mining boom of the mid-1890s and the collapse of the Argentinean bond market a few years before that. When I expressed my disquiet at this temporary breakdown of the efficiency of the stock market to my mentor, Nobby Dilhorne, he smiled at me benevolently and poured us both a glass of dry sherry.

"My dear chap, the chaos you refer to is due to a wind that rushes through the market from time to time and against which no man can keep his footing. I have seen it happen many times in my career and no doubt so will you. I began working in the City in 1866 and experienced a baptism of fire when later that year the collapse of Overend, Gurney and Co, the large bank, set off a major panic. This led to the collapse of most of the joint stock companies operating at that time and large-scale unemployment. Of course, many investors lost their shirts but eventually the panic subsided, the economy recovered, and it was all soon forgotten. I doubt if one person in a hundred of your generation has even heard of Overend, Gurney and Co. Long experience of such crises equips the professional stockbroker to be more phlegmatic in a panic and our role, often without success I'm afraid, is to attempt to dissuade our clients from losing their heads, for their shirts will surely follow. But all too often they will be caught up in the maelstrom and follow the herd instinct to disaster like lemmings off a cliff. Whatever our own disposition we must, at the end of the day, act on our clients' instructions and we are unable to stop a fool from being parted from his money if he wishes to be so. Those who invest must always try to cultivate the virtue of patience: 'fools rush in where angels fear to tread' is a useful motto for investors but one that is rarely heeded."

# V

# *BLOOMSBURY*

IN MY MID-TWENTIES, DESPITE THE ENJOYMENT of building my career in the City and pursuing my sport and other leisure activities, I found myself preoccupied with the thought that I might be missing out in some way. There developed an uncomfortable feeling that at least some of those paths I had chosen not to pursue might have contained promises of fulfilment or personal satisfaction in ways I couldn't have imagined.

When I tried to find something concrete in my amorphous collection of hankerings after something, it was easier to know what I didn't want rather than what I did. There was no profession for which I had discovered a sudden vocation, no intense passion for a particular field of knowledge that I might wish to pursue for the rest of my life, no desire to travel to the far reaches of the earth or climb the highest mountains. I came to the conclusion that I wished I was more like Maynard, or at least more like my image of Maynard. I followed his career with interest, impressed by such titbits as I gleaned from Saxe. Maynard had enjoyed a brief but successful period in the India Office and was back in Cambridge as a lecturer with a prize fellowship in 1909. It wasn't a case of hero worship; more I saw in him something of a role model, someone I might seek to imitate to some degree. I realised I had neither the intelligence nor the drive to become an authority in all the areas that he seemed destined to conquer, nor to move in the circles to which he was invited, but I aspired to have perhaps a second or third division version of his role in life. Not a polymath to whom all the right doors are open but perhaps a dilettante to whom not all the right doors are closed.

Given this new-found aspiration, I was delighted when, early in 1912, Saxe invited me to a party at 38 Brunswick Square, Bloomsbury, perhaps opening one of the doors I referred to. It came about after I telephoned him at his office in the Treasury to invite him to a race meeting.

"I thought you might be interested in a National Hunt meeting in the next couple of weeks?"

Saxe was silent for a few moments and had it been anyone else I may have thought the line had gone dead. Eventually, he said, "May I think about the race meeting? Why don't you come to a party I'm invited to in Bloomsbury and we can talk about it then?"

"Are you sure? I don't like to just turn up without an invitation."

"I am certain you will be welcome. You know some of the people who live at Brunswick Square already: Leonard Woolf and Maynard Keynes have rooms."

The opportunity to meet Maynard again was not to be missed and I readily agreed.

I was delayed in attending the party and when I rang the bell of the handsome four-storey house the door was opened by a flushed-looking young man in a dinner suit.

"Party's upstairs," he said. "Jolly warm so taking a breather. Do I know you?"

"Lewis Durrington."

"Sorry, don't think I do." He turned to his companion, an attractive young woman of twenty or so, dressed in the latest style of evening gown, sleeker and less heavy than in earlier years, with a square neck and raised waistline. Her head was adorned by a band to which was attached an upright peacock feather.

"Now, where were we?" the young man said, his arm going round her waist, causing her to giggle.

I went round them and mounted the stairs towards the sounds of laughter and chatter. The large drawing room, elegant but with artistic flourishes, was occupied by over twenty people. I noticed Saxe immediately. He was playing the piano, rather well, I thought. A woman of about thirty was leaning on the piano and saying something to Saxe which made him smile. Around the room were groups of people, generally in their late twenties and thirties, the men mostly dressed like me, in a dinner suit, and the women in evening dresses or gowns. A few young men were dressed in a more casual style, bordering on the bohemian. I presumed them to be of a poetic or artistic bent, though uniform in their unconformity both in dress and in their slightly emaciated-looking visages. They were reminiscent of Bunthorne, 'the one foot in the grave young man' of Gilbert and Sullivan's *Patience*. All were engaged in animated conversation which, from the participants' expressions and posture, ranged from humorous and light-hearted, through coquettish and flirtatious to serious and perhaps profound. One conversation appeared to be bordering on an argument between two young men who were unable to see each other's point of view. A waitress or maid was walking round the room, offering the guests canapés and other titbits. A long-faced, fair-haired man of my age looked over at me and smiled; it was Adrian Stephen who had been at Trinity at the same time I was at Caius.

"Lewis, good to see you again. How are you?" he asked, extending a hand. "Saxe told me you were coming."

"I do apologise for taking the liberty," I said.

"Not at all. At least somebody invited you and that's not always the case," he replied, smiling.

"It's a fine house. Several of you share it, I think Saxe said."

"That's right. After our parents died all four of us Stephen children moved to Gordon Square. Then Thoby died and Vanessa married and we two younger ones came here. We had more space than we required and Duncan needed more room for his work so he and Maynard, who shared his old flat, took the rooms on the ground floor. We have the second floor and this floor we use for entertaining and that sort of thing."

"And Leonard is here too?"

"Yes. He was looking for a place when he returned from his post in Ceylon and we were all glad for him to take rooms on the third floor. He is an old friend of the family, after all. You know Duncan?"

"Only by sight, really."

"Have you met my sister, Virginia?"

"No, I haven't."

"Let me introduce you." He led me over to the piano and the woman leaning on it straightened up.

"Virginia, this is Lewis Durrington. We were at Cambridge together."

"How do you do, Mr Durrington?" she said pleasantly.

"I'll get you a drink, Lewis. We've got a hefty punch on the go."

"I believe you are a friend of dear Saxe," said Virginia.

"He is indeed. Thanks for coming, Lewis," said Saxe, glancing over his shoulder while continuing to play a Chopin nocturne.

I noticed how sublimely he played and how relaxed the two were in each other's company. My thoughts were interrupted by Adrian returning with a glass of punch.

"Give it some respect, old chap, it's deceptively sweet but danger lurks within."

"That warning might equally have been given to the Captain of *HMS Dreadnought* when you went on board," I said. "Cheers!"

Virginia smiled wistfully. "I'm afraid that may be the only event for which we are remembered."

I thought she had a pleasant voice and spoke slowly, almost deliberately, as if she were savouring every word she uttered.

"Well, it made all the papers," I said. "I still can't believe you got away with it. Five people dressed supposedly as Abyssinian princes, including one who is actually a woman, and nobody suspects anything, even when you are received by the Captain and Admiral, C-in-C Home Fleet, with an honour guard."

Adrian laughed. "Don't forget that our cousin, Willie Fisher, was serving on the ship and he spoke to us without recognising us at all."

I shook my head. "It's quite extraordinary that you got away with it, especially after you had already pulled the same stunt at Cambridge. I forget; what were you supposed to be that time?"

Adrian laughed. "The Sultan of Zanzibar. Different place and different names, old boy. But you're right and that time none of our fellow students recognised us. It's about being believable and once you overcome that hurdle, nobody challenges you even if they have their doubts."

"The secret to any successful hoax lies in the planning," said Virginia. "Of course, if a group of people just turn up unannounced claiming to be royal or famous in some way, they will attract suspicion. But Horace Cole arranged for a telegram to be sent, supposedly from the Foreign Office, to the Admiralty, telling them to expect a visit from these royal personages and it was not queried. Then he had a fake Foreign Office official order a VIP train at Paddington and the station master obliged. When we arrived at Weymouth and alighted from a special coach we were immediately regarded as genuine and the rest was plain sailing, one might say." She and her brother laughed at their memory of it.

"Very embarrassing for the Navy and they took a lot of stick from the newspapers. I felt rather sorry for them," said Saxe.

"It was just a joke, Saxe," said Virginia, "No harm done to anyone. We cannot be held responsible for the dimness of some navy officers. I do hope you are not in the Navy, Mr Durrington."

"No, I'm a stockbroker."

"Really? Then you must be used to seeing the wool pulled over people's eyes." She smiled.

I returned the smile. "I believe you are a writer?"

"I do write, but I don't know if I count as a writer as I am yet to have my work published."

"If you write, you are a writer," said Adrian, smiling at her encouragingly.

"Yes, one must write primarily for oneself," observed Saxon. "Only if you find it satisfactory can you expect it to be worth reading by others. Every artist must be true to oneself."

Virginia did not answer and nor did Adrian. Knowing him as we did, I think we were all surprised that Saxe had ventured an opinion so soon in the conversation or even at all.

"Well, you are working on a novel: publication will come," said Adrian.

"We shall see," said Virginia, fingering her beads.

This apparent self-doubt about her writing career exhibited by Virginia was heard by Leonard Woolf whom I saw standing nearby. In the pause after Virginia's comment, he edged over. "Come now, Virginia. Maynard has been published and so have I and you have more talent than both of us put together," he said, a reassuring smile on his lugubrious face.

Virginia laughed and we all joined in her laughter. "That's the difficulty of being surrounded by successful people; they put so much pressure on one," she observed.

"Or artists put pressure on themselves when they see the success of others," said Adrian. "In an artistic environment rivalry is probably inevitable."

Leonard put his hand on Virginia's shoulder. "You must remember that we all struggle as writers, my dear, especially early in our careers," he said. "Look at Strachey."

Virginia released her shoulder from his grip. "Maynard didn't struggle," she said.

"Maynard's work arises from his expertise, not from a literary perspective, so he is accepted as an authority and people must buy his work," said Leonard.

I wasn't sure if that was a compliment to Maynard or a veiled insult but nobody commented. I thought it rather charming that Virginia's friends seemed keen to support her writing ambitions since I knew that, as Apostles, they tended to be associated with mastery of the barbed comment more than the gentle encouragement. The discussion was interrupted by the advent of one of the other guests, whom I didn't know. He was in his early twenties, bespectacled, with a slightly hawkish face.

"Ah, I heard the name 'Maynard' mentioned. Is he not making an appearance this evening?" He was holding a cigarette in his thumb and forefinger and spoke in a rather mannered way.

"No, he couldn't get away from Cambridge; something cropped up," replied Leonard.

"Or someone," said the young man.

Leonard turned to me, "Do you know Francis Birrell, Lewis?"

I shook my head. "Lewis Durrington," I said, offering my hand.

Birrell transferred his cigarette to his left hand and shook my hand fleetingly. "Which of these literary luminaries was your entrée to this great gathering?" he asked.

"Saxe invited me," I replied.

"I haven't written anything since those bits for Euphrosyne," said Saxe.

"Would that be Euphrosyne the opera, the publication, the legendary virgin or the Byzantine Empress?" asked Birrell.

The others laughed but Saxon merely shook his head and turned back to the piano.

Birrell turned to me again. "How do you know Saxe?"

"We were both at Cambridge."

"As was I. What did you read?"

"Economics."

"Ah, the dismal science; there's no shortage of the dismal here. Pity Maynard's not coming. Are you one of his admirers?"

"Very much so, but only from afar."

"So, not an intimate acquaintance?"

"No."

"How rare," he said, smiling and turned his gaze to Virginia. "And how is life for the vacillating Virginia? Have you agreed to let Leonard make an honest woman of you yet?"

"Don't be ridiculous," snapped Virginia and, patting Saxe on the back, she walked over towards the group of young artistic types standing by the window.

Unfazed, Birrell nodded to Leonard, "You will have to be more imperative with her. Some women need a firm hand, I believe."

Leonard ignored the remark and traipsed after Virginia; his serious expression more serious than usual.

"That was not very kind, Francis," said Adrian.

Birrell ignored him and walked off to seek amusement elsewhere.

I looked at Adrian quizzically and he smiled. "I ought to circulate a little, Lewis. Perhaps I could introduce you to some more of our friends."

"You go ahead. I want a word with Saxe, anyhow." I took Saxe's glass and my own and recharged them. When I returned, Saxe brought his musical interlude to a conclusion.

"Virginia seemed a little upset. I hope all is well," I said.

"Leonard and Virginia have known each other since she was very young and he has always taken a fancy to her. I believe they have a tacit understanding, though nothing has been said as yet. Perhaps Leonard is further advanced in that belief than Virginia and she is in no rush to make a decision on the matter. Others adding pressure on her to do so will serve no purpose."

"Of course. Now, about the trip to the races I mentioned when I telephoned you. Are you going to Aintree for the Grand National meeting?"

"I have no plans to."

"Oh, you must. I am going with a couple of friends; why don't you accompany us?"

"I've never actually been to a race meeting."

"Well, you can't start with a better one than the Grand National. I'll telephone you next week and see how you are fixed."

Saxe finished his drink and returned to his piano and I circulated a bit among the other party members. I passed a pleasant evening with the residents of 38 Brunswick Square and their guests. In my conversations I became involved in a myriad of topics, some of which I could only listen to, partly comprehending and nodding sagely in my ignorance. However, when a subject like the price of artworks cropped up I could hold my own, as the one matter in which I was an expert as much as any of them was the nature of markets. One of the younger artists bemoaned the fact that so many painters do not receive recognition until late in their careers and some not until long after they have died.

Duncan Grant smiled. "We can't expect the intrinsic value of our work necessarily to be recognised by others and even if they do, they might not wish to pay for the privilege of owning it."

"The art critics are the ones you have to win over," muttered a young artist whose name I forget.

There followed a brief outpouring of vitriol on the influence and taste of critics and Duncan observed that it was just as well that Clive Bell wasn't present.

"Surely, the critics serve a purpose in guiding potential art buyers to worthwhile investments," I said.

"But art collectors buy for the wrong reason," someone replied.

"If you want to sell something, whatever it is, I don't see why you would be concerned by the motive of the buyer, unless it were malicious in some way," I answered.

"He's right. If someone offered me a thousand guineas for one of my paintings, I wouldn't care if that person had no taste whatsoever," said another.

"If they offered a thousand guineas for one of your paintings, they would have no taste whatsoever," said the sceptic who had first raised the influence of the art critic.

Amid the laughter someone said, "The difficulty of finding a monetary value for art is surely that any price attached to an artwork is purely arbitrary and driven by factors outside the work itself and the craft and inspiration that has gone into it: the fame of the artist, fashion, taste, etcetera."

"Precisely," I said. "If you want to sell a painting you find a buyer and the more highly rated the painting is in terms of its current and future market value, the more potential buyers there will be and the higher the price will be bid for it."

"There you have it," said Duncan. "Get your work praised by a critic, then accept commissions from people who want to buy something of yours and make sure they like what you produce. Singer Sargent could give you a few tips, I'm sure."

"I'm going off to paint *Bubbles*," said one of the group and the laughter signalled a change in conversation.

Duncan turned to me. "Thanks for your comments there," he said. "We can get wrapped up in our own view of the world and forget that it's not always so. We have had that conversation many times; it's a frustrating life, that of any artist, in the quest for recognition, especially as so many receive none at all and even those that do are often already dead."

I nodded. "The price of most things goes up when the supply runs out so the dead artist has an advantage over the living."

Duncan smiled. "Not much of an option."

After I left that evening, it didn't occur to me that many of the people I met were some of the luminaries of what would within a few years be widely referred to as the 'Bloomsbury Group'. Bloomsbury had been the location for their regular meetings to discuss art and literature at the home of the Stephen family in Gordon Square, which contributed several of the original members. Most of the coalescing set were interested in pursuing careers in art or literature or activities associated with the arts in some way. The lifestyle of many of them, though I didn't know it at the time, was decidedly bohemian. They adopted unorthodox political and social attitudes and many were libertarian in their sexual behaviour. Not all of them lived in Bloomsbury all of the time and living in Bloomsbury did not guarantee entry to the group, though presumably as the group became more famous many an aspirant with literary or artistic pretensions would have been prepared to move there in the hope that they might share in the glamour. Certainly, the group would grow over the years and Leonard Woolf would take the trouble to distinguish between 'Old Bloomsbury' in regard to the original members and those who came afterwards or who were associated with the group via their working or sexual relationships. Whatever their radicalism and progressive attitudes in other matters, the Bloomsbury set never lost its awareness of status.

At the time, I regarded the Bloomsbury Group members I met as a mutual support society, all with ambitions in the world of art or literature but as yet, despite being thirty years old or more, most not particularly successful, apart from E M Forster who was an established novelist by then and Maynard Keynes, a published academic. Hence, the grooming of each other's egos at this time, one session of which I had observed that evening. By the time I saw them again en masse, they would have achieved much, become famous and have egos which no longer needed massaging. Over the years, my rare contact with members of the group would come only through my friendship with Saxe. Other than that, I played no regular part in the world of Bloomsbury and had neither the qualifications nor a particular wish to do so.

The week after the party, I telephoned Saxe and, rather hesitantly, he accepted my invitation to accompany me and my friends to Aintree for the Grand National on the 27th March. Saxe had a flat in Great Ormond Street, Bloomsbury, and on the morning of the trip I collected him on the way to Euston Station, only a ten-minute walk from his flat. When we arrived at Euston, Lyndon Ashley and another old friend of mine from Cambridge, Neville Plaice, were waiting for us.

We had a very pleasant trip to Liverpool, with much to talk about and a good lunch in the dining car. Even Saxe was fairly talkative at times, especially when Neville outlined his use of form books and other technical matters which Saxe found fascinating. A taxi from the station took us to the racecourse and we were in position to watch the first race. March that year was very wet and the course was quite saturated. We ran through the card with fairly small wagers and differing degrees of success, until the big race arrived and we were more adventurous. With the course over four miles long and the going very heavy, the runners struggled and they fell, pulled up, or dismounted their riders with alarming regularity, including mine at the third. Only seven horses finished the race, which was won by *Jerry M*, the joint favourite, by six lengths, ridden by the famous Ernie Piggott. None of us had backed him and the day belonged to Saxe who placed a bet of ten pounds each way on the horse which came second, *Bloodstone*. With odds of 40/1 he made a tidy profit. The journey home was filled with discussions of 'what might have beens' and amusing anecdotes about the day and some of the characters we'd seen on both sides of the rails. Saxe insisted on buying all the drinks.

The following day Saxe telephoned me to say how much he had enjoyed the day and I suggested we might do it again some time. However, it was to be a long time before we went to the races again together and the next time was not just to watch the racing.

# VI

# *EGYPT AND HOME*

UNDER THE WISE TUTELAGE OF NORBERT DILHORNE my career developed incrementally as I gained both depth and breadth in my expertise as a stockbroker, building an interest in specific sectors of the market and particular forms of investment. Soon I was able to make recommendations and give advice to clients and look forward to becoming a full partner. Then, as happens in life as well as in the stock market, the unexpected happened in the form of the Archduke Franz Ferdinand's chauffeur taking the wrong road in Sarajevo straight into the path of a surprised but prepared assassin and the Great War followed. In a beautiful summer the blissful period of civilised peace and progress came to an abrupt end.

Not quite thirty on the outbreak of war and sound in body, I felt I should do my bit. But I was sound in mind too and mature enough for the call to arms fervently heard by men ten years or more my junior to be somewhat muted when they reached my ears. In any event the financial crisis which followed the outbreak of war preoccupied me for the time being and I put to one side any thought of volunteering, especially as Nobby Dilhorne had recently retired and I felt my firm had the greater need of me.

Since the introduction of the electric ticker tape system in 1870 it had been possible to relay information from trading floors continuously and simultaneously all round the world. As a consequence, price changes were known almost immediately and trading in currencies, stocks and shares could be undertaken instantaneously in any exchange from another financial hub anywhere in the global financial system. There was a fear when war broke out in 1914 that, while the major economies were on the gold standard, the international trade in securities could lead to vast sums of capital shifting between countries as the war moved in favour of one side or the other, thus threatening to undermine the entire world financial system. In consequence, all the major stock exchanges closed soon after the outbreak of war while they sought to make alternative arrangements in order to manage volatility in the markets. The United Kingdom, among others, left the gold standard to protect its gold reserves during the crisis. This was not, as one might expect, to prevent a flight from paper money to gold among the public, but from the joint stock banks who initiated a run on the Bank of England, converting their holdings at the Bank into gold, as fear of losses trumped a sense of responsibility.

Overnight my firm, like all the other stockbrokers, returned to the old practice of 'selling on the street' whereby jobbers offered a market in securities and brokers would buy and sell stocks and shares 'over the counter', not exactly back to the days of trading in the coffee houses but not far from that. It was extraordinary how quickly the 'new' system operated efficiently, showing that when there's money to be made a way will be found. The need to match sales and purchases and settle net outstanding debits and credits worked satisfactorily, although liquidity sometimes threatened to be a problem for some firms. I enjoyed the novelty of the new regime at first but it inevitably placed some curbs on trading and I was glad when, the government having reduced the risk of financial turbulence by placing restrictions on the movement of capital, the London Stock Exchange was able to re-open in January 1915.

With something approaching normality in the financial system my thoughts once again turned to the need to do my duty to King and Country. My mother tried to dissuade me as the hopes of a speedy war had by now evaporated. My father said that while he was proud of me for considering joining up, he would think none the less of me if I remembered that "discretion is the better part of valour". But eventually duty got the better of me and, with even less enthusiasm than the previous year, I joined my local cavalry regiment, the Berkshire Yeomanry, later in 1915.

Napoleon is said to have asked about a colonel recommended for promotion to general, "Yes, I know he's good, but is he lucky?" and I certainly felt that luck was the main factor in my coming through the war unscathed, rather than any merit on my part. I was extremely fortunate to miss the Gallipoli campaign which took place before I completed my training. The regiment fought as a dismounted unit and suffered over fifty per cent casualties killed, wounded, or taken prisoner before eventually being withdrawn in November 1915. I was stationed for most of the war in Egypt, with nearly a quarter of a million other British and Empire troops, preparing and waiting for the attack on Ottoman Turk forces in the Middle East. I spent the long periods of military inaction on exercises, languid hours in the officers' mess and touring the country, especially the many archaeological sites. I didn't cut all ties with my old life, instead using my free time to catch up on the news of economic and industrial events and keeping an eye on the markets, admittedly always a couple of days late. The regiment went over to camels for part of the time I served in Egypt and I got used to riding my new mount, perched on high while he moved at his own speed with a rolling gait, rarely giving me a sense of total security and occasionally hinting at his displeasure at being forced to carry me on his back. Like a thousand others, I had the obligatory photograph taken, wearing a sun helmet and astride my camel, with the pyramids and a sardonic looking Sphinx in the background. One member of my troop asked me if the pyramids were natural, "like the Giant's Causeway in Ireland" and I let him down as gently as I could.

I got on well with my fellow officers and a few became good friends. One in particular, Tommy Felstead, was a kindred spirit. Like me, Tommy had been very active in sports at university, having boxed and played rugby and cricket at Oxford. To the delight of his troop, he participated in the regimental boxing competitions and showed himself to be a light-footed and rapid punching middle-weight, which his opponents admired though not always appreciated. Even though he wouldn't dream of laying a finger on the men outside the ring, his boxing reputation must have contributed to his having few disciplinary problems. After the war we would keep up with each other socially, especially at the Varsity matches and at Lord's during the cricket season.

Eventually, in July 1917, under our new commander, General Allenby, there were three months of intensive preparation for an autumn offensive. In the first few days of November, I saw action in the third battle of Gaza when we attacked the Ottoman rear guard and afterwards in the harassing of the retreat of the Turkish troops as we moved on towards Jerusalem. I saw the full ravages of war in the field for the first time and the beginnings of the final disintegration of the Ottoman Empire. Viewing the lines of their dead bodies I was unable to fathom why the Turks had entered a war that was not theirs and from which they would have gained little but now would lose everything. There was nothing to see but the futility of their dead and the waste of life they had inflicted on our forces. These thoughts dominated my mind, though of course were absent from my expressions of sympathy as I wrote my letters of condolence to the families of my lost comrades.

While stationed in Egypt I met Merelina Adleigh, the daughter of one of the senior British consular staff who ran Egypt at this time. She was staying for a while with her parents and I met her at a diplomatic function while acting as adjutant to my colonel. Merelina was twenty-three, a blonde and very pretty in an elegant, slightly unapproachable way which belied her friendly, outgoing nature, once you got to know her. Instructed by the colonel to mix and mingle as much as possible, I got as far as Merelina and made little attempt to go much further, until eventually I was dragged away by the hostess to meet some of the other consular staff. At the end of the evening I sought out Merelina and she agreed to see me again later that week.

"But do call me Lina in future. Life's too short to have to keep saying 'Merelina,'" she said as we parted.

We hit it off quite quickly and I saw her as often as my duties and her obligations would allow over the next few weeks and, before she returned to England, we had come to a tacit understanding. Conscious that war can lead to people making the rashest of decisions, especially in affairs of the heart, we decided not to announce our engagement until we were sure our ardour wouldn't cool, and we corresponded regularly for a year while we were separated by the wartime situation.

I finished my war service on the western front when in May 1918 the Yeomanry were amalgamated with the Machine Gun Corp and shipped to France. Although late in the day, I was glad to see some action on the western front. It salved my conscience to at least be able to say I knew something of that theatre of war in which better men than me had lived, and too often, died. At the Battle of Scarpe in August we supported the Canadian Corps who fought magnificently and won two Victoria Crosses. Then we advanced into Belgium and were in Courtrai when Armistice Day came. Relieved it was over, it was only in the weeks that followed that I realised the extent of the losses among those I had counted as friends, or at least had some regard for. Five of those who had played for Cambridge against the WG Grace XI had died, as had a similar number from the football club. Ralph Talbot, whom I had toured Italy with, and several others I had known well had also not returned, including one from my office. I knew this was a pattern repeated throughout the country and those who had died had not been especially unlucky. With a life expectancy of six weeks for a new infantry officer on the western front, only the extremely lucky survived. I was thankful for my good fortune but could not escape entirely the feelings of guilt which attacked most of those who had come through the war unscathed. I was grateful that my mind was soon preoccupied with plans for the future.

As both Lina and I were certain we felt the same, we made our relationship public while I was still in France and we married after I returned to England. Having not yet resigned my commission I was able to marry in my uniform which pleased both our fathers. My best man was Tommy Felstead, my closest friend in the regiment, while my other fellow officers mounted a guard of honour. With my wife's 'dowry' we bought a not very large but extremely pretty house on the

Thames near Hurley in Berkshire, where we put down our roots. We live there still.

After demobilisation I returned to my old firm and, to my surprise, I was accorded a new level of respect by virtue of my war service, even though I hardly deserved it, having endured none of the horrors of Gallipoli or the western front, let alone given my life as had one of our clerks. I soon settled back into life as a stockbroker, though the situation had changed. I was now a long-established junior partner and, counting myself well-informed in certain sectors of the market and particular forms of investment, felt as confident as one can ever become of giving advice to clients and assisting in the management of our wealthier customers' portfolios. Sadly, it did seem to me that the City had lost some of the buzz of the pre-war years and it would be several years before the volume of trading in stocks and shares was as high again. Society as a whole seemed to have had the stuffing knocked out of it by the war and I sometimes felt the high jinks that went on in the 1920s were a sign of people trying too hard to recapture a lost joie de vivre. Perhaps it was merely a sign that I was on the cusp of middle age.

Towards the end of 1921, Lina gave birth to our first child, a girl whom we named Catherine Beatrice for our two mothers. She missed my own birthday by three days and Lina commented what great celebrations we would have in November in the years to come.

I have never been a great one for introspection or reflections on the meaning of life. As the saying goes, we are dealt a hand in life and we just have to play it as well as we can in the way our nature takes us. For me, Polonius puts it best in Hamlet: "To thine own self be true". I believe that any regrets one has will be as nothing compared to those which result from being false to oneself and half-heartedly following a path chosen by others or acting against our better instincts. I am well aware that I was dealt a pretty good hand at birth and in the years that followed have had more than my share of good luck but however kind fortune has been to us we must still play our cards well. We have all heard the hard luck stories of people who made a hash of their lives and in my own business I have come across too many who managed to lose a fortune through carelessness or stupidity. It is difficult for the poor to rise up the social ladder but it is relatively easy for the rich to fall off the top.

Perhaps it was the birth of a child or the approach of a new year or who knows what that conspired to make me take stock of where I was as I entered my late thirties. I had already made one gesture to the passage of time by retiring from club cricket at the end of the previous season. It wasn't that I couldn't do it anymore; I just wasn't as satisfied with my performance at either bat or ball as much as I had once been and I was unable to turn things round. It's odd when you look at the statistics how many sportsmen know it's time to go at about thirty-five, whatever the sport, and I knew it was my time too. I suppose the fire starts to go out except for that special few who can play at the top of their form into their forties or even fifty. I had already given up soccer a few years before with a dodgy knee. Another sign of my approaching middle age was that I had begun to lose the thrill of gambling. I still enjoyed the odd wager from time to time but nowadays, apart from the occasional race meeting, I preferred the markets, where I felt my knowledge and experience gave me an edge.

Despite a vague awareness of gently subsiding physical powers as witnessed by my retirement from playing the sports I loved, I did not anticipate middle age with a sense of dread. The disruption caused by the war ensured that life would never return to its old ways and, however much change had been for the better, it ensured that I already felt a little anachronistic and therefore middle-aged. I watched with benign bemusement as my much younger wife embraced the emancipation of women delivered by the war. She was determined not to be constrained by marriage and motherhood from playing her part in the community. For me, nothing could symbolise the change in the status of women more than the end of the hobble skirt from just before the war and the ease of movement and greater comfort of the rapidly shortening dresses of the post-war period.

I was extremely fortunate in having a happy marriage and hoped Lina felt the same way. Having never much thought about fatherhood I was surprised how much I enjoyed it, especially as the months passed and Catherine's personality developed as she embarked on childhood. Financially I was very comfortable and saw this as unlikely to change as my income always exceeded the relatively modest demands my wife and I made upon it. I had a diverse and enjoyable social life, was on good terms with both my family and my business partners, had work I enjoyed and excellent health. Concerned that I might come across as rather smug, I revealed the findings of my mid-life audit to Lina while we were having dinner one evening.

"I have nothing to complain about and am unable to detect a cloud on the horizon, though there must be some. I have come to the conclusion that I must be a self-satisfied bore."

Lina laughed. "Don't be silly: you are by nature an optimist. It's not as if you go around like Pangloss, telling everybody how wonderful life is and saying how happy you are all the time. There will be some people in exactly the same position as you who would run through a long list of their problems and why their life is dreadful. To make it worse, they don't keep it to themselves but load their woes onto everybody else. If it's any consolation, I haven't got any complaints either." She picked up Catherine and held the baby above her head, moving her gently from side to side. "Have I? No. I haven't." She brought Catherine down till their faces were a few inches apart and the baby giggled. Then she looked over at me, "Mind you, it may just be that I am a self-satisfied bore too, so I wouldn't notice."

I laughed as I knew that was certainly not true. Lina is one of those people who lights up a room when she enters and I have noticed many times in our marriage how her relaxed temperament, genial style and witty conversation drew people to her at any social or business event. But, of course, I am biased.

Catherine's first winter was a mild one, which I thought to be beneficial for her health though my father was of the opinion that a child benefitted from a cold first winter as it "hardened them off, like plants" as he put it when he and my mother came to stay for a few days over Christmas. My father had retired long ago but still traded from time to time in the markets on his own account and we made a point of steering clear of such matters when with our wives to avoid being tiresome and receiving approbation of one kind or another.

One quite warm day in January Lina and I went to the ballet to see Diaghilev's staging of *The Sleeping Beauty*, under the pseudonym of *The Sleeping Princess*, at the Alhambra. During the interval, as we made our way to the bar, I was surprised to see Maynard heading in the same direction and waved to attract his attention. Unfortunately, he didn't seem to notice me but, quickening my step and pulling Lina along with me, I caught up with him as he reached the cloakrooms.

"Maynard, how are you? You look very well."

He looked at me rather blankly.

"Lewis Durrington. We were at Cambridge at the same time."

A flash of recognition went across his face. "Ah, Lewis, of course. You were friendly with Saxe, I remember. It must be?"

"Fifteen years."

He smiled and shook my hand, then looked over at Lina.

"Sorry, of course you don't know my wife, Lina. This is Maynard Keynes."

"How do you do, Mr Keynes? Lewis often mentions you."

"How do you do? Really, in what context?"

"I have followed and admired your career as an economist as I take a keen interest in such matters," I explained.

He nodded. "I'm flattered."

"Shall we have a drink?" I asked.

He hesitated for a second. "Er, yes, why not?"

I herded Lina and Maynard into the bar and a waiter took our order.

"Are you enjoying the performance?" Maynard asked Lina.

"Yes, very much: and you?"

"Yes. Lydia Lopokova is wonderful, isn't she?"

Lina reached for her programme, unable to remember which dancer she was.

"The Lilac Fairy," Maynard said.

"Yes, she's excellent," Lina replied, remembering that Lydia had danced a solo.

"I have seen this production several times and she sometimes performs Aurora, in which role she is just as good," said Maynard.

While we were talking, the bell went for the end of the interval.

"It was good to see you again, Maynard," I said.

"You too, Lewis. Give my regards to Saxe. Mrs Durrington." He bowed his head slightly to Lina and was gone.

At the end of the show, we left the theatre and hailed a taxi in Leicester Square. Lina said she had enjoyed meeting

Maynard and thought he had seemed much warmer than she had expected. "I thought he would be very serious, even dour and rather unworldly. Instead, he was friendly and not in the least unnerving."

"He is very pleasant in a social context but in different circumstances he can be quite intimidating without necessarily meaning to be. I've heard him speak at Cambridge and he explains very difficult ideas very clearly and patiently but he's not averse to displaying his knowledge. You would have to be a braver man than me to challenge him when he is in a particularly authoritative mood."

Unfortunately, the consummate delight experienced by Maynard from his regular attendance at the Alhambra was not universally shared by London audiences and the show closed earlier than expected, not long after Lina and I had attended.

Maynard's mention of Saxe made me realise that I had neglected to see him since my wedding, when I hadn't spent more than a few minutes with him, and I hadn't had a lengthy conversation with him since before I joined up. I finally got round to visiting him in Great Ormond Street not long after the trip to the Alhambra. His accommodation consisted of a large living room and a small, dark and dingy bedroom. Rather oddly, there were two pictures, one either side of the fireplace, and both were exactly the same farmyard scene. This fact was invariably commented on by those who visited Saxe though the picture itself was rarely thought worthy of discussion. Saxe apparently had some good works by other artists but these were not on display. He loved music and was an excellent pianist so that not surprisingly there was also a large piano in the room. The rest of the furniture was functional but not particularly memorable.

I found Saxe much changed when I saw him in 1921. Physically, he looked as if he'd had all the stuffing knocked out of him. Always reserved and with a tendency for understatement, he seemed now to look even more emptied of any sense of enthusiasm in his life. He asked after Lina and was pleased to hear that we now had a child. He congratulated me and said that he did not believe that he would ever be so fortunate.

"Why is that? You are still a young man."

"Forty-one."

"That's not old for a man to marry for the first time: I was nearly thirty-five."

"I thought I might, but not now. You see, I think I must be one of those people for whom there is only one person they could ever marry."

I was inclined to dismiss that idea but held my tongue; if he believed that, nothing I said would change his mind.

"I met her and I asked her to marry me but she chose another." He looked down at the floor and his tone was very sad.

"I'm sorry," I muttered.

"She is a painter named Barbara Hiles. Do you know her?"

"No, I don't believe I do."

"I got to know her through our mutual association with the Bloomsbury set. I have a picture of her somewhere." He rose from his seat and went over to a desk, finding the photograph immediately in the top drawer. "It was taken in 1917," he said, handing it to me.

I looked at the sepia photograph. A young woman with dark hair, parted in the middle, her expression pleasant but not quite a smile, was sitting in a deckchair, facing the camera. In the background, lying on the grass but looking up at the camera, was the smiling Saxe. With his neatly parted hair and military moustache he looked quite dashing and appeared happy. When I examined the photograph, I thought it confirmed my impression as to how Saxe had changed; the spark detectable even in this inanimate portrait was no longer in this living person before me.

"What happened?" I asked.

"It was all very civilised. I like her husband Nick Bagenal and I think he likes me. He was ready to stand back and let me marry her but I couldn't interfere with their happiness. Barbara chose him but she offered to have some sort of ménage à trois with both of us. I thought that suggestion too much like the Judgement of Solomon."

"Yes. You can't resolve matters of the heart like a diplomatic treaty."

"It's not the sex I care about: I wanted to share my life with her. That's the problem with the Bloomsbury Group; I do believe they think sex is the answer to everything. Anyway, let's not rake over old coals: I am past that now and I am still friends with both Barbara and Nick, especially Barbara."

I could tell he wasn't truly resigned to his fate and it is the merest flicker of hope that continually turns the knife in the wound but I was glad to drop the subject too. I invited him out to lunch but he declined the offer and I was not sorry; sad people have a way of lowering one's own level of optimism and resilience to the misfortunes of life. There's always the slight dread that a joyless temperament might be catching and it pushes people away. I didn't stay much longer but left with the sense I was abandoning Saxe and I made it my business to stay in touch with him over the years, come what may.

Knowing his fondness for music, I always coaxed him into playing the piano whenever I visited. As he played a piece of Chopin or Schubert, perhaps Beethoven or Brahms, his expression would take on a more relaxed tone and he would seem revitalised, if only for a few minutes, before he fell back into his realm of quiet despondence. I determined each time to see him more often, but of course I didn't.

# VII

# *NEW YORK*

MUCH AS I HAD OFTEN CLAIMED TO KNOW Maynard, I didn't really get to know him properly until the 1930s. Even then it was only through a fortuitous sequence of events that our relationship was formed. In the 1920s I was busy building my career and, with Lina, raising our family which, by the end of the decade, had grown to three children: a son, Charles, and another daughter, Lilac, in addition to Catherine.

If you mentioned the word 'Charleston' to most people in the 1920s they would assume you were talking about the dance which took its name from that of a tune written by James P. Johnson in 1923 for a hit musical, *Runnin' Wild*. It would certainly have been my first thought too as that dance seemed to epitomise the so-called 'Roaring Twenties': that decade after the post-war depression. The economy boomed for nearly a decade and social and cultural change, epitomised by trends in fashion, design, new technology and entertainment, were rapid and radical. Of course, not every industry recovered its pre-war strength, nor did everybody enjoy better living standards. It was a change in the tempo of life and social attitudes for some, as long as it lasted, while for most it made little difference to their lives. Later, 'Charleston' would take on a different connotation for me when I resumed my association with Maynard Keynes.

As is so often the case, not least in the financial markets, there is a tendency to become complacent in life, to assume that an upward trend, once established, can be expected to go on indefinitely. The wise caution of 'saving for a rainy day' is accepted in principle by most but frequently neglected when times are good. Add to that the herd instinct which manifests itself in so many aspects of human life and we have a recipe for the frequent bouts of irrationality which bedevil the stock markets. A rising market builds confidence upon confidence and too many investors are ready to buy as the market nears its peak. Investors see a share which rises in price day after day, sometimes quickly, and they assume the price will continue to rise indefinitely. This leads many of them to buy just as the price levels off. When the price moves downwards, they lose faith in their judgement and sell at a loss. I am sure many investors repeatedly buy at the top and sell at the bottom when of course we should be aiming to do the exact opposite. Basing future expectations on past performance may work for a time, even a long time, but not necessarily and never forever. My role at such times, as impressed on me by my old senior at the firm, Nobby Dilhorne, is to add a note of caution to my advice and to warn that the next correction in the market will come one day, probably when we least expect it. Later my role will be to help those who got in a jam because they ignored my advice to salvage what they can from the ruins of their over-confidence.

Perhaps because the roaring twenties were associated with faster economic and social change and get rich quick schemes it seemed to me that as the decade went on, people were less prepared to wait and more willing to take on risk to achieve their social and financial ambitions. This was especially the case in the United States, where those who watched the ever-rising stock market but were unable to share this rapid accumulation of wealth because of a lack of funds, were enticed to join the ever-growing ranks of people borrowing money to buy shares. This practice had long been established in the United States but now it boomed as more and more people developed an insatiable desire to 'get a piece of the action' as they often put it. The borrowing usually took the form of leveraged purchase of shares in which an investor would have to find only a fraction of the cost of their purchase, say ten per cent, and the rest would be borrowed at a reasonable rate of interest. As long as prices continued to rise all was well. For a fraction of the full cost the investor could make a substantial profit. The more people buying shares, the higher the demand and so prices continued their upward trend, with everyone making a profit. But, as in the game of pass the parcel, if prices eventually fell, any leveraged investor still holding the shares when the music stops suffered a loss often much higher than their original investment.

I first became aware of the extent of this risky activity of leveraged share purchase when I went to New York in May 1928. It was primarily a short holiday for Lina and me to coincide with her birthday. Between two four-day journeys by liner across the Atlantic there was the opportunity for a few days' sightseeing, a shopping expedition for Lina and a show on Broadway for us both. We sailed on the *Aquitania* and enjoyed the benefit of its exquisite interiors fashioned after English stately homes. On Broadway, we saw *Animal Crackers*, starring the Marx Brothers, which they would later make into a film. We both enjoyed it immensely once we had acclimatised to the Marx Brothers' style of humour and their anarchic, though not entirely preposterous, view of the world.

On the day that Lina went shopping, I paid a courtesy visit to one of the New York brokers who acted on our behalf for the purchase and sale of New York securities. Bernard H Meadows was the senior partner and my opposite number in the New York firm, and I had the pleasure of meeting him in the flesh for the first time, though we had spoken frequently on the telephone. He showed me round the Stock Exchange, that fine classical building already dwarfed by its later additions. Then we went back to his office. Against a background of clacking ticker tape and the shouting of orders on the telephones in the outer office, Meadows, a balding man of extremely large proportions and a jovial manner, spent over an hour explaining the recent history of the market in New York and we discussed the differing practices of the London and New York exchanges. His firm had a private restaurant attached to the boardroom and, over a very good lunch at which he exercised his excellent appetite, we discussed the opportunities for stockbroking and related activities arising from changing investment trends and the growth of overseas opportunities.

By the time coffee arrived we had turned our attention to the continued buoyancy and upward trend of the New York market and the growing practice of leveraged investments, but not before I sampled the excellent brandy he poured for me.

"This is very good. How do you manage to serve good wines with lunch and now brandy without falling foul of the prohibition laws?"

Meadows smiled. "It is illegal to buy alcoholic drinks but not to drink them and alcohol bought before the law came into force can be drunk legally. Shall we say that I laid down some substantial stocks before prohibition was introduced? Sooner or later, someone will get rid of this ridiculous law which has been a blessing to those who like imposing their values on others and a boon to the criminal element, but a confounded nuisance to everyone else."

"I see the New York market is continuing its good run," I observed.

"Yes, since 1920 the market has risen on average nearly twenty per cent a year," said Meadows, lighting a large Havana cigar.

"That's extraordinary. You are not worried about a bubble?"

He sipped his brandy and dragged on his cigar while he pondered the question for a few moments. "Can't say I am. From the start of this decade the American economy has grown year on year and had some very good years indeed, and the market is reflecting that. We may have entered a new economic era and, as always in the past, we don't usually recognise a major change when it happens. It's only looking back that we recognise it for what it was."

"But in the market leveraged investment is presumably behind some of the rise in demand for stock?"

"That is true. Leverage has been a major contributory factor to the growth of the number of retail investors and the rise of a shareholding democracy," he said. "I believe it's a good thing for ordinary people to have a stake in the economy, not just as a worker, but also as a part-owner of the companies that drive the economy forward. It's a healthy development that capital ownership is more widely spread."

"You are not concerned that people will get over-stretched?"

"Not if they act wisely and know their limits."

"Perhaps the smaller investor might be better off putting his money in an investment trust to spread the risk."

Meadows smiled. "Actually, those trusts use leveraging themselves to invest in stocks and in other investment trusts. It's rather like the evolution of the banking system. As I'm sure you know, banks at first only lent out a portion of the deposits made with them. But they knew that when a borrower spent the loan it was paid back into the bank as a new deposit and some of that was lent out too. Soon the banks realised that they were lending the same money out over and over again. As not every customer draws their money out at once, banks need only keep a small proportion of deposits in cash while continuing to expand their loans."

"The system works as long as there is not a loss in confidence and a run on the bank."

"Quite so. As long as the market rises, taking into account the regular minor corrections, the system will be able to support leveraging. We have no reason to think that won't be the case in the future as the economy continues to grow. Another brandy?"

I had enjoyed the day and meeting Meadows and some of his colleagues and I had learned a lot too. Yet I found myself repeatedly going over in my mind my conversation with Meadows about the extent of leveraged investment in the US stock markets. I had seen it so many times in my own career when a rising market led to over-confidence and a bubble which would eventually burst but this boom was built on a massive expansion of risk-taking and borrowing. I was very troubled. While not having experienced a loss of any kind that day, I nonetheless felt that my financial position was less secure than I had considered it a few hours earlier, a feeling not eased by Lina's shopping bills when we met later in our hotel.

Over the next few months, despite my principal concern being the London market, I kept my eye on the US market and tracked its continuing upward trend. By the summer of 1929 I was no longer troubled; I was extremely alarmed. In the previous ten years the US economy had grown by about sixty per cent, a very creditable performance. The US stock market index could be expected to have grown too as it to some extent reflects the growing value of its constituent companies. But the index had actually grown by nearly six hundred per cent in that same ten-year period. I immediately issued a circular to all our clients, warning them of the danger of over-heating in the US market which could negatively affect share prices in London if there was a severe fall or even a serious correction. I advised them to ensure that their finances would be able to withstand any major downturn in the market. I didn't consult with my partners about this and one or two thought I had been guilty of panic-mongering. It is true that by no means everyone agreed with me, one of my colleagues telling me to my face that I had lost my nerve, perhaps even my sense of proportion. Many commentators thought the market, which always anticipates future trends in the economy, was not excessively high because the economy could be expected to continue its rapid growth: the same argument put forward to me by Meadows in New York. Such views were ignoring the fact that the market has its own momentum independent of the pattern of economic activity.

# VIII

# *CHARLESTON*

Because of our friendship, though not knowing the details of his private investments, when I called round on one of my infrequent visits to Saxe, I advised him of my concerns for the over-heated stock market.

"That's very kind of you to think of me, Lewis, but most of my money is in gilts and longs of one sort or another; I don't tend to play the whole field in my investments."

"Talking of playing the field, I am going to the next Brighton meeting. Would you be interested?"

"Thanks for the offer but I don't think so. Actually, I am going down to Sussex on Saturday week, to Charleston. I haven't visited there for a while."

I smiled. "Gosh, it's ages since I have seen any of the Bloomsbury set, not counting you of course; I bumped into Adrian Stephen a few years ago but that's about all since before the war. Oh, I saw Duncan Grant at an exhibition too several years ago."

"Why don't you come with me?"

"I don't suppose they'd be interested in seeing me."

"Nonsense. I'm sure they'll be delighted to make your

acquaintance again, especially as you are one of my old friends."

"May I bring my wife?"

"I don't see why not. People call in for no particular reason all the time."

I accepted the invitation readily, for myself as a possible opportunity to meet Maynard again and for Lina because I guessed she would be pleased to meet some more of this exotic group of which Saxe was a member. When I arrived home, I told her of our invitation.

"To have tea with some of the Bloomsbury Group?" Her face lit up.

"That's what he suggested."

"I would love to," she said.

I was pleased that she was pleased. Lina had read both *Mrs Dalloway* and *To the Lighthouse* by Virginia Woolf and when she had discussed the first of these with me, I had mentioned that I had met Virginia before the war, as well as knowing Leonard and Adrian Stephens.

She recalled that conversation now. "I was so jealous when you told me you had met her. Especially as it was before she was married and become famous. You went to Bloomsbury when they were just getting started and you know Duncan Grant and Leonard Woolf and Adrian Stephens. You are very nearly one of the group yourself."

I smiled. "I don't think they would agree."

"I do hope we have an opportunity to meet Virginia and Leonard, I'd love to tell her how much I enjoy her writing."

"She might not be there."

"No, of course not." There was a flicker of disappointment but then her expression brightened again. "Still, it will be interesting to see any of them."

Saxe had planned to go by train on that Saturday and stay

until Sunday but I offered to give him a lift. We picked him up from his flat in my new Humber and we stopped for lunch on the way down. Saxe and Lina had met only a couple of times so most of the initial conversation was funnelled through me until we stopped at an inn on the A22. Over a lunch of beef and kidney pie with a pint of ale, a half in the case of Lina, Saxe gave us the background to Charleston farmhouse and its place in the Bloomsbury Group. It had been the home of Clive and Vanessa Bell since the Great War and Duncan Grant had shared their home since that time. Maynard had also spent many weekends there since the end of the war. He had found it peaceful and idyllic there and took advantage of the Bells' generosity to do much of his writing at Charleston, away from the hurly-burly of London and the demands on his time when he was at Cambridge. After his marriage to the ballerina Lydia Lopokova in 1925, Maynard took a lease on Tilton, a farmhouse near Charleston, as his country retreat. This added to Charleston becoming something of a country hub for the Bloomsbury Group since, as Saxe had intimated, it was common for large numbers of the group and their acolytes to descend on Charleston at weekends, especially as Virginia and Leonard Woolf also had a house in the area, Monk's House, in Rodmell, only eleven miles away.

"My particular reason for going down this weekend is that one of my oldest friends, Lytton Strachey, will be there, and Dora Carrington, the painter, who is a companion of Strachey."

I wondered what he meant by the word 'companion' but left it to one side. "I remember you and Lytton were in the Apostles together," I said.

"Yes, and we bought the Mill at Tidmarsh together in 1917. Lytton and Carrington lived there until they moved to Ham Spray House a few years ago. I liked Tidmarsh very much and used to stay there on occasion."

I glanced at Lina and could tell she was as puzzled as I was by the domestic arrangements of the people involved. I thought she looked beautiful sitting there, in her very pretty printed summer dress, and wearing a large straw hat, which she thought appropriate in case she met "any of the bohemians" as she put it.

Saxe went to the bar to order some more drinks and Lina said, "I wonder who else we'll see."

"Any one in particular you are hoping will be there, apart from Virginia Woolf?"

She pondered for a moment. "Well, perhaps E M Forster; I have read some of his books too and Lytton Strachey and of course Maynard, I have at least met him before."

"Not the artists? We are more likely to see those as Charleston is occupied by artists and owned by an art critic."

"Yes, but I don't know them at all whereas I feel I have some vague idea what the writers might be like from their books."

"Personally, I think they are a rum old lot. If it hasn't happened already, they are in danger of being more famous for the lives they lead than for their accomplishments."

Lina laughed. "The more eccentric they are the better; after all, we don't have to live with them."

After we left the inn, we motored on and a few miles after driving through Lewes we turned off the main road, took the back road for a short distance and then off a fork which took us onto a rough farm track. At the end of the track was the farmhouse.

"I suppose this is what is meant by 'far from the madding crowd,'" I muttered, as the track gave the car's springs a tough time and Lina, I thought unnecessarily, laughed when she turned and saw the grimace on my face.

When we came to a halt outside the house, I was unable to stop myself from testing the suspension and having a quick glance underneath the car, again to the amusement of my dear wife, which in turn gave me the opportunity to exercise my powers of self-restraint. Saxe stood watching me for a moment.

"Trouble with the car?" he asked.

"No, it's not used to going cross country; just checking it's not too upset," I said.

Despite my friendship with Saxe Sydney-Turner, I was still only vaguely aware of the full composition of the Bloomsbury Group. Saxe was not forthcoming on such matters but he had mentioned a few names in passing and I had met some of the core members at the party in Brunswick Square in 1912. The group and its associates had so grown over the years that I did not hazard a guess as to whom we might meet when we followed Saxe into the garden, he not bothering to go to the front door. I glanced at the house as we passed. It was a good size and, although unpretentious, had lots of windows, which I assumed would be important to painters.

It was a warm, sunny day and several people were seated in deckchairs. I recognised one straight away from Cambridge days, reinforced by a photograph I had seen recently: Lytton Strachey, the biographer of, among others, Queen Victoria. He was wearing a light-coloured summer suit and Panama hat and sported a long rust-coloured beard. He held a slim book in his long slender fingers. I also recognised Duncan Grant, having seen him relatively recently. The other man I thought might be Clive Bell but the two women I had not met, though I guessed one must be Vanessa Bell. A young girl of eight or nine was seated on the grass, reading a book.

"Ah, look who's here!" cried Strachey, in his familiar, rather high-pitched voice.

"Good afternoon," said Saxe, glancing round at the group. "I have brought two friends over to see you: Lewis and Lina

Durrington. You will remember Lewis from Cambridge, Lytton?"

Strachey stood, placing his book carefully on his chair, and shook hands with Saxe. Then he peered at me through his bookworm spectacles. "Can't say I do. I never remember a face." He laughed briefly in his screeching voice and shook hands with me, "Of course. I trust you are keeping well, Durrington?"

"Yes, thank you, and you?"

"Quite well, thank you." He turned to Lina and nodded slightly.

While we were being introduced to Strachey, a youngish looking woman jumped up and embraced Saxe. "How lovely to see you, Saxe," she said.

Saxe introduced her to us as Dora Carrington. She smiled and corrected the introduction to "Carrington, I don't use Dora." Despite this abrupt opening statement, she seemed very friendly and appeared more youthful than the others with her pretty face topped by a mop of red-gold hair.

Duncan Grant walked over and greeted me warmly. "Lewis, so nice to see you again, it must be a few years," he said. He retained his dark, slightly dishevelled hair and was wearing a white shirt without a tie underneath a linen jacket which looked as if it had been put through a mangle.

"I don't think you know Vanessa?"

"No, we haven't met."

"How are you?" she said with a pleasant smile. "Did you have a good journey down?"

"Yes, thank you."

"How did you get to know Saxe?" she asked.

"At Cambridge. He was a few years ahead of me but he came back to Cambridge regularly for meetings of the Apostles and we met at a bridge party."

In appearance she was quite different from her sister, Virginia. I found her very attractive, though her sultry looks had had the edge slightly taken off by middle age and her clothes were comfortable rather than fashionable. I wondered how it was that she and her husband had shared their home for so long with Duncan Grant and what was the precise relationship between Vanessa and Duncan.

This sense of puzzlement was only enhanced by the presence of Clive Bell, who I remembered vaguely from Cambridge but hadn't seen since. He was polite but again did not engage us in conversation. I felt by his expression that he cultivated the look of an intellectual and by that I mean someone whose thoughts rarely dwell on the mundane. This look was assisted by a high forehead, itself accentuated by a receding hairline, which was revealed when he removed his hat. He was smoking a pipe, an accessory which further adds to a man's ruminative appearance.

"I'll make some tea," said Vanessa, Dora offering to help and accompanying her into the kitchen.

Lina looked down at the young girl, who had watched our arrival with interest but had not been included in the introductions.

"Hello, what's your name?"

The girl sat up. "I am Angelica Bell."

"Well, I am very pleased to meet you, Angelica Bell. I am Lina Durrington. What are you reading?"

"Just a book," said the girl and trotted off to join her mother.

"What a sweet girl. Your daughter?" asked Lina of Clive Bell. He responded with a nod.

While refreshments were being prepared, Duncan went off to fetch some more chairs and Saxe gave us a brief tour of the garden. He explained that it had been laid out by Duncan and Vanessa in the ten years they had lived at the farmhouse. It was truly a work of beauty with a rectangular lawn and its gravel paths leading the visitor round flower beds displaying Mediterranean influences among its mixture of English cottage plants. There was also a large, attractive pond, a shaded orchard, and a kitchen garden where they grew their own vegetables and herbs.

"They were helped in their design by Roger Fry," said Saxe, "but the final result is very much down to them."

Having thought I was beginning to understand the make-up of the household of Charleston, I was thrown into some confusion again.

When we had all taken our seats, tea was served by Carrington and a young maid named Grace.

"Did you enjoy your walk round the garden?" asked Carrington of Lina, as she served her with tea.

"Yes, it's delightful."

"Isn't it? It always gives me such joy. It's so beautiful and inspires one to want to paint. My friend, Barbara Hiles, is a painter and used to like to camp in the garden." She laughed.

At the mention of Barbara Hiles I remembered her name then realised she was Saxe's lost love and I cast him an involuntary glance but he appeared unperturbed.

"You are a painter too, I believe?" asked Lina.

"I do a bit," said Carrington.

Clive Bell removed his pipe from his mouth and leaned over. "Like so many of the great painters, Michelangelo, Titian, Raphael, Rembrandt and so forth, Carrington is known by just one name. Unlike them, she hides her light under a bushel."

Carrington looked a little flustered and I, presumably Lina too, did not quite know what to make of that statement but let it pass.

Lytton Strachey turned to me. "And what do you do these days, Durrington? Are you still something in the City?"

"Yes, I'm a stockbroker."

Strachey joined his long fingers together in front of him. "Ah! The black arts of the world of the markets. A tiresome business: having to attend to the financial matters of moronic rich men."

"I do not delve into the intellectual capabilities of my clients but if they are wise enough to pick me as their advisor, their intelligence can hardly be faulted."

Strachey smiled and turned to Lina. "How do you occupy your time, Mrs Durrington?"

Lina stared at him for a moment as if she wasn't sure this was a question worth answering. Then she ignored the possibility of a veiled insult and replied, "Nothing out of the ordinary for a woman with a comfortable income, a good husband, three lively children and an interest in the local community."

Strachey was unabashed. "Very good, and where is this community?"

"We live on the Thames in Berkshire, near Hurley, between Maidenhead and Henley."

"I know Hurley well, a charming village. The Thames divides for a while there doesn't it? One can find oneself on an island without realising it."

"Are you from Berkshire?"

"No, I was born in London but I lived in Berkshire, at Tidmarsh, for some time. A fine county, especially since most people are unable to locate it."

Lina nodded. "Yes, Saxon told us you lived in Berkshire. You live in Wiltshire now, I believe?"

"Generally speaking, yes."

The small talk continued over tea and cake, punctuated by the odd aphorism, epigram or veiled criticism shared by one to another of the intellectuals seated around us, only to be interrupted by the arrival of Maynard and Lydia Keynes.

"Thank goodness, you have arrived, Maynard. Now Lewis will have someone who can talk his language," said Clive Bell.

"Hello, Lewis, how are you? I think we last met at the Alhambra, and Mrs Durrington, delighted to see you again. I don't think you know my wife, Lydia."

Lydia was not quite what I expected. She had a sparkling demeanour and I thought her charming as we exchanged some pleasantries. Her face was round and, though quite slim, she had always lacked the sylphlike figure one associates with the great ballerinas. I congratulated her on her fine performance at the Alhambra but she smiled a little wistfully and said that it was a long time ago. Her career had widened to include acting as well as ballet and she now presented programmes too, on the BBC, which Lina and I had enjoyed.

Lydia began talking to Lina and various other conversations resumed in the garden. Maynard pulled up a chair near me. "What do you think of the markets at present?" he asked.

I knew that Maynard was a professional investor, having been told by Saxe that he managed the substantial investments of King's College, as well as managing his own portfolio. "I believe they are overheated," I replied.

"Surely not; the commodity markets have had substantial falls lately."

"That's precisely my point. If the real economy is weakening, how can the stock markets continue with their inexorable rise?"

He didn't reply, merely stroking his moustache while he considered my conundrum.

Having hesitated for a moment or two before expounding my much-derided view of the markets, I now plunged in. "The nub of the matter is that earlier this year I visited a fellow stockbroker in New York and we discussed the rapid growth in the prices of New York stocks over the past decade, which far outstrips the growth of the US economy. I am certain that the recent rapid growth in stock prices, especially in the United States, is the consequence of a bubble and the higher it goes, the greater the danger of a major fall in the market. A rapid rise in stock prices is further fuelled by the herd instinct as investors become afraid they will be left behind, believing those already in the market must know something they do not, whereas that is not necessarily so. In addition, there is a greater tendency in New York for people to borrow money to buy shares, thereby becoming too leveraged if things go wrong. I accept that the London market is not built to the same degree on such speculation but 'when New York sneezes, London catches a cold' as the saying goes. I have offered all my clients my advice to be prudent and watchful and beware of being overstretched."

"It's very kind of you to share your concerns with me, Lewis, and I do respect your expertise in such matters. Perhaps my position puts me less at risk because I have disposed of most of my American stock holdings."

"May I ask why?"

Maynard smiled. "I can't claim excellent foresight. The fact of the matter is that I have suffered a setback due to the recent heavy falls in commodities, especially in tin, rubber and cotton. I attempted to recoup my early losses through leveraging to enable me to finance further purchases of commodities, so far without success, so that I am down quite a bit in those areas."

"I think you should seriously consider reducing your positions even if that means accepting further losses."

"Really, Lewis, I can't agree. I am down on my commodity holdings so to realise my losses while the stock market is rising would surely be a dangerous strategy."

"I understand your reluctance but a heavy fall in the financial markets is almost certain to reduce confidence in the real economy, especially commodities, so it might be wiser to sell now and buy back in the future when prices fall, especially as you are highly leveraged."

Maynard smiled. "The world economy will continue to grow, and industrialisation will grow at a faster rate so, even if there is a setback in commodity prices in the short term, I am prepared to wait."

I had heard this argument before many times and merely shrugged. "It's just my view. In the long run you may well be right."

"I am most grateful for your advice, but I have my own views on the market cycle too," he said, a little condescendingly.

I felt I had no further advice to offer and the conversation came to an abrupt end. Maynard rose from his chair and walked over to speak to Lytton while I listened in to the various other conversations taking place in search of one I found particularly interesting. Because of the Bloomsbury Group's reputation for intellectual but witty conversation, I assumed there would soon develop a grand debate over some philosophical, ethical or aesthetic principle and I was ready to be a mere spectator to a session of high-powered verbal cut and thrust. But nothing of the kind developed over tea this afternoon. Even Maynard, who from my limited experience was not really one for small talk, said nothing of importance. Instead, the interchange of chit-chat continued, though always laced with witty or controversial comments and the occasional sardonic or slightly insulting turn of phrase. This state of listless calm was interrupted by the arrival of two young men, neither of whom I recognised but whose arrival injected a shot of electricity into the proceedings.

Their sudden appearance was most remarkable in the reaction generated among the rest of the guests. While Lina and I stared inquisitively, and the Bells and Duncan Grant smiled in welcome, Carrington jumped up and retreated into the background, Maynard flushed and looked slightly embarrassed, Lydia huffed and walked off into the house and Lytton Strachey chortled, "The phrase that comes to mind involves a cat and pigeons."

Ignoring or oblivious to the new undercurrent, Duncan walked over to his new guests and greeted them both. "Sebastian and Stephen, glad you could both make it. Do you know Lewis and Lina Durrington?" He gestured to Lina and me.

"No, I don't think so," said Sebastian and he shook hands with me in a rather diffident way.

I smiled. "I'm sure we haven't met and if we have, we have both forgotten. This is my wife, Lina."

He laughed, "Sebastian Sprott," he said, giving Lina a charming smile. May I introduce Stephen Tomlin, an old friend?"

While Sprott was tall, elegant and had a calm demeanour, Tomlin seemed the diametric opposite: short, with a large head and thick neck, he seemed almost to exude energy. Sprott nodded to us and went to speak to Maynard.

"Lovely to see you again, Maynard. How are you?" He seized Maynard's right hand and clasped his shoulder with his other hand. He greeted Lytton warmly, if less effusively. The three of them exchanged a few pleasantries.

Carrington smiled at Tomlin and said, "Stephen is a very fine artist and sculptor. He will achieve great things."

Before anyone could comment, we were joined by Lytton who asked Tomlin, "How is my niece?"

This apparently bland question resulted in an anything but bland reaction. Carrington gave a gasp. "You can be so beastly," she said and went running off into the house.

"What did I say?" said Lytton.

Tomlin shook his head. "She doesn't need always to be reminded."

We took the silence that followed as an opportunity to resume our seats and Tomlin and Strachey walked off, speaking sotto voce.

The arrival of Sebastian acted as a catalyst to give a faster tempo to the conversation as he was asked about his recent social engagements. He mentioned a visit to Lady Ottoline Morrell at her home in Gower Street.

"How is she?" asked Duncan, "I haven't seen her for ages."

Sebastian shook his head in resignation. "Poor Ottoline, life has not been as kind to her as she was to others. You know she had to sell Garsington Manor?"

Duncan nodded. "Yes, Carrington told us it was on the cards."

"Well, now she has fallen ill. Cancer of the jaw I believe."

"Oh dear," said Duncan, "I am sorry."

This revelation brought an end to all the other conversations in the garden and there followed a general reminiscence by most of those present of the pleasant times enjoyed at Garsington Manor. Strachey, Grant, Bell among many others had taken refuge as pacifists during the Great War, nominally working on the estate but actually enjoying the largesse of Lady Ottoline and her husband, the Liberal Member of Parliament, Philip Morrell. Ottoline had held great lavish parties and soirées after her move to Garsington Manor and the house had become a magnet for artists, writers and others who called themselves her friends. As a patron of the arts, she had encouraged and supported young new artists: Stanley Spencer, Mark Gertler and Carrington among others.

"It's very sad," said Sebastian. "Illness befalling her on top of financial difficulties and the problem of her husband's mental illness."

"Can nothing be done about Philip?" asked Clive Bell.

Sebastian shook his head. "It is difficult to discern the exact cause of his illness."

"Sometimes, he is quite lucid," said Carrington. "Poor Ottoline, she has still to support him when there is none to help her. She could not afford all the support she gave to artists and writers and all the wonderful entertaining, but we all just accepted her generosity."

"We didn't know," replied Duncan.

"We didn't ask," said Carrington.

There was silence for a few moments. Even Lina looked down, as if it were her shame too, then Sebastian asked me, "Did you see active service, Lewis?"

"Yes, I was stationed in Egypt and saw some action in Gaza and Palestine."

"Ah, Egypt. How wonderful. I love the culture and the exotica of Egypt and the Maghreb; so close to Europe but a different world and, marvellous though it is, you must keep your wits about you. I remember a very strange incident when Maynard and I were on holiday in Tunisia and Algeria. You know what I'm referring to, Maynard?"

"I could hardly forget it," Maynard smiled.

"What happened?" asked Lina.

"When we were in Algeria, Maynard and I used the services of a street urchin to clean our shoes. He did a good job and we gave him a tip but he complained the tip wasn't enough and when we went to walk off he and his friends began pelting us with stones. I was worried the situation might get out of control and suggested Maynard give him some more money to get rid of them."

Maynard laughed. "I knew the tip we had given was the going rate and they were just trying it on, so I refused."

"Quite right too," said Strachey. "I believe in some Arab

countries one is likely to be stoned for rather more interesting offences than refusing to give a tip."

I noticed Lydia was not amused as she rose and took her cup and plate into the house.

There followed an entertaining and relaxed exchange of tales from travels in the north of Africa while we finished our tea.

Despite Vanessa's gentle protests, Lina insisted on helping to clear the tea things away and followed Grace into the kitchen, holding a tray of crockery. Vanessa and Duncan went off with Saxon, though without explanation, and I was left with Bell, Sprott, Tomlin, Lytton and Maynard. I was merely the silent, though amused, audience as they exchanged some thoughts about Bell's critique of a couple of recent exhibitions he had attended, their repartee richly embroidered by an interchange of pithy and witty comments, light-hearted insults and arguments. As I half expected, my silence eventually provoked a question as to my particular interests in art from Clive Bell.

I thought for a few moments before being as honest as I could. "I fear that I have very little artistic appreciation, certainly in the pictorial arts. Although I often admire the technical expertise displayed in a picture or a sculpture and find it visually pleasing, I hardly ever feel moved by one in any way. This would not always be the case, say, with a piece of music or a poem or even a passage of prose."

All four of them were momentarily silenced: Maynard with a slight smile on his face, Lytton a quizzical expression, Sprott grinning, Tomlin impassive and Bell thoughtful.

I noticed that Lydia had reappeared from the house and was listening to our conversation with a wry smile.

"Do you regret that without the pictorial arts something is lacking in your life?" asked Bell, leaning towards me.

I smiled. "Doesn't an aesthete believe in 'art for art's sake' and that it need deliver no social or moral purpose? I suppose my answer to your question is 'not really' as I don't believe in art in that way. Nor do I regret that I derive no pleasure from certain pastimes or hobbies for which I have no emotional attachment, just as a true atheist has no regret for not having a faith."

"Point well made, Lewis," said Sprott.

Maynard laughed. "You can't argue about art with an intelligent Philistine, Clive."

"Lewis is not so different from you, Maynard, my darling," chided Lydia, squeezing his hand. "Were you ever emotionally moved by one of your paintings as much as when you watched the *Sleeping Beauty* so many times?"

Maynard smiled but said nothing.

"It was not the music so much as the dancer," observed Bell.

"I see Saxe is here. Have you seen much of him at Ham Spray lately?" asked Tomlin of Lytton.

"Not very much. He seems more than ever withdrawn into himself."

"Gerald Brenan says he's one of the greatest bores he's ever known," said Tomlin, looking round belatedly to be sure Saxe was not in earshot, "virtually no conversation and forever showing endless snapshots of his holidays in Finland."

There were one or two sniggers and nods of recognition but Lytton who, throughout the time of my visit had been either acerbic or witty or both in his comments, sat up and retorted angrily, "Brenan and others who speak like that don't know Saxe and what a fine person he is. When we were first at Cambridge together he was full of the joy of life: a poet, a raconteur, a wonderfully erudite and charming speaker on so many subjects."

"I don't remember him like that, I'm afraid. What

happened to change him?" I asked.

"I fear I must bear part of the responsibility for it," replied Lytton. "I have always had an interest in psycho-analysis, as you may know. When we were at Cambridge several of us, Leonard, Saxe and myself included, experimented with what we called 'The Method'. It was a way of helping each other to go further into understanding our true self and Saxe appeared to embrace the idea too much, becoming more and more introspective and perhaps inwardly obsessed. He appears to have retreated from those around him to an extent I find hard to understand. Whatever the reason, he seems unable to find joy in his life anymore."

There was a long silence which was broken by Sprott. "It is extremely dangerous to experiment with psycho-analysis, if you are not qualified to do so. Lytton knows my views on the matter."

"Could nothing be done for him?" I asked.

"He would have to be prepared to engage in some form of analysis and I am not sure he is willing to do so," replied Sprott.

"Whatever sadness afflicts his life now, he has never stopped being a loyal friend," remarked Bell. "He has always been generous with his time and his kindness has been a support to us all."

Someone changed the subject and Lytton picked up his book and our brief sortie into the past lives of the Bloomsbury set was over. I glanced at my watch; it was a quarter to five. I wandered towards the house in search of Lina, feeling restless and ready for home.

At that moment, Lina, Vanessa and Duncan emerged into the warm afternoon, their eyes squinting in the sun. Lina smiled and walked over to me.

"I thought we might be on our way soon," I said to her, as

she linked her arm in mine. "Do you know where Saxe is?"

"He's talking to Carrington in the house at the moment, or rather listening to Carrington. Oh, there he is now."

I checked that Saxe hadn't changed his mind about staying for the night and then we slowly took our leave of the Bloomsbury members. None of them, apart from Saxe and Carrington, expressed any wish to see us again but I was neither surprised nor particularly disappointed; it was not my world.

"Well, what did you think of them?" I asked, as we walked over to the car and I prepared to put the springs through another shake-up.

"There was so much to take in. Carrington is very pleasant and Sebastian too. I had quite a talk with Lydia after everybody had arrived. I had the impression she doesn't like some of them very much."

"Why not?"

"She feels they are rather patronising towards her and rarely engage her in a serious conversation. She thinks perhaps they don't consider her worth it. She said they cannot be bothered to talk about matters they really care about to you unless you are the right kind of person. I think I know what she means, they only chattered about this and that when I spoke to them. I felt rather sorry for her; she is a cultured person and worthy of being treated as such. When I said that to her she said that for them, it is not enough even to be able to do something in the artistic field, you have to be able to talk about it *forever*." Lina raised and lowered her arms in a flamboyant display of resignation, impersonating Lydia.

I laughed. "Poor Lydia."

"It's a bit much," said Lina. "How dare they be so dismissive."

"I think I gave the game away regarding my lack of culture when I told them I didn't have much feeling for painting."

Lina stared at me for a moment. "That's not strictly true and anyhow that should have been an opening to a conversation rather than the end of one."

I started the engine, put the car into gear and we slowly set off on the way back to a proper road.

"Well, that was quite a day," said Lina, holding on to the safety strap by her head as we pitched and rocked along. "I had a lovely time and, despite what Lydia said, I quite enjoyed meeting the Bloomsbury Group. It was enough to see them in their natural habitat, as it were, and to look round the house and exchange a few platitudes. I think I would've found some rambling debate on the relative merits of Rubens and Botticelli or the use of blue by Vermeer beyond me and consequently quite tedious, let alone a full-scale philosophical debate."

"Yes, they are an odd lot, perhaps more eccentric than when I first met them," I said vaguely, my mind still engaged on the business of reaching the Lewes Road, which moments later I did with a sigh.

"But I do understand why Lydia sometimes feels uncomfortable and out of place," continued Lina. "There *was* an atmosphere at times and strange, knowing looks were passed one to another when something was said. Why are some of them unkind about your poor friend Saxe? He's one of the set after all."

I shrugged. "Saxe is different from the others; I think they have diverged away from him in some ways. I am surprised Maynard is so close to them still as his career has developed very differently from the rest."

"Lydia says his interest in the arts is so important to him and they are part of that interest. They also find him useful."

"Useful?"

"Well, as you say, his professional life is very different to theirs. He is a wealthy man and he picks up the bills for some of their projects and other expenses. He pays more than his fair share to be part of the group."

"Well, Maynard is surely too astute to be taken for a fool; he must be doing it out of kindness and friendship."

"I suppose so. As some of them obviously took advantage of Ottoline Morrell, I think they have a sense of entitlement. Others should be pleased to bestow favours on them because of who they are. She told me one or two other things while you and Maynard were talking about financial matters. I didn't quite know what to make of them."

"What sort of things?"

"The various complicated relationships within the Bloomsbury Group. Do you know anything about them?"

"Not really. Saxe did tell me that many of the Bloomsbury people are somewhat fluid in their sexual relationships; I think, for example, that there is an odd situation to do with the Bells and Duncan Grant."

Lina laughed. "You might say that. Charleston is the home of Duncan and Vanessa who live as husband and wife. Clive Bell doesn't actually live there at all. He just visits from time to time, to see the children obviously. The Bells keep up appearances for the sake of their children."

"I thought there was something odd going on when Duncan played the host, and the garden was all about Duncan and Vanessa. Well, poor Clive."

"I don't think you need worry about him. He has a lady friend, Mary Hutchinson, who is also something to do with the Bloomsbury Group. She's a niece of Lytton and is also involved with Aldous Huxley and his wife. Lydia mentioned various other relationships between just the ones that were there today: Lytton Strachey is linked in some way with Carrington, who was in a relationship with Stephen Tomlin who is now married to Julia Strachey who is the niece of Lytton Strachey. That's why Carrington didn't like Lytton mentioning his niece. I got the impression that the Bloomsbury Group is one large merry-go-round: every time it stops, they change partners if they wish. It's enough to make your head spin."

We both laughed and I thought how strange it is that whereas even a minor infidelity may be seen as a serious matter in the normal state of affairs, when a group of people are engaged in complex and frequently changing sexual partnerships the result is regarded as comedic or even farcical.

After thinking about this for a few moments, I said, "Perhaps it is all these complicated relationships that cause the undercurrent you were speaking about; sexual resentment or jealousy about the different relationships that overlap each other. Personally, I find that, whatever their pretensions to be an intellectual group preoccupied with the fine arts and the great philosophical questions of life, their petty obsessions with jealousy about others' success and sexual infidelity undermine their whole image and make them a laughing stock."

"You don't think Lydia is jealous because of Maynard's involvements?"

I was sceptical. "I don't think so. Certainly, Maynard has never given me any suggestion that he is in a relationship with someone else: he always seems absolutely devoted to Lydia."

"I'm glad," she said. "She loves him very much. Did you go into the house?"

"No. What was it like?"

"It was incredible. It is a rather old-fashioned place with limited amenities and simple furniture but quite large. Everywhere there are paintings: on the walls, on easels, leaning against furniture and the fireplaces and some of the walls are painted too. All in all, it is a decorated chaos, but it seemed right for them."

I nodded. "Well, given their Bohemian lifestyle, it would

have been a surprise if they had lived in a dull, conventional home. Did you like the paintings?"

"I didn't have the opportunity to look at them properly. There were lots of portraits, many of them of Bloomsbury Group members, modern style. I liked some. There's a nice one by Vanessa of Saxon playing the piano."

I never saw the paintings as that was to be my one and only visit to Charleston and that night I lay awake, troubled by my visit. Despite my admiration for Maynard, my attempt to help him with financial advice had ended in what seemed a terse and abrupt conversation. I had no particular interest in the eccentric coterie with whom he shared his cultural passions just as, I'm sure, they had little time for me. Yet, much as I tried, I couldn't square the Maynard I knew with his close and enduring association with the Bloomsbury Group. Of course, he shared their love for the arts but what of their chaotic lifestyles and attitudes to morals? Was his devotion to Lydia as I imagined it or did her dislike for them emanate from Maynard's own leanings towards a more nuanced view of faithfulness? After grappling with this conundrum without a clear answer, I finally found some resolution in concluding that, as with Saxon Sydney-Turner, Maynard must be the exception which proves the rule.

# IX

# *ARMAGEDDON*

Despite my own forebodings for the stock markets, the general view was either one of 'wait and see' as practised by Maynard or 'follow the herd instinct' and hope there would be time enough to sell when the market did turn, as practised by many of my clients. A market crash is one of those events which is never forgotten by those caught in it. Whereas a bubble builds over time and is accompanied for at least some people by periods of euphoria and excitement, a crash happens rapidly, and the dominant emotions are those of extreme fear and panic. The first sign of the crisis came in London. On 20th September 1929, Clarence Hatry, a prominent British investor, and several of his associates, were jailed for fraud and forgery over their investment activities. This led to a fall in confidence and a crash in the London market. Optimism among American investors as to the strength of London and other overseas markets declined and the Dow Jones index came under increasing bouts of selling and volatility.

Like a dam developing a crack, the US stock market was subject to an accumulating build-up of selling pressure over the next few weeks. A few of my clients got out but too many hoped this was a minor correction. The crack developed into a breach on 'Black Thursday', 24th October, when a major sell-off occurred at the opening bell and the market fell by eleven per cent almost immediately. The repair team arrived in the form of senior bankers and financiers and they tried to stabilise the market through large purchases of stock in the biggest companies, as they had done with previous heavy falls. In response, the market rallied a little, keeping the fall down to around six per cent on the day. Some of my junior colleagues allowed themselves a sigh of relief but I advised my clients to consider the closure of any US positions on Friday, though trading was difficult during the current chaos.

The weekend gave everybody with a stake in the market time to reflect and when the Stock Exchange opened on Monday it was fear rather than stoicism which dominated proceedings. Heavily leveraged stockholders, fearful of being unable to cover their positions, small investors worried about their life savings, investors still able to take profits built up in the previous three months: all sold. The dam burst and there was a total panic. Even optimists who considered battening down the hatches for better times which would surely come, could not stand by as their wealth shrank and they joined the rush for the exit, though there was often nobody prepared to buy their holdings of stock at any price. I remembered Nobby Dilhorne's remark, 'a wind that rushes through the market from time to time and against which no man can keep his footing' and used the phrase myself to one of my junior partners who sought my opinion. The word 'black' was used again to describe that Monday and the following day as the New York exchange fell nearly a quarter over those two days. Despite the odd short rally and faux recovery in the weeks and months that followed, the trend was steadily downwards from 1930 to 1932.

The Wall Street crash led to markets falling worldwide, especially in London and the rest of Europe. In the days that followed, our offices were bombarded by investors seeking to get out of the market before it was too late. For most it was already too late to recover more than a fraction of their original investments. Market makers failed to answer calls; why would they buy shares for which they had no likelihood of finding a buyer? The floor of the Exchange was often almost deserted and there was little need for the waiters to sweep the floor; some would soon be laid off anyway. Our staff, themselves often carrying losses from their inevitable dabbling in the market, were either idle through a lack of orders or subject to a barrage of frustration from clients unable to sell their holdings or hard-luck stories from clients who were nursing huge losses. During a particularly slack day two junior clerks launched a large, reinforced-paper aeroplane from the top-floor window of our offices in Old Broad Street while another waited to catch it. Unfortunately, it sailed over his head and knocked the top hat off a partner from one of the discount houses and he didn't appreciate the joke. Asked by their manager to discipline those involved, I ticked them off with a light scolding; I knew at least one of them would be out of a job by the end of the year.

In the long period of doldrums in the market following the crash, many investors were wiped out financially. Several of my clients were ruined, one of whom shot himself, while another died in an inexplicable car crash. I offered nothing but sympathy to those who had ignored my warnings. The last thing they wanted to hear was, "I told you so". When they asked for my advice now, I could only suggest that the time for selling had been missed and that they should hang on and wait for the good times to return, which they would, though we could not know when. In the meantime, they must hope that the companies in which they owned shares did not go under. As to those who held foreign government bonds, they would have to put their faith in future governments not to default on their commitments; our safe was full of the ornate certificates of Imperial Russian bonds whose holders had almost no hope of receiving so much as a kopeck.

In the United States the effect on investors was generally worse due to the heavy commitment to leveraged purchases of stock. Many investors did not merely lose their life savings but lost everything. I paid a visit to New York in 1932, on the *Britannic,* the new White Star liner, which was barely a third full, such had been the impact of the economic depression on transatlantic travel. I went to my old colleague, Bernard Meadows, and found him a much-diminished figure, if not physically at least so far as his optimism and confidence were concerned. He recounted to me some of the worst horrors of the crash and the sense of complete hopelessness that accompanied his attempts to mitigate the collapse of his customers' and much of his own wealth. He said he was still haunted by the telephone calls he had received from clients before they had taken their own lives, one of his closest friends among them.

"I see you have not exhausted your cellar," I said as he poured us a drink from a fine champagne cognac.

He smiled. "If ever people needed a drink to steady their nerves in peacetime, it has been during the last three years and not a legal bar open. I can't help feeling some of my clients would have panicked less, maybe even despaired less, if they had been able to fortify themselves with some Dutch courage, I think you call it in England."

"You kept your nerve I'm sure, Bernard."

"I've seen crashes before, though never as bad as this. You think the market has hit the bottom and there's a slight recovery and then it drops heavily again. One day, it will come back; it always does. Either that or in ten years you'll be able to buy the whole Ford Motor Company for a nickel. It's like life in general: there is always a very bad moment when you want to throw in the towel, maybe jump off the cliff, but if you can accept the fact that it can't get any worse than this you are through the worst. That's what I told my clients because I believed it myself. Some could never see beyond the abyss." His voice faded and he stared into the distance.

I didn't interrupt his silence and when he spoke again, I could hear once more the old optimism in his voice. "Of course, the greatest irony is that when the market hits rock bottom or somewhere near it, those who have the money can get in at giveaway prices and wait for the recovery. Joe Kennedy seems to have timed it right, getting out before the crash and now waiting for the economy to pick up; he and others like him will be very rich when the wind blows the other way."

On my way back to my hotel I saw everywhere signs of the impact of the depression on those who had no stocks nor any interest in the financial markets but had been swept out of their jobs by the collapse in the real economy which followed the market crash. Central Park was full of little shanty towns occupied by those who had lost their homes, queues were waiting by a lorry distributing food, longer queues formed at restaurants serving free meals. Surprisingly, many of the queuers were well-dressed, the raiments and the remnants of their former status. There were people sleeping on the streets and others with placards begging for work in a city where one in three had lost their jobs and half the factories had closed.

Of course, there were similar scenes in Britain, especially in those industrial areas which had never recovered from the post-war depression. But I doubt it was ever on the scale witnessed in parts of the United States where the "Dustbowl" drought of the early 1930s led to a collapse of agricultural production and employment and added to the Great Depression already prevailing in manufacturing and other sectors of the economy.

I had said nothing about my own position to Bernard but, when I returned to London, I would follow a similar strategy to Joe Kennedy, though on a smaller scale, and I enjoyed a successful decade in the 1930s. Having sold my personal investments before the crash, I invested in the US stock market near its bottom in 1932 when it was forty-one per cent below its peak and I benefitted from the slow recovery after that. It was not that I was clever or gifted with a special foresight. I made my decision on the basis of probability that, having fallen four years in a row, itself unheard of, the Dow Jones might fall another but was extremely unlikely to fall more than five years in a row. I did not mention my success to anybody other than Lina and my parents because I was embarrassed by my own good fortune. It could only appear as schadenfreude or gross self-satisfaction to reveal that one had made the right choice when those one spoke to had not, especially when I had warned them. It was like being an undertaker during a plague; a success story nobody would cheer.

I suggested to those clients who had some capital that now was the time to re-enter the market while to my more risk-averse clients I advised buying gold, which will always maintain some value. One of my clients purchased exquisite Persian rugs which I was pleased to store in our strong-room, aware that everyone must do what they think best in uncertain times. However, I gently reminded him that he had replaced fear of the uncertainty of the stock market with fear of the uncertainty of the market in Persian rugs as well as fear of the moth.

# X

# *LONDON*

SOON AFTER MY RETURN TO LONDON, I WAS surprised to receive a letter from Maynard. It was an invitation to lunch at the Café Royal in the next couple of weeks. It was the first time Maynard had initiated the contact with me and I was highly flattered. I accepted without delay.

We met in the bar and when I arrived he was drinking a Champagne cocktail. He ordered another for me and gave me a warm welcome. We went through the usual small talk and over lunch he told me of his experiences in the crash.

"It was quite bad," he said, ordering more drinks. "I lost about eighty per cent of my money in the collapse of the commodity markets." He smiled, "Pride comes before a fall. I have only myself to blame."

At first, shocked by his revelation, I said nothing. I thought back to the warning I had given him at Charleston about the weaknesses in the stock market. How strange that this most illustrious lecturer in Economics, former prominent Treasury official, bestselling author and prescient critic of the Versailles peace conference had been unable to avoid the disaster of the Wall Street Crash.

When I did respond, I managed to avoid gloating and offered my sympathy. "We all make mistakes. I hope your college investments were not too badly affected?"

"Not too badly. I have always been more conservative when dealing with someone else's money so though they are down, nobody has done anything worse than reach for the smelling salts. But you were so right; I should have realised that a financial crisis will reverberate through all aspects of the economy."

"It is raining, but I do not believe that it is raining," I said.

Maynard smiled questioningly. "'Moore's Paradox'. You think it applies?" He was referring to a philosophical principle formulated by G E Moore, a member of the Apostles, in which an apparently absurd sentence can still, paradoxically, be true. I had just quoted Moore's most famous example.

"Yes, though perhaps not precisely in the sense Moore used it. From your own sophisticated understanding of markets, you knew that a major fall in the US stock market would affect the commodity markets but you chose not to believe it. You were in effect saying, 'The US stock market is falling and all other markets will also fall, but I do not believe the commodity markets will fall'."

"Why do you think I thought that?"

"Because you wanted to be proved right or because you could not bear to take a loss at that moment. Subjectivity was stronger than your objective understanding of the situation."

Maynard raised his eyebrows but said nothing.

"I know because I have done the same thing myself. I have yet to meet an investor that has never been overcome by emotion or wishful thinking," I said, a little disappointed that even the great Maynard Keynes had been unable to avoid some of the subjective pitfalls of the private investor.

Maynard nodded. "I know you are right. I will try to

rebuild again and I think these events have helped me reassess my investment strategy. I have been too analytical in the past, trying to predict market cycles and so on. I realise now that an intellectual, measured approach cannot withstand the overwhelming force of an irrational market."

I smiled inwardly as he repeated the argument I had tried to impress on him without success at our previous meeting. I waited for him to continue.

"My former approach took no account of the ability of the market to become irrational through the cumulative action of thousands of individuals behaving irrationally. In future, I must accept that reading the economic situation correctly does not guarantee success in the markets in the short run, but it will open up opportunities where wrongheaded pessimism about the true situation has created bargains."

I nodded. He was now following a strategy more familiar to the professional investor and this change in tactics, combined with his own talents and the avoidance of foolish errors, would enable him to make another great fortune in the 1930s. In the next ten years, his reputation as probably the greatest value investor of all time would be established and I would watch this happen as he entrusted my firm to take on much of his stockbroking services.

"The economic situation across Europe and America is dire," I said, changing the subject. "I'm surprised you haven't been drafted in to help."

He smiled and shook his head. "Governments are stuck in the old ways. They believe recessions are caused by deficiencies of supply and that the economy will right itself in the long run. In the meantime, their role must be to balance the budget, raising taxes and cutting expenditure. I don't believe there is any law of science that guarantees that the economy will eventually right itself with full employment; it can just as easily stabilise with much of the capacity of the economy idle. No, the real problem is a deficiency of demand and so they should get rid of the straightjacket of the gold standard and allow the currency to find its true level, as Britain finally did last year. Then boost demand by raising government expenditure. They have resorted to lowering interest rates but this does little to boost investment when business confidence is low. Unfortunately, at the moment they are not listening and probably won't until they have failed with the wrong policies for so long they feel forced to try something new." Unperturbed by his grim assessment of economic policy, he tucked into his saddle of lamb.

In the silence, I returned to my sole meuniere and savoured the taste of the excellent Pouilly Fumé. "How long do you think it will take for the world economy to return to full employment if governments persist with current policies?" I asked.

"Oh, in the absence of the Black Death or a major war, a hundred years, give or take twenty."

I laughed but he didn't.

"I am serious. Our government is still cutting capital expenditure and reducing the wages of teachers and public servants. How is that supposed to stimulate an economy on its knees?"

"You have to keep grinding away at them. They eventually listened about the gold standard."

"Don't worry. I will. Perhaps you would like to attend my Tuesday Club when you can. It involves bankers, financiers, Treasury officials, businessmen and academics and so on and has provided a useful exchange of views for policy-makers involved with economic and business matters."

"I'd be delighted to act as an observer."

"Feel free to contribute. I'm sure your experience will be invaluable."

After this lunchtime meeting, my friendship with Maynard began to flourish. Over the next five years I was the occasional consultant about the market, the regular collaborator at meetings of the Tuesday Club and a conscientious follower of his achievements. His 1930 book, *Treatise on Money*, had influenced government thinking on the gold standard and in the 1930s he became the world's foremost economist and an advisor to political leaders on both sides of the Atlantic.

The year 1934 stood out for me as the year when I felt closest to Maynard and his world. Franklin Roosevelt had been elected US president in 1932 and Maynard was a keen supporter of his efforts to revive the US economy in his 'New Deal', which aimed to reduce the massive unemployment of that period. In May 1934, Maynard visited Roosevelt and they exchanged views on the progress being made in regenerating the US economy and, by implication, the recovery of the world economic system. When he returned from America, Maynard spoke on the New Deal at a meeting of the Tuesday Club, held appropriately enough on the 4th July.

This meeting was referred to as a forum and a number of guests were invited, in addition to the regular members. Once again, Maynard spoke warmly in support of Roosevelt and his achievements. He pointed out that what some had referred to as a Bolshevik administration had saved the capital financial structure of the United States with that country's output now between twenty and thirty per cent recovered from its low. He said that any shortcomings which he had observed in the New Deal could not detract from what it has achieved. "The extent, variety and spread of the recovery is outstanding in economic history." He worried for the future of liberal democracy if it could not act to save the societies in which it operated while the dictatorships of Nazism and Communism were showing that their absolute power enabled them to do whatever was needed to revive their economies. He concluded that, "only the United States is bold and hopeful and has already made a great start towards solving the world's problems in liberal terms."

As I listened to Maynard, the master of his subject, educating and entertaining his audience with the depth of his knowledge and the breadth of his wit, I reflected how blessed I was to be able to count him among my friends. It's an odd experience to have known a great man from before he was famous or renowned. Some can't really accept it and forever after begin their recollection with, "I knew him when he was a nobody," as a way of asserting their own importance. Others are envious or otherwise feel inadequate and belittle the person's achievements with a disparaging remark. There are also those who admire, to a greater or lesser extent, their friend and feel proud to have known him and perhaps feel the warmth of his reflected glory. I like to think of myself as being in the last category with regard to Maynard, though only in terms of admiration for his achievements and contributions to society, for which I deserved no recognition, reflected or otherwise.

I realised my friendship with Maynard was somewhat peripheral to his life as there were so many demands on his time and I saw him only rarely. After the end of the forum, I waited, reading the newspaper, while Maynard was surrounded by the admiring audience, showering him with congratulations. A few journalists were there, seeking a quote or snapping a photo with a one-use flashbulb. As the crowd thinned, I offered my own appreciation and invited him and Lydia to dinner the following week. I was pleasantly surprised that, given his commitments, he accepted my invitation.

Lydia and Maynard arrived in good time and our children, old enough now to appreciate the visit of a famous person, were delighted to meet them. Lydia spent some time talking to young Lilac, now aged five and a very serious little girl who kept her parents perpetually amused by the solemn attitude to her toys or the games she played, uttering a statement to a doll of great gravitas or immense profundity that one would normally associate with a statesman commenting on a diplomatic crisis or the state of the economy. She similarly amused Lydia by testing her on the five positions of ballet, as she had been told that Lydia was a dancer. While they talked, Lydia had a large smile on her face throughout but when Lilac went off to bed Lydia fell silent for a while and she appeared lost in her thoughts. Our other two children were more impressed and less forthcoming with our guests, though Charles asked Maynard to sign his autograph book.

"I'd be delighted to," he said, taking out his fountain pen and signing where Charles indicated.

"Your signature is readable," Charles announced. "Some people just do a squiggle."

Maynard smiled. "Would you like Mrs Keynes's signature? She is very famous."

Charles nodded and took the pen and book over to Lydia. He looked at the signature. "You have a different name," he said.

"It's my stage name. The name I use when I dance."

Charles nodded.

"What other autographs do you have?" asked Maynard.

"A few cricketers and footballers that my father got for me. One used to be captain of the England football team. I have a judge, who is a friend of my father, and also I have Mr Somerville."

"Who is he?"

"He is our member of parliament. He put MP after his name."

"Would you like the autograph of the Chancellor of the Exchequer?"

"I'm not sure what that is," said Charles after thinking for a moment.

"He looks after the government's money," said Maynard.

"Yes, please," said Charles, and handed the autograph book over. Then he and Catherine were sent up to bed.

It was a lovely evening; warm but not as hot as earlier in the month. After dinner, we sat in the garden, overlooking the river while we had liqueurs and brandy. It was the fourteenth of the month, Bastille Day in France, and I referred back to Maynard's speech at the Tuesday Club forum. "Do you think Roosevelt has saved liberal democracy from revolution?" I asked.

"Probably in America, although I doubt it was ever on the cards there; they've had their revolution. But other countries will have to find similar will and imagination to get through this crisis."

"What is Mr Roosevelt like?" asked Lina, a question I knew she had been itching to ask Maynard since I had told her he was coming to dinner.

"Well, I got on with him pretty well. I had assumed he would be more fluent in the use of mathematical concepts but he's no mathematician."

I laughed. "I don't suppose he claims to be. How is he on economics?"

"He understands the economic concepts well enough." Maynard stroked his moustache with just the hint of a smile showing in the corners of his mouth.

"But what is he like as a person?" insisted Lina, smiling at him as she topped up Maynard's glass.

"I found him to be friendly and charming with a lively mind that sends his thoughts off on tangents when he is discussing any serious subject. He has a positive outlook and a powerful self-belief, qualities which I think endear him to the American people. Above all there is a certain nobility about him."

"Why do you say that?" I asked. I had not expected such a tribute for somebody whom Maynard had found a little wanting in his grasp of the great economic issues of the time and who was a politician, a class he had little time for.

"I suppose one might describe him as a patrician, not just because he is from the upper class but because he is noble in his ambitions and cares for all his people. His overriding aspiration is to bring the nation through the current crisis and I believe he has the capacity and the will to achieve this. But, more than that, he has an indomitable spirit which enables him to endure his hardships and trials with patience, humour and resilience and without any apparent self-pity or self-doubt."

"It must be difficult to carry on with all the burdens of office knowing so many people depend on you," said Lina.

Maynard shook his head. "Perhaps a lesser man would buckle under the strain but his endurance knows no bounds. The man suffers from a severe physical impediment which he bears with great fortitude."

"Is he ill?" I asked.

"Not exactly. He has paralysis of some kind in his legs, polio or something of the sort. I thought it strange that he didn't stand when I was shown into his office and he made some reference to it during our conversation when he was talking about the difficulties of obtaining work for those who are less than fully fit. Naturally, I was taken aback as I had no idea about his physical difficulties. He explained that considerable efforts are made to keep it out of the public eye as many Americans would be uneasy about having a President who could walk only with great difficulty. Even the press is inclined to collaborate with this policy."

"Poor man," said Lina.

"I didn't hear him complain. Though he doesn't advertise his condition he doesn't deny it either; it's more a case of not drawing attention to it. Some years ago, he set up a hospital for polio victims at Warm Springs in Georgia, which he regularly attends, especially at Thanksgiving. It's as if everyone knows and accepts the situation but admiration and affection for the President prevents anyone mentioning it. I don't know what he's like when alone or with those closest to him but in public he is always cheery and positive and all those he comes into contact with are carried along on his wave of optimism."

"How wonderful," said Lina. "From what you say, he sounds like a great man."

"I think he probably is a great man," Maynard replied simply.

This was the last time I saw or even heard from Maynard for some time, other than the return of Charles's autograph book which now contained the signature of Neville Chamberlain, then the Chancellor of the Exchequer.

Maynard became extremely busy in his efforts to promote a planned economy in Britain to deal with the Great Depression, as a member of the MacMillan Committee in the early 1930s and subsequently as a member of the Economic Advisory Council. He expounded his arguments in a book, generally regarded as the greatest economic text of the twentieth century, *General Theory of Employment, Interest and Money* which was published in 1936. By this time some governments, most notably that of the United States, had begun to adopt policies which were, to some extent, in line with his principles of economic regeneration by government intervention, though not always to the extent that Keynes thought necessary to produce the hoped-for results. Though not always appreciated during the 1930s, his theories would be adopted by most capitalist economies in the post-war period.

I endeavoured to keep up my friendship with Maynard, attending his Tuesday Club meetings as often as I could and contributing more often to discussions from my position as a stockbroker and market analyst. Unfortunately, Maynard was usually too busy to stop for a drink after our meetings. His career had broadened to include campaigning and policy-making for the Liberal Party, publishing the weekly Liberal magazine *The Nation,* which would later merge with the *New Statesman,* as well as his on-going academic writings and business activities. My main contact with him was as a client of my firm. He would occasionally adjust his portfolio of stocks and shares and at such times he would consult me regarding recent analysis of particular companies and ask for any statistical information or research material about a specific sector. I was always willing to oblige and usually took the opportunity to monitor Keynes's trades as they more often than not could be worth a consideration for my other clients.

But then disaster struck.

# XI

# *RUTHIN CASTLE*

IN 1937 MAYNARD FELL SERIOUSLY ILL AFTER HE was struck down with septic tonsillitis. There is no doubt that he had been overdoing it, working all the hours in the day without sufficient rest and his resistance to infection was weakened. His condition gradually deteriorated as the bacteria from the infection seeped into his heart valves, causing bacterial endocarditis which damaged the heart and lungs and was potentially fatal. At the time, before penicillin and modern remedies, there was no cure for this condition. So, as was the usual practice for that period, Maynard was sent to a sanatorium where he would get plenty of rest and quiet in a fresh, peaceful environment and be treated for his life-threatening illness.

Ruthin Castle in the Vale of Clwyd in North Wales had opened in 1923 as a hospital for the treatment of internal diseases about which little was known. As the name implies, it was built in the grounds of a semi-ruined old castle which still featured castellated ruins and a moat. New rooms for patients, often facing south, were added and built in sympathy with the original architecture. As well as medical treatment, dietary regimes and physiotherapy, the clinic provided outdoor pleasure pursuits such as tennis and croquet, fishing and shooting. All in all, it was an attractive location for medical care and recuperation, except for one problem: there was no specific treatment for Maynard's condition. This was despite there being a highly-qualified medical team with expertise in areas as diverse as dietetics, radiography, bacteriology and heart conditions. So Maynard was treated with the traditional remedy of peace and rest in a fresh climate and the experimental one of trying various chemicals like iodine and arsenic. The first didn't work because Maynard refused to stop working and rest and the second didn't work because they were not the answer.

I first knew that Maynard was unwell when Tuesday Club meetings were suspended and I telephoned Lydia who told me he was seriously ill and she agreed to my suggestion that I might visit him. The hospital informed me that his condition was such that visiting was not encouraged but I was permitted to see him for an hour one afternoon the following week. I telephoned Saxe to let him know how serious was Maynard's condition and he asked if he might go with me. After a check with the hospital that this was in order, I readily agreed. The only access to the castle was by car from Chester so we chose to motor all the way, a journey of several hours in my Rover 10. Saxe was his usual quiet self, making little conversation and responding to my occasional remarks with a muffled monosyllabic response. He spent much of the time reading his newspaper, particularly the racing page. We stopped for a break at a pub and had a glass of beer and a nondescript cheese roll.

When we arrived at the sanatorium in the early afternoon, we were given instructions by the doctor on duty not to tire or excite Maynard as he was still very ill, whatever his protestations to the contrary. He suggested we see Maynard separately but relented in view of the long journey we had undertaken. We were taken up to Maynard's room along corridors which bore that strange hospital concoction of smells combining sanitation with treatment which Saxe described as bleach and embrocation.

The nurse knocked on the door and when Maynard responded she ushered us in and left us alone. We found him lying on the bed in pyjamas and a dressing gown. Not having seen him for a couple of years or more, I was rather shocked when I saw him. He had lost a great deal of weight; his cheeks were sunken and there seemed nothing of him under his clothes. Rather contradictorily, his face had a high colour. He was holding a copy of *The Wall Street Journal* and there were other periodicals, newspapers and reports of various kinds spread all over the bed.

"Hello, Lewis, and Saxon too. How kind of you to come all this way." He smiled faintly and held out his hand. "Lydia told me you were coming. She spends a lot of time down here but I managed to get her to take a break for a few days."

I took his hand, which felt cold and bony. "How are you, Maynard?"

"Oh, not too bad; I think I'm improving. It's this damned infection; they haven't an answer at the moment so I go up one day and down the next."

I pulled a chair over to the bed and sat down, Saxe standing behind me. "You have rather a high colour."

He nodded. "The infection causes me to have regular fevers; very wearing."

"You should be resting." I pointed to all the papers in front of him.

He smiled a little sheepishly. "I'd go mad just lying here or reading light fiction. I can't do any work but I try to stay abreast of current affairs, even if I receive the papers two days late." He pointed to the date on *The Wall Street Journal*.

"Presumably, they are still exploring treatment options?"

"I think they have run out of ideas but can't face telling me."

"Do you see much of the other patients or are you isolated here?"

"Not all the people here are ill. There are lots of upper-class gentlemen hoping to lose some weight and I see them from time to time. They are quite competitive in their race to lose the most but, judging by the size of them, at the moment they are all coming last."

I laughed, pleased his sense of humour was intact.

Maynard looked over at Saxe, who had his newspaper under his arm. "Have you finished the crossword this morning, Saxe?"

"Er, yes, Maynard."

"I couldn't get thirteen down."

Saxe looked up his own copy. "Avaunt," he answered.

Maynard nodded.

There was a knock on the door and a different nurse brought in some tea and small delicate cakes which she placed on the table. She took Maynard's arm and walked with him to the table and we sat down too.

Over the pleasant afternoon tea we recalled the old days, even Saxe joining in. I steered clear of any serious matters for fear that Maynard would exert himself but even light-hearted conversation seemed to tire him very quickly. After about forty minutes I looked at Saxe and he nodded; it was time to take our leave. We escorted Maynard back to his bed. He gently dismissed all offers to help him.

As we took our leave, I pleaded with Maynard not to return to work until he was fully fit.

"At the moment, I would settle for half-fit," he said, as I shook his hand.

"Very kind of you to come too, old friend," Maynard said to Saxe, shaking his hand.

Saxe smiled and wished Maynard an early return to health.

We stopped at the door and waved but Maynard's eyes were closed.

On the drive home I experienced that sinking feeling all too common when somebody one cares about is slowly slipping away and there is nothing to be done, even when the patient has access to the best and most expensive (not necessarily one and the same) treatment.

Saxe clearly felt the same. As we drove out of the gates of Ruthin Castle he said, "Do you think Maynard has a chance?"

"Of course, he's a tough old bird and he comes from strong stock," I replied, though I thought otherwise.

"I wish it were me rather than him. He has so much to live for, so much to give."

I did not know what to say in response to Saxe's sad self-deprecation and could only pat him on the arm.

In September, Keynes went home to Tilton, not recovered but probably thinking he would be as well looked after there as at Ruthin. Lydia was indeed a tireless and devoted nurse but he hated being an invalid. He had never by nature been comfortable with a life of relaxation and the enforced inactivity of convalescence he found dispiriting. Many of his friends, including me once or twice, called in and Lydia was always walking the thin line of encouraging visits because he so looked forward to them and limiting the length of them because they tired him. He always appeared to be in good spirits, though he was clearly frustrated by the inability of his body to support the ambitions of his mind. With no significant progress in his recovery, I was not alone in believing it unlikely that he would ever be able to resume anything approaching a fully active life again, especially after his period of convalescence stretched throughout 1938 and into 1939. Then a semi-miraculous change in fortune occurred.

In March 1939, Lydia engaged the services of a new physician, Janos Plesch, a Hungarian Jew who was a prominent figure in Germany but had fled Berlin when the Nazis took over. An expert on blood circulation, he had invented the first reliable machine for measuring blood pressure. He had since become qualified to act as a medical practitioner in England and had his own practice in Mayfair. Regarded by Maynard and Lydia as a hard taskmaster, he made radical changes to Maynard's regimen. Instead of one based on complete rest he instituted a more exercise and body restorative plan. He also tried various steps to reduce the bacteria in Maynard's chest. The decisive step was Plesch's introduction of Prontosil, a drug containing sulphonamide, which acted as a kind of antibiotic and destroyed the streptococci in Maynard's throat. This hastened an improvement in Maynard's condition, although it was unable to cure the infection in his heart valves. His weakened heart would remain a permanent hindrance to a recovery to full health, though he refused to accept the status of an invalid. Coincidentally, the drug Prontosil was given at around the same time to Lady Ottoline Morrell, after she suffered a stroke, but this appeared to hasten her death rather than effect a cure.

Feeling well enough to return to work, Keynes was able to go back to something approaching his old working regime by the time war broke out in September 1939. He was soon recruited to the Treasury as neither a minister nor a civil servant but as an adviser and problem-solver, especially on the thorny question of how the war could be financed, in particular negotiating lease-lend with the United States. He was also appointed to the court of the Bank of England as well as various parliamentary and other committees, signs of his indispensability as one of the guiding lights of the economy through the war and into the post-war period. Unfortunately, no attention was paid to the strain on his physical strength which would have been demanding of a fully fit man. He was now the principal architect of the post-war arrangements which would aim to ensure a stable system of international currencies and world banking. In recognition of his work he would receive countless honours, including a peerage, so that he could speak on behalf of the coalition government in the House of Lords.

His health would never recover fully and, although his energy and determination disguised his weak constitution, each year drained him further as his workload and the calls on his time far exceeded the moderate commitments his doctors thought him safely capable of.

Much as I would have liked to, I was not in a position to counsel Maynard to spare himself a little from his wartime commitments. He knew that he had to pace himself but chose to cut back on his social activities and I, like many of his friends, saw very little of him in the war years as the range of his official activities continued to expand. In any case, I was fairly busy myself. By 1939 the stock market had recovered much of its losses from the early 1930s and I began to think of retirement. After the outbreak of war, however, I recalled the financial crisis of the last war and decided to stay in my post as a steadying hand on the tiller, as it were. As it happened, the financial ructions were not as serious as in 1914 and the Stock Exchange was closed for only six days during the war. I also joined the Home Guard and, restored to my substantive army rank of captain, commanded a platoon for the duration. In the early days we prepared for the possibility of invasion, drilling with wooden rifles till the real ones were delivered and acting out guerrilla scenarios with petrol bombs and other makeshift weapons. Then gradually the fear of invasion subsided and the drills became a matter of 'just in case' rather than 'when'. My most difficult task was preventing an over-enthusiastic member of the platoon from shooting a Polish pilot who crash landed in a field near the village and whose command of English was proving insufficient to convince my platoon member that he wasn't a German. Charles, my son, was too young to be called up in 1939 but he later saw service in Italy. Lina and my elder daughter, Catherine, were involved in a convalescence home for wounded soldiers which was established at a grand house not very far from us and Lilac, itching to do her bit, eventually assisted there too in the last year of the war.

Despite carrying considerable burdens, what with his government duties and weakened health, towards the end of the war Maynard found the time and energy to support his great love for the arts. He became the first chairman of the Arts Council of Great Britain and used his influence to secure a high level of funding for the performing arts, despite the parlous position of government finances. His pet project was the restoration of the Royal Opera House, which had been converted into a dance hall during the war. Not surprisingly, due to his own love for ballet, he gave equal weight to it with opera when he installed Ninette de Valois's dance company in Covent Garden as a putative national ballet company. Lydia was involved in some of the fund-raising events to support the Arts Council funding and Lina and I attended a couple of these, though I rarely got the opportunity to have more than a word or two of greeting with Maynard when I saw him.

# PART II

# *THE FOLLOWERS*

# XII

# *THE DILEMMA*

My reflections on what I knew of Maynard's life and career had brought me up to the present day. I sat back in my chair and I still couldn't, for the life of me, think of anything that Maynard had done which could be the cause of his being blackmailed. His whole life had been dedicated to academia and public service of one kind or another. I could not imagine that he would have used his connections in government or the business world to feather his nest through corruption or fraud. Perhaps there had been some form of insider trading, using his privileged position in government to buy or sell before the news was made public, but I knew full well that this would be hard to detect and even harder to prove. In any case, he didn't want for anything financially. I could testify to his success as an investor and he was now a very rich man with, as far as I knew, relatively modest demands on his income. As to sexual peccadillos, he had always seemed devoted to Lydia since the early 1920s and any odd indiscretion before then would surely be stale news.

I supposed there could be salacious stories about Maynard which were unknown to me but from what I knew of him he was something of an idealist when it came to morals and ethics, almost to the point of naivety. More than once we had expressed different opinions as to what, for most people, constituted the pursuit of happiness. While I accepted the presence of aesthetes, philanthropists, ascetics, perhaps even saints in our society, the majority of people appeared to have an insatiable desire to indulge material pleasures, including the accruing and possessing of wealth. Maynard believed that as people became financially better off they aspired to higher pleasures like beauty, fellowship and altruism. He was sure they would derive greater pleasure from generosity to others and in good works rather than the miserly hoarding of wealth or spending on extravagant fripperies. I wished him well with his view based on his attraction to Platonic philosophy. My assessment was based on the observation of my fellow human beings, specifically those with whom I came into contact through my profession. Even when he put forward examples of philanthropy in the great national and municipal works financed by the wealthy over the centuries, I was sceptical enough to think that many of these good works might have been undertaken in the pursuit of prestige, public honours, or pride, as much as philanthropy.

Like all decent people, Maynard could not fully understand that not everyone shared his ideals and valued the pursuit of virtue and that in fact some people are just bad. I think it was Plato, a rational, good person, who came up with the phrase 'honour among thieves' to illustrate that nobody is beyond some virtue. On closer inspection the concept is nonsensical. If a man shows no honour to his victims, why should he show honour to another thief, other than for his own purposes or to his advantage? It is the tragedy of good people that, in thinking the best of others, they lay themselves open to be exploited by those who are not so generous. Personally, I have always tried to keep my cynicism finely tuned and I have found it becomes easier the older I get.

I finally went to bed after two o'clock, expecting to have questions about Maynard's past whizzing round in my head but I was fortunately intellectually exhausted and was asleep almost immediately, only to be wide awake an hour and a half later. It was nearly four, that time when to be awake is to be filled with worries which did not exist during the day and which now manifest themselves as unsolvable problems. Lina's arm was out of the bed and I touched it with my fingers: it was as cold as ice and momentarily I felt an unthinkable dread until I heard her breathing and I pulled the covers over her, leading her to turn round and sigh in her sleep.

I lay on my back, the issue of Maynard's blackmail coming into focus. My first thought was that I must help Alec. Maynard was my friend but, even more, he was also my hero, someone I revered and had always looked up to. How could I not do all that was in my power to save him from this scum who, with his scurrilous claims, threatened to ruin Maynard's reputation and his career with all its consequences for the post-war settlement? Yet I demurred. What would it mean for me to become involved in Alec's plan – whatever that was? It was certain to mean engaging with a criminal, directly or indirectly, possibly involve criminal activity and sure to be unpleasant and probably sordid in some way. But there was worse: if the blackmailer did have evidence of wrongdoing, Maynard was not the man I thought he was. Perhaps my whole picture of him was flawed and he did not deserve my help. Even if I did wish to help him why should I put myself at the service of Alec, whom I hardly knew and whom I had no reason to trust? The more I thought about it, the whole business seemed fantastical and I knew I would be a fool to get involved, a view clearly taken by Maynard's closer friends.

The pendulum swung backwards and forwards in my mind: sometimes I would be the brave, resourceful friend riding to the rescue of a great man and perhaps helping to save the country from disaster, and at other times I would be the sage man of caution, controlling the situation, reserving my position until I had the whole truth and then advising without becoming involved. Eventually, the turmoil unresolved, I fell asleep and woke again at seven, the pendulum pulled by gravity into the central position of total indecision.

Over breakfast, Lina noticed my unusually laconic mood and asked if there was anything wrong. I smiled and said I had a lot on my mind and hadn't slept well. I didn't take up her offer to talk it over, saying it was an investigative research matter which I would resolve when I went into work. She gently reminded me that I was supposed to be taking things easier and went back to her newspaper.

At the office that day, my mind would continually return to the issue of Maynard and Alec's predicament and slowly my decision began to emerge. That evening, as agreed, I called on Alec once again. We went through the same rituals of greeting and courtesy as before, even to the glass of brandy, this time with soda. However, something had changed. The previous evening, we had met as acquaintances but now we were co-conspirators. We sat in silence for a few moments, I waiting for Alec and he, presumably, hesitating to put the question. He looked at me and I smiled.

"You'll help?"

"Yes, but with reservations. I will give you any advice I can and swear I will not divulge what you tell me without your consent. But I won't commit to any actions on my part until I know exactly what Maynard is supposed to have done. On that basis, I will do whatever I can."

"I understand and I am extremely grateful. Thank you."

"I spent most of last night wracking my brains without success as to what exactly Maynard is supposed to have done."

"It is of a sexual nature."

I laughed. "What nonsense. I have known Maynard for forty years. He has been happily married for over half that time and I have never had any inkling of a tendency for his eye to wander, let alone his hand or anything else. As to youthful excesses, I hardly ever saw him look at a girl, he seemed quite abstemious so I hardly – oh!" The penny dropped. "Not women?"

"Not women. Are you shocked?"

"No, just surprised. When he was at Cambridge, he proclaimed the principle of 'Higher Sodomy' as the Apostles called it: the chaste love of another man. I remember he wrote a paper on it for the Apostles, I think, which was highly praised. Wasn't a similar argument used by Oscar Wilde in his defence?"

"Wilde obviously preferred 'Lower Sodomy' as the Apostles called it and apparently so eventually did Maynard. As he said in another context: 'When the facts change, I change my mind.'"

I smiled. "As you say, 'another context' as that was said in reference to the economic situation. What facts changed regarding his attitude to sexual relations between men?"

"He tried it."

I laughed.

"Like the Classical Greeks in so many ways, he was clearly not averse to the beauty of the male form and what it had to offer."

"So, what the hell, it's common for the young to experiment when the sexual urge is awakened."

"Did you?"

"Not of that nature, no, but that's not the point. Everyone has the occasional indiscretion in one's youth and is hardly likely to be called to account for it forty years later. I'd call the blackmailer's bluff."

Alec shook his head. "It was not an 'occasional indiscretion'. I gather that he was quite rampant, occasionally with women but mostly young men. His behaviour could best be described as promiscuous: pretty well anyone, if not quite anywhere, and he was not careful. I have been told by those who knew him before the Great War that there were letters and other writings and now there are demands for money." There was just the merest touch of criticism in his voice but essentially it was a statement of fact.

"I had no idea."

"Why would you? You once told me that you have only known Maynard well since the early 1930s. His relationships with men came to an abrupt end after he married and, as far as I know, Maynard has been faithful to Lydia throughout his marriage."

"A life of two halves, so far as his sex life is concerned," I said, perplexed by the whole business.

I must confess: *now* I was shocked. Many men find it difficult to control their sexual urges throughout their lives but clearly this was not a particular challenge for Maynard. How then, had he been so reckless in his private life to leave a trail of indiscretions that could now prove an embarrassment or worse? I could only put it down to the arrogance that bedevils many great lives.

Alec eventually broke my reverie. "I can tell from your silence you are quite disturbed by what I have told you."

"I wouldn't say disturbed, but certainly perplexed. Despite my own, admittedly fairly unadventurous, sexual habits, I know enough about the world to realise that the different sexual practices are probably more numerous than Heinz varieties. While some of them may not appeal to me, such preferences are a personal matter and nobody else's business, provided of course, they are conducted in private: mustn't frighten the horses. What does surprise me is that a man in Maynard's position was not more prudent, given that his particular inclination is against the law."

"It was a long time ago, when he was not such a public figure."

"He was already well known in the early 1920s. He's always been such a moralist in his pronouncements on ethics and what it is to lead a good life. I'm afraid it lays him open to the charge of hypocrisy if nothing else."

Alec offered me a cigarette. "He has never regarded one's sexual behaviour as coming within the realms of other people's moral judgement."

"That may well be so but lack of discernment may indicate poor taste and certainly poor judgement. In any event, society generally does not take the same view. Lloyd George was for a time considered a great prime minister but many thought his sexual promiscuity made him untrustworthy. Unfortunately, others judge us by their moral code, not ours."

I realised I sounded rather petulant. I was still coming to terms with being asked to get involved in issues of a criminal nature connected to Maynard's past life, without previously knowing anything about it. Not only was I not sure that I was willing to be involved, but I wondered how many other people Alec had approached before turning to me. I thought it served no purpose to ask and went back to the matter at hand.

"There's no point in us quibbling about personal morality. Let's take it back to the beginning," I said. "What was the first inkling you had of this blackmail?"

"A letter came through the post to this office, marked 'private and confidential'. Fortunately, as Maynard is not employed in the civil service, none of his mail is opened in the mail room."

"But you opened it?"

"Yes. He believes that usually such mail is a ruse to get his attention. Anyone who is writing to him privately should know his home address or could have a letter forwarded via this office."

"What did the letter say?"

Alec went over to a desk, unlocked the drawer, took a letter from a wallet and passed it to me.

I unfolded the sheet of good-quality writing paper and found a cryptic note which was written in block capitals and with neither heading nor date.

*"Lord Keynes,*

*I know about your criminal sexual activities involving male prostitutes and innocent, impressionable young men and I have letters and other material to prove it. I enclose part of one of several sent to the person concerned. I have many others.*

*Though you don't deserve it, I am willing to remain silent if you pay me £5,000. If not, I will send the letters to the police.*

*When in disgrace with fortune and men's eyes*
*I all alone beweep my outcast state*

*Wait for further instructions.*
*Gaius Praetor"*

I threw the letter onto the coffee table in disgust. "I don't recognise the quote. Do you?"

"No. Another letter came yesterday morning. You saw me open it. Maynard is expected to ring a number to receive further instructions. I realised I couldn't ignore this any longer." He took the letter from his pocket and offered it to me to look at but I waved it away.

"What happened to the portion of the letter he referred to?" I asked.

"I destroyed it because I didn't want anyone else to see it."

"I would have liked to have reassured myself that it was sufficiently incriminating that we need to act."

Alec nodded. "I was rash, I'm sorry. It did not include a signature but, given the places and people named, and knowing what I do of Maynard's past private life, I am pretty sure it is genuine. Some of the content is salacious; some might find it shocking."

"I knew nothing of this."

"Outside his own circle, not many people did. Maynard has always tended to maintain strict barriers between the various aspects of his life, whether it was to protect his private life or career or to avoid embarrassment or difficult questions, I'm not sure. I assume in the early years he felt safe in his sexuality; both his brother and his sister are homosexual so his parents must have had some idea or chose not to know. Then he moved in circles like the Apostles and the Bloomsbury Group where it would not have aroused objections or chastisement: quite the opposite, in fact."

"So, his Bloomsbury friends knew about it?"

"Yes, many of them were directly involved. He had affairs with some of them: the Stracheys, Duncan Grant, and others. One of the people I sought help from told me that Maynard had been warned several times about bragging of his sexual conquests and putting such adventures in writing but he was apparently quite heedless of the risks."

Momentarily, my mind went back to that party I had attended all those years ago in Brunswick Square when

Maynard and Duncan had lived there and how naïve I was and must have appeared then to those sophisticates. My mind returned to the business at hand. "From what you say, all these affairs ended a long time ago. As I said before, he should call the blackmailer's bluff and go to the police."

Alec shook his head. "I don't know if people are less tolerant now or if it was the war that changed things, but it seems the police take a lot more interest in harassing and prosecuting homosexuals than was the case twenty years ago. Some of Maynard's sexual partners were male prostitutes and soldiers and most were very young so there is also the question of whether he was leading the easily-influenced astray: that would be sure to guarantee conviction. Even if his influential friends and a good barrister could keep him out of gaol, there would at the very least be a scandal and it would get into the press, his enemies would see to that."

"Who are his enemies?"

"Every great man has enemies, especially among those who profess to be his friends."

"What a bloody mess. Well, if you won't tell Maynard and you won't go to the police, I don't see how that leaves you many options. Are you thinking of paying the £5,000? It's rather a lot of money."

Alec did not look in the least alarmed and I realised he hadn't invited me here to find a solution: he already had one.

"I did have a thought," he said.

I smiled, thinking we were building up to the point when he would ask me to pay the blackmailer. I was wrong.

"If we pay the blackmailer, that will not be the end of it. Sooner or later, he will come back for more and even one payment would be a confession of guilt and make it impossible to get help. The answer is to turn the tables on the blackmailer and somehow get the letters without paying for them."

"But how exactly would you do that?" I could feel the blanket of involvement beginning to enfold me as I allowed him to draw me into his confidence.

"Since I opened that first letter, I have been thinking about the process of blackmail a lot. It seems to me that the blackmailer has two weaknesses. The first is that his power lasts only until he carries out his threat. Therefore, he will not do that until there is absolutely no chance that he will be paid. The second is that he must find a way to receive the money without any danger to himself and that is not straightforward. Either he, or someone else on his behalf, has to meet his victim to collect the money or he has to set up a dropping point where the money can be left. Each option carries dangers with it. Both of these weaknesses can be turned to the advantage of the victim. The first gives the victim the opportunity to delay settlement of the payment and time to find out more about the blackmailer which could be put to his own use. The second may present the victim with the opportunity to set a trap to apprehend the blackmailer or to double-cross him."

"I understand the weaknesses but presumably you have also considered the *strengths* of the blackmailer?"

"Yes. The two greatest strengths of this particular blackmailer are, first, that we don't know for certain who he is and, second, that we are unlikely to go to the police. However, if he believes the latter to be true, he may be less cautious about protecting his identity."

"Presumably, 'Gaius Praetor' is not his real name? He would be very stupid to sign the letter if it were."

"Quite. Purely on the off chance I did check the London telephone directory and there is nobody named 'Praetor' in it."

"But why sign the letter at all?"

Alec took the glasses and topped up our drinks. "I don't

know. Perhaps it is nothing, a joke at our expense in some way or a play on words. I haven't been able to work it out."

I nodded. "Have you decided what to do?"

"I have a number of ideas. Obviously, which one I decide to pursue will depend on the blackmailer's moves as well as my own. The problem is that, knowing nothing about him, I have no way of anticipating or even guessing his reaction to any steps I take. My initial thought was to delay making any payment and to try to find out who the blackmailer is or the address from which he operates. Without a clue as to who he is or where he lives, I will have to find a way of bringing him out into the open and then consider my options."

"Right. How do you plan to achieve that?"

"I hoped you might be able to help."

At last, Alec had got to my role in this escapade. "What did you have in mind?"

"I would like to make use of your gift for mimicry."

Once again, I was caught off-guard by his suggestion. I was completely dumbstruck by the idea. "How do you know about that?" I said.

"Maynard mentioned it to me once, when we were talking about Marshall and one or two other lecturers."

I laughed. "I know I could do a fair impersonation of some people at Cambridge but it was just a party piece. I never expected that it would be of use for anything."

"I'm serious," said Alec. "In the letter which arrived today he gave his instructions. We have to contact him by telephone and he insists that he will speak to Maynard and nobody else. Maynard's voice is well-known through his radio broadcasts so not just anyone will do. The blackmailer must believe he is dealing directly with Maynard but, as I've already stressed, Maynard must not be dragged into this business for the sake of his health. The solution is that you impersonate his voice."

"But I've never even attempted to impersonate Maynard."

"It will be on the telephone; it doesn't need to be perfect."

Against my better judgement, I found myself taking the bait. "What do you want me to do exactly?"

"Initially, I want you to ring the number and pretend to be Maynard. Then take down any instructions or other information you are given."

"Just a minute. If he has given a telephone number, isn't he worried about the number being traced?"

"I have already had the number traced. It is a public telephone box; one of the block outside Charing Cross Station."

"But what is to stop us identifying him or having the police on hand to apprehend him?"

"Perhaps you should read the latest letter."

I leaned over and picked the letter up from the table. Alec had given me the gist of the first two sentences. The third answered my question. "I have photographic copies of these letters in envelopes addressed to the Metropolitan Police and all the main daily newspapers. These will be posted next Monday if I do not give instructions to the contrary. You would be foolish to detain, obstruct or apprehend me in any way."

I read the whole letter again and shook my head. "I am still uncomfortable about not speaking to Maynard about this. If we concoct some scheme to try to foil the blackmailer and it goes wrong, Maynard could be ruined without even having had an opportunity to express his own views on the matter."

It was the first time I heard Alec raise his voice. "We cannot burden Maynard with a personal crisis at this time. I don't think anyone realises how important he is for everyone's economic future. Without him, how else will we avert the regular international financial crises which have plagued the world economy for decades?"

"I understand that but..."

He waved away my interruption and carried on. "On top of that he is leading our government's attempts to secure American financial support after the war, without which we are sunk. This is not merely a matter of one person's career or his reputation. If he is distracted from his work the consequences would be disastrous for the whole world. As it is, his commitment to his work is placing a tremendous burden on his health and any more strain could kill him."

His voice broke a little as he spoke and I knew there was nothing I could say that would change his course of action, whether I helped him or not. But I made one last attempt to persuade him to seek the assistance of the appropriate authorities.

"If he is so important to the government, surely strings could be pulled at the very top to deal with this problem without involving or implicating Maynard?" I suggested.

"I wish that were true but the risk of something going wrong is too great. The Establishment has a softer spot for Nazis than it has for homosexuals. Do you remember Gottfried von Cramm?"

"Yes, Wimbledon finalist several times before the war."

"In 1938 he was arrested and convicted of having had a homosexual relationship with Manasse Herbst, a young Jewish actor and singer; he was sent to prison for a year. Herbst and he were definitely friends and he had helped Herbst to leave Germany by illegal means before the noose tightened on the Jews. The exact nature of his relationship with Herbst was equivocal. Probably the prosecution against von Cramm was at least partly motivated by a wish to punish him for his involvement in helping a Jew and any sexual transgression was secondary. Von Cramm was released after six months in prison and resumed his tennis career. Despite winning the Queen's tournament in 1939 he was refused permission to compete at Wimbledon a few weeks later purely because of his criminal conviction. Yet other German players who had the approval of the Nazi regime were allowed to take part."

"No two cases are the same. Maynard would have more support, would be able to pull more strings than Von Cramm."

"Perhaps, but once this matter of Maynard's being blackmailed finds its way onto government files and is whispered in gentlemen's clubs, it will eventually come to the notice of those who, for whatever reason, dislike Maynard. Even if they let him finish his work, as soon as it is completed, they will make him pay in one way or another. All that he has done for his country will count for little; there is nothing people like more than building somebody up and once he's at the top, bringing him down. I can't let Maynard suffer that, so I have no choice but to save him from it. Will you help me or not?"

I could tell Alec was pleading rather than giving me an ultimatum and I relented. "Yes, of course," I said, despite my misgivings.

Alec's plan of action was straightforward, perhaps simplistically so. At the allotted time, eleven o'clock the next day, I was to ring the telephone number we had been given and Alec would be at Charing Cross Station to follow events, with the intention of finding out more about the blackmailer, perhaps by following him. We would plan the next step after that.

I heard him out but shook my head. "I have no experience or expertise in this situation and would guess neither have you. If something doesn't go according to plan we won't be in a position to work together. As for me imitating Maynard and fooling the blackmailer, the whole idea is preposterous."

"If you have a better idea, I'd be glad of it."

I shook my head again.

Alec nodded. "He won't see you and he can't be sure you are not Maynard. I shall be very careful at my end, cautious rather than impulsive; it will work."

I shrugged and said I would do it and, after another drink and one more run-through of our scheme, including an attempt to rehearse my conversation with the blackmailer, I went home.

# XIII

# FIRST CONTACT

By the time I walked through my front door, the initial misgivings about my active involvement in Alec's plan had grown into a full-scale regret. Doubtless there are many who, in my position, would have jumped at the chance of being involved in a spot of clandestine heroics with very little risk to themselves but I was not one of them. Perhaps I might have been when I was younger; age rarely makes us more adventurous. I was not fearful for myself, nor did I have any moral qualms. Maynard was undoubtedly a good, as well as a great, man and any blackmailer is beyond contempt. Yet, that evening, as I walked round the garden trying to develop my knowledge of Maynard's way of speaking into a passable imitation of him, I felt a great unease, without quite understanding why. When I came in from the garden, Lina and I sat down with a glass of sherry before dinner and talked over our day, as was our custom.

"Are you all right?" Lina asked.

"Yes. Why?"

"Well, it's not like you to wander round the garden when you come in, especially in February when it's so gloomy. I happened to look out the window and you seemed to be talking to yourself. I thought you might be worried about something."

I laughed. "I may well have been talking to myself. I needed to sort something out in my mind, nothing important." I mentioned that I had seen Maynard but that my invitation to lunch had been put on hold. Naturally I said nothing of my conversations with Alec.

"It's a pity Maynard is so busy all the time. I'd have thought he could fit you into his schedule."

"He's backwards and forwards across the Atlantic at the moment."

"Still, a couple of hours for an old friend." She changed the subject then and we talked about the war and how it was going in Italy. The fighting was still fierce and our worries surfaced about Charles, who was serving with an infantry brigade.

"I can't understand why they are still fighting in Italy," she said. "At this rate, the war will be over in Germany first."

"It'll be over in a few weeks," I said, in hope more than conviction.

Perhaps it was Lina's brief and slight criticism of Maynard or the fog in my mind clearing, but by the next morning I felt even more disquiet over what I was about to do. I had to face up to the reality that the reason Maynard and I rarely saw each other was because I wasn't a particularly close friend, despite my attachment to our friendship. I had always suspected as much but had chosen to ignore the fact until it had surfaced when the previous evening I reviewed my extremely sketchy knowledge of his past life. Now I was discovering whole areas of his past that I knew nothing about. This was of no consequence: I was old enough and mature enough not to experience jealousy or loss of self-esteem about my relative lack of importance to Maynard. My disquiet arose from doubt as to whether I was the right person to be taking on this task. Surely it should be one of his closest friends, a confidant, one who would know Maynard's mind on this matter and would behave appropriately. Where were all these close friends who had shared his past and perhaps an intimate relationship which meant they had empathy with his predicament? Time and again I came back to the thought, *Why me? Why should I be sticking my head over the parapet and getting involved in something that has nothing to do with me?*

There was also a part of me that was irritated by Maynard's reckless arrogance which I had seen flashes of from time to time in his investment decisions and risk-taking. Now it had led to me being asked to help clear up the mess he had left as a consequence of his wild disregard of the danger his behaviour had led him into. In short, I had given my word, but I went unwillingly into the fray.

My doubts about the wisdom of this venture led me once again to consider the possibility of consulting Maynard about this business and offering him the chance to make a decision himself or at least get his approval for what Alec and I were about to do. Despite Lina's protestations about dinner being ready, I telephoned Tilton Farmhouse and the telephone was answered by Lydia.

"Hello, Lewis. How nice to hear from you. Maynard mentioned you had been to his office. How are you?"

"Fine, thank you, Lydia. Something rather important has cropped up and I wonder if I might speak to Maynard, preferably in person. I could drive down this evening, if it is convenient."

"Oh dear! I'm sorry, Lewis, but that's not possible. Maynard is not very well at the moment; he couldn't see anyone this evening."

"I'm sorry to hear that. I hope it's not too serious?"

"It's his heart again. He had one of his bad turns this morning and he'll need to have at least another day before he can get up. He can't have any excitement or pressure when he's in this condition."

"No, of course not."

Lydia offered to help if she could but I told her not to worry, that I could deal with it through Alec and to give Maynard my best wishes. Circumstances had left me no choice: I would have to co-operate with Alec without Maynard's knowledge or his blessing. I told Lina that I had called Lydia just to find out how Maynard was. She nodded when I told her he was very unwell and expressed her wish he would retire and save his dwindling strength.

The next day, I toyed with the idea of staying home in the morning to make the phone call but decided I ought to be relatively close at hand should Alec need help. Nor did I make the call from the office for fear of a bored or inquisitive telephonist listening in, so I went out to a local shop which I knew had a public telephone. Armed with my sketched-out script of likely questions and answers, I walked into the cabinet and dialled the contact number.

The phone was answered after one ring. "Hello?" The voice was quite high and quiet, but not a woman's: it sounded like a boy. "Hello?"

Momentarily surprised by the voice, I had to take a moment before replying. "This is Maynard," I said, in my version of Maynard's clipped, clear way of speaking. I used his middle name as the person on the other end of the line would know who I meant and anyone else would hardly know I was referring to Maynard Keynes.

"Take down this telephone number and call it immediately," the voice instructed, without any of the niceties of conversation.

I wrote down the number as it was dictated and before I could say anything else, the call was ended. Feeling slightly unnerved by the abruptness of the call, I took a few moments to calm myself before checking my notes and dialling the new number I had been given. The telephone rang twice.

A man's voice answered this time. "Who is that?"

"Maynard," I replied.

"Have you got the money?" His tone was neutral and he spoke in a soft, gravelly voice. I wanted to tell him to clear his throat.

"Not yet."

"Why not?" He sounded more menacing this time.

"You can't expect me to pay over the money without agreeing the terms of the contract."

"The what?"

"You are demanding payment of £5,000 which is a considerable sum, but what will you do for that exactly?" I was managing to speak calmly, maintaining my version of Maynard's voice, but I could feel my heartbeat quickening. The irritation I had felt towards Maynard earlier that morning was now channelled into anger at the person behind the voice.

"I will give you all the letters I have."

"But according to your letter you have made copies. How do I know that you won't ask for more money in the future?"

"You will have to trust me."

I didn't answer. Whatever he said, I knew there would come a day when the thought of some more easy money would be a temptation too hard to resist. Once again, he would find the copies of the letters and Maynard or Alec would be contacted. There could be no trust between us.

"I am sure you will understand that I need more reassurance than that," I said, eventually.

"The copies are photographs. I could let you have the negatives as well as all the copies." He sounded slightly irritated now.

"Very well. But you are asking me for a lot of money and most of mine is tied up in investments. It will take me a while to get it."

"Borrow it; you're a rich man."

"It will still take me a few days."

"Find it by the weekend or the price goes up."

I found his dismissive impertinence extremely annoying but still I showed restraint. "How will we make the exchange?" I asked.

"I will send a letter to your office with the arrangements. Once again, do not try anything clever or it will all come out. Remember, you need your reputation more than I need your money." He put the phone down.

I replaced the telephone in its cradle. Things had not gone according to plan, at least not our plan. As I came out of the telephone booth, I glanced at the shop assistant and wondered if she had been able to overhear my conversation but she smiled innocently. I walked back to the office, hoping that Alec had been able to make more sense of the morning's events than I had.

Twenty minutes later Alec called. "It did not go as well as I'd hoped," he said.

"I guessed as much when I telephoned the number you gave me and was immediately forced to ring a different number."

"Can we meet later?"

"All right, but somewhere quiet. I'll see you at Cleopatra's Needle in an hour."

Alec was waiting for me when I arrived and, as I approached, I noticed he appeared fidgety and uncomfortable as two day-trippers stood next to him, while they examined the ancient Egyptian obelisk, apparently more interested in the German bomb damage of the Great War than the hieroglyphics. He noticed my arrival with relief and we walked along the Embankment towards Northumberland Avenue while Alec told me what had happened.

He had arrived early at Charing Cross Station to make sure he knew which telephone box had the right number. Then he had taken up his position across the road, waiting to see who used the box. At about five to eleven, a young boy had entered it and Alec had feared that he might prevent the blackmailer from using the telephone. But then the boy had answered the phone and Alec had realised he was my contact. Not sure what to do when he saw the boy, he had waited for him to leave the telephone box and followed him to a newsagent. The boy walked in the shop and came out with a comic. Alec had considered challenging him but had thought better of it in case the boy reported to the blackmailer that we were on his tail.

"So, I had to let the boy go," he said.

I nodded, sympathetically. "You were in a difficult situation. He was probably just being paid to take the call or it could be a case of Fagin and Oliver Twist."

"How did you get on? Let me have the second telephone number and I shall be able to trace it."

I gave him my note with the second telephone number and told him of my conversations with the boy and the blackmailer. I said he could expect another letter the following day, outlining the arrangements for the payment of the £5,000 and the return of the letters. "The trouble is that we don't know how many letters there are, so he could retain some for further demands later on. There's also the question of photographs and probably negatives."

"What sort of person do you think he is? I mean his background?" asked Alec.

"An odd, scratchy kind of voice but well-spoken; I would think he is quite well educated. I had the impression that, for him, this was not merely business; he takes pleasure in his work."

We walked in silence, thinking about our next move.

Eventually, Alec spoke. "When we get the next letter, I will have to work out some way of tracking him down."

"What if you can't track him down; where will the money come from?" I asked him.

"I'll find a way."

# XIV

# *THE EXCHANGE*

I SPENT THE REST OF THE MORNING ON tenterhooks, going through the motions as best I could and frequently having to ask colleagues to repeat what they said as my mind was almost permanently elsewhere. At last, Alec rang to say the promised letter had arrived in the second post. At lunchtime I went over to his office and he showed me the latest instalment of this grim saga. As before, it was all written in capital letters and was to the point, signed once again by 'Gaius Praetor'. We were to pack a brown holdall with the money in five-pound notes and leave the bag in the large waste bin facing the Duke of York steps on the other side of The Mall, at nine o'clock the following Monday morning. The letters and copies would be found in the same bin in a similar bag at ten o'clock.

"Why there?" I asked.

"It's a place that's difficult to hang around without being seen, I suppose," Alec muttered.

"Do you have a plan?

"Yes. Carry out his instructions, but without the money; just newspaper."

"He won't like that very much."

"I assume he is aware that something of the sort may happen but won't be too concerned. After all, he will still have the letters until he has seen whether the money is there. The point is that we have one more chance of finding out who he is."

"If he discovers that he has been fooled, that might make it more difficult to deal with him in the future."

"I hope that we will have the upper hand if what I have in mind works."

"What is your plan, exactly?"

"I thought I would try to follow him if he arrives by foot and have the back-up of someone in a car, ready to follow him if he uses a car himself."

With that word 'someone' I felt a twinge of concern that I was about to be involved in an expedition fraught with potential disaster. But it was a fleeting moment. Having allowed myself to be drawn into Alec's schemes, I was unable to extricate myself honourably. In any case, I was ready to commit fully to this venture. It was becoming for me a personal matter; I wanted to bring the swine down.

"What do you want me to do?" I asked.

He smiled in gratitude, or was it relief? "Perhaps you could arrive by car and wait to see what happens. If he arrives by car, you could follow him as he goes off. If he is on foot, you could help give chase."

"He'd better not be young if I have to run after him: I'm sixty, you know, and not exactly at the peak of fitness. We should have engaged the services of a private detective or something of the kind."

"I would have if I knew one. I can't be sure that we can trust just anyone in the telephone directory. The fewer of us involved, I'm sure you agree."

"Of course. By the by, did you find out where the second telephone number I had to ring was located?"

"Yes, another telephone box; this one near Hyde Park Corner, so no help there."

After further discussion, Alec set off to buy a cheap brown holdall while I went to the bank to draw out two hundred pounds in five-pound notes, which we would wrap round the wads of newspaper and perhaps fool the blackmailer long enough for us to hunt him down. It was no small sum but I was pleased to do this in the hope that the blackmailer might be lulled into a false sense of security. It was later that day that I had what I thought was a brilliant idea and telephoned my old friend, Lyndon Ashley, a man I knew I could trust.

Very close at Cambridge and on our long holiday on the Continent, Lyndon and I had kept up our friendship ever since. Sometimes we'd see a lot of each other over a short period and then not for months, perhaps even a year or two. Not exactly rushing into a career, he had spent a few years after Cambridge as an amateur county cricketer before eventually working in Malaya for a time. He was now an overseas representative in the tobacco industry, spending his time in Rhodesia, Turkey, and various other places. Two qualities I had always been sure of in regard to Ashley: he could take care of himself and he would stand up for the underdog. There was a particular episode I remembered now which had occurred when I was out with him one evening in London just before the Great War.

We had had dinner and were taking a short cut through an alley to his club for a drink or two when we came across a man being beaten up by a group of three young men. By the time we arrived on the scene, the victim was on the ground and a couple of his assailants were kicking him. While I stopped aghast, Lyndon went straight at them, punching one of them in the solar plexus and another on the jaw, the first doubling up and the second falling backwards against the third thug, the two of them falling in a heap.

Lyndon was magnificent, standing his ground, fists raised and ready for more. "You cowardly bastards, three against one. How do you fancy it, now we're even?" he growled at them.

I rushed forward now to stand between the man who had been attacked and the bullies to make sure he was not assaulted again.

One of the thugs did swing a punch at Lyndon but he blocked it with his left and delivered an uppercut which sent the man reeling. Another made a comment about "sticking up for a poof" but backed away as Lyndon moved towards him. Lyndon laughed. "You're nothing but a bunch of nancies yourselves."

If they were stung by the remark, they looked to have had enough but I thought it time to end proceedings so we could see to the poor chap on the floor. "Now you've had your fun, clear off," I said, giving them an out. They took it and wandered off, mouthing obscenities about their victim and his rescuers.

I bent down to talk to the young man, who was in his early twenties. He was now sitting up. He had a bruised eye, a cut lip and a bloody nose but seemed alert. He was using a handkerchief to stem the flow of blood from his lip.

"How are you, old chap?" I asked.

"Oh, not so bad. They wanted to do some damage but they didn't give me the full force of their kicks. I shall be bruised tomorrow in the ribs but nothing broken." He tentatively checked his nose and his teeth. "Pity about the suit, though," he added, looking down at his torn jacket pocket.

Lyndon and I helped him up. "Thanks awfully for packing them off." He smiled at Lyndon, "You were brilliant."

Lyndon grinned. "The element of surprise is worth two good punches. Once I had them on the run, they hadn't the heart for it. What happened?"

The young man hesitated. He seemed wary of recounting his experience. Eventually, he told us.

"I had a couple of drinks with a friend and they were in the same pub. I suppose they were strangers and didn't know it is a regular haunt of – people like me. They noticed my friend and I were very close and took offence. When I left the pub, they followed me. It started with a bit of baiting and when I told them where to go, they let me have it."

He wasn't far from his flat and we took him home and left him, once he'd assured us that he could manage. He said he had someone who would come round. We went off to the club. Lyndon being the modest man he was, never mentioned the incident again.

It was recalling this fracas that led me to telephone Lyndon and tell him I'd like his help for a friend who was in a spot of trouble. Lyndon didn't hesitate nor ask the nature of the problem and we met in the private bar of a pub in the City which was always quiet after the rush hour.

"Good of you to be willing to help," I said, after buying a round.

"What's this about? Money problems or got themselves in a jam of some sort?"

"Blackmail," I said quietly.

Lyndon's expression changed from curiosity to amusement. "Somebody caught with their trousers down with somebody else's wife?"

"Something of the sort. The person being blackmailed is Maynard Keynes. You remember him?"

"Of course, one of the blue-eyed boys at Cambridge when we were there. He has done very well for himself. So, what has he been up to?" Though he asked the question, I detected a look of distaste from his expression.

"Someone has some incriminating letters about his youthful activities."

"Something that happened when he was young? No one gets blackmailed for sowing a few wild oats, unless it was with his sister or his mother." He waited expectantly.

"He was indiscreet and careless in some affairs with men and someone has written evidence of it."

Lyndon banged his fist on the table at which we sat. "I knew it!" he exclaimed.

"Did you?"

"He was an Apostle, wasn't he? Half of them were at it all the time but he was careful, or I thought he was."

"You knew?"

"I didn't exactly know but I could tell. Do you remember asking Ralph Talbot why he didn't join the Apostles and he gave a vague, evasive answer? Well, he told me it was partly because he detected an undercurrent, perhaps more than an undercurrent, of it at the meeting he attended and he felt uncomfortable. People like Lytton Strachey were quite open about it apparently."

"Why didn't he tell me?"

"He knew you had friends among the Apostles and Keynes was a bit of a hero of yours and he thought it better to leave you in blissful ignorance."

I thought, *How often I have been kept from the whole truth about Maynard.* "But Maynard was careful; he was so explicit about resisting the temptations of the flesh," I said.

Lyndon smiled. "Yes, I know, the paper he wrote about chastity in love and all that. At the time, I thought he must have at least considered the physical option. The fact is that while these great intellects espouse a higher aspiration for life than we lesser mortals through the arts, philosophy, virtue, a nobility in their conduct, in reality they are no better than the rest of us, governed by self-interest, vanity and sexual appetites. Wasn't it Oscar Wilde who said, 'We are all in the gutter, but some of us are looking at the stars'? The truth is these intellectual friends of yours are more likely to be looking up a skirt or whatever Maynard would be after."

"Be that as it may, Maynard mustn't be exposed or his career could be in jeopardy and it could affect our position in negotiating the peace agreement and the post-war settlement."

Lyndon sneered. "What utter tosh. Nobody is indispensable, the war is nearly over and, just like the last one, we shall end up paying for it and the Yanks will profit from it."

"But it's not right that Maynard should endure a public calamity for what he did in his private life as a young man; he has done no harm."

"Not a bad pint," said Lyndon, looking at his glass. "I haven't much sympathy for Maynard," he said.

"That's rather harsh. After all, he has done nothing regarded as universally wrong," I said. "I remember you helping that young man in Piccadilly that time when he was set on by some thugs."

"It was nothing to do with how he conducted his life. He was being attacked because of what he was, rather than what he had done and he was outnumbered. They were the sort of cowardly scum who take out their own inadequacies on somebody they judge to be worth less than them because of his sexual leanings. They were merely looking for a pretext to justify their pathetic need to give somebody a thrashing and I would stand up against them every time."

"But Maynard."

"I haven't got anything against him personally but, as I said before, I haven't much sympathy. To be quite frank with you I find the idea of sex between men quite disgusting and although there is no way of stopping it, I don't feel inclined to encourage it by treating Maynard as a victim. After all, we don't show any compassion to other people who are driven by their inner compulsions, such as kleptomaniacs or obsessive gamblers: they have to control themselves or pay the price."

"Those things can affect others but what one does in private with another when both are willing should matter to nobody else."

Lyndon scratched his head and paused as he gave the subject further thought. "You have a point there but it is illegal and consequently he *has* committed a crime. If someone is trying to use that fact to blackmail him, any understanding he comes to with the blackmailer results in him being acquiescent to another crime. He should go straight to the police. Anyhow, what has brought him to this position? He knowingly committed a crime and then boasted about it and wrote about it, without any regard to the consequences. To do so is either stupid or arrogant enough to believe the law doesn't apply to you."

"Perhaps it shouldn't be a crime to do what he did."

"Perhaps it shouldn't but it is. I might think speeding in my car shouldn't be a crime and act accordingly, but to overtake a police car over the speed limit and give a rude sign to the policeman as you drive past is asking for trouble. Look, I don't wish Maynard any harm, but if you want me to help him evade the clutches of a blackmailer using nefarious methods yourself, I'm afraid I'm not your man. Another pint?"

We had another drink or two and dropped the subject of Maynard. When we left the pub, Lyndon wished me well in my effort to save Maynard and we parted on the best of terms, our friendship unaffected by our difference of opinion, as true friendship always is.

Despite the setback of Lyndon's refusal to help, I revisited Alec's plan with him and we agreed a refinement to it, which I organised just in time for it to go into action. The following Monday morning, at five minutes to nine, I watched Alec walk to the recently emptied waste bin on the edge of St James's Park where it fronts The Mall, surreptitiously drop the smallish holdall in the bin and briskly cross the road towards the Duke of York steps. I had already been parked for some half an hour or so about fifty yards back towards Admiralty Arch, keeping down in my seat to give the impression the car was empty but able to see the bin quite clearly. Nothing happened for what seemed like an hour, but was actually only ten minutes, when a taxi drove past me and pulled up a few yards past the bin. While I waited to see if a passenger alighted from the taxi, a man passed by my car, walking rapidly down The Mall towards the Victoria Monument. He was a few years younger than me, dressed in a three-quarter length topcoat and cap. He was looking to left and right as he proceeded and then slowed when he neared the waste bin. As he came to a halt, I saw from the corner of my eye another man, dressed in an overcoat and bowler hat, his face hidden by a scarf and dark glasses, nonchalantly walk across the road from the Duke of York steps.

Then everything happened at once. The man who had stopped by the bin pulled out the holdall and unzipped it to take a brief look inside. This galvanised the man crossing the road into action and he began running towards the bin, his arm reaching out for the bag. Immediately, the man with the holdall turned away and made to run off, only to be caught by his pursuer, and a fight ensued. It was brief. As the man in bowler hat and glasses lunged for the bag, the other pushed him away and, dropping the bag, he hit his assailant with three good punches: a left jab to the temple, a straight right to the midriff and, as the head came down, a crunching uppercut to the chin. The man's hat and glasses flew off and he hit the ground, banging his head. He lay still. The other man picked up the holdall and ran off into the park, while I got out of the car and went to the stricken man. I was joined first by Alec who witnessed the incident from wherever he had been watching, and then the driver from the waiting taxi. Arriving first, I pretended to check if the man was all right while feeling over his chest for a wallet. This was my first proper look at him. He was in his late forties, perhaps fifty. His dark hair was greying and was parted low over one side of his head. I suppose his features were, objectively, not unpleasant: a firm, slightly dimpled chin, thin lips, a longish nose and heavy brows over deep-set, currently closed eyes. However, confronted with my enemy I sought and found an unpleasant visage: a tight-lipped, cruel mouth, a beak-like nose and undoubtedly the eyes would be those of a scavenger.

"Would you mind calling an ambulance," I said to the taxi driver, "and perhaps the police?" The taxi driver nodded and crossed the road to where there was a telephone box.

While Alec shielded me from view, I searched the unconscious man's jacket and removed a wallet. When I stood up, I surreptitiously secreted it in my overcoat pocket. By this time, there was a small huddle of people watching events from the other side of the road but none sought to approach us or to interfere.

"I'll deal with this," I said to Alec.

"I'll go after him," he said and began running into the park, apparently after the thief.

With nobody else close by, I checked the man's pockets for any other clues about him. There was a bus ticket, which I ignored, and a folded sheet of paper with some names and numbers written on it: 'Anna, Charles Jackson – Trixie

Saturday lunch, 1, 2, 3, 8, 4, 1, 2.' For a moment I was tempted to keep the piece of paper, then thought better of it and, memorising the notes as best I could, returned it to the pocket. I stood up, took my notebook out and recorded what I'd read.

Having finished his call, the taxi driver emerged from the phone box and was surrounded by the bystanders, a couple of whom asked him questions. He shook his head and walked back to the scene of the fracas.

As I looked down at the man he came round, his hand reaching for his sore chin. I helped him sit up.

"What happened?" he asked.

"I don't know exactly. I just happened to be walking by when I saw you grappling with a man who then knocked you down and ran off. I think you may have been robbed."

The taxi driver had returned by this point. "You all right, guv?" he asked. "There's an ambulance on its way."

"I don't need an ambulance," said the man.

"I've called them now," said the taxi driver, sullen in his insistence, his good deed in danger of being turned into no more than a nuisance call. "You'll want to report this to the police, being beaten up and robbed and all. I saw him run off with your bag."

I ignored the taxi driver's assumed but incorrect version of events. Glancing behind me I saw a five-pound note which presumably had fallen from the holdall and was held from flying away by a stout weed. "He must have dropped this when he ran off," I said, retrieving the banknote.

The man was fully returned to his senses now and I could almost see the cogs in his brain whirring as he contemplated a conversation with the police. I saw, fifty yards away, a policeman strolling down The Mall towards us and the man saw him too. There was fear in his eyes. "It was of no importance," he said.

"Take me to Victoria Station, please," he said to the driver. He took the fiver I held out to him and thanked me.

The taxi driver looked a little stunned himself. "Are you the gentleman that ordered the taxi?"

"Yes. Let's go now." He quickly walked over to the taxi and climbed in.

The taxi driver looked at me and shrugged. "If he doesn't want to speak to the police it's up to him." Then he followed his fare to the waiting vehicle.

As I watched him shuffle off I knew we had our man as I had recognised the impatient, gravelly voice of our blackmailer. I looked round. The last two stragglers had accepted that the excitement was over and moved on. The policeman was sauntering along, still some way off. Even if he had been asked to look into the melee he would not be too put out if it was all over by the time he arrived. I walked back to my car, started the engine and eased away, down The Mall, turning right into Marlborough Road and then Pall Mall and back to the City. My original plan had been to follow the blackmailer but it was unlikely that he would use the taxi to take him home and there was always the danger that he might begin to put two and two together if he saw me following him. Anyhow, I had his wallet and that might be all we needed.

That evening I went straight to my club after work. Tommy Felstead, my old friend and comrade in arms in the Berkshire Yeomanry, was waiting for me, the holdall he had taken from the blackmailer under his arm. After Lyndon's refusal to help me, I had rung Tommy and he had come straight to my office. We hadn't seen each other for over a year and he had retired, but he had agreed immediately when I asked for help to get a friend out of a jam. I had described the situation as a matter of blackmail over a sexual indiscretion and he had asked for no further details. "There, but for the grace of God and all that," was his only comment.

Now, I shook his hand warmly and took him into an empty library where we ordered drinks. "Tommy, you were splendid," I said. "I'm sorry it wasn't as straightforward as I had expected."

"My fault entirely. I was hanging around so that I didn't arrive just after the money was dropped in the bin; it would have been too much of a coincidence. Another minute earlier and I would have had a head start on the villain."

"Well, it worked out very well as I was able to get a good look at him while he was dazed. You haven't lost any of your timing."

Tommy smiled. "I try to keep fit." He showed me his bruised right knuckle. "I think I hit him too hard with the uppercut. Was he all right?"

"Yes, he went off under his own steam and should be none the worse for it, at least physically."

He handed over the holdall. "Here's the bag. Everything going to plan?"

"I think so. We'll know later, especially if this helps us track him down." I showed him the dark crocodile leather wallet I had taken that morning. "I hope you understand me not giving you all the details, Tommy, but the fewer people who know more than they need to, the better."

"Absolutely agree, old boy, the less we know, the less we can tell. Bloody awful business blackmail, glad I got the chance to biff the blighter. Hope that you can frighten him off now; these people cause untold misery."

I smiled in admiration at Tommy, not only because he had done exactly as I had asked of him but also because he had acted on trust and my conviction that it was the right thing to do, no questions asked. Such faith is not easy to come by, though it is all too easily betrayed.

"One of the fivers fell out the holdall and I gave it to him, which added another note of authenticity. You are welcome to have the rest of the money in the holdall as your 'purse', if you like," I said.

He laughed. "Wouldn't dream of it. I rather enjoyed it: the tension before the action started, the shock of his arrival, the combat and the running for dear life. I remember my heart pounding when I stopped running and laughing out loud when I realised I had succeeded. I knew someone had chased after me but he soon gave up."

"That was my colleague. It was to add an air of authenticity and also to give him a chance to escape the vicinity."

"Clever. As I stood there with a big grin on my face, I saw a couple of women staring at me and moving on sharply in case I was one of those weird characters you always come across in parks. That made me laugh again. At our age, the moments when we feel alive, fully alive, get fewer and further between but this was certainly one of them. When it's all done with, you can tell me as much or as little of the story as you like over dinner at Claridge's."

"That's a date," I said.

We had another drink and updated each other on our latest news before we parted. I insisted on buying him a bottle of best brandy from the bar as I saw him off. Then I made my way to Alec's flat.

When he opened the door, Alec's face broke into a broad grin and he shook my hand vigorously. As he ushered me to a seat he said, "That was a brilliant idea, Lewis. He may believe we have tricked him but he can't be sure."

I smiled. "Sometimes I think he must know; it was too much of a coincidence. But you are right, there is sure to be a doubt in his mind and we must act as if we kept our side of the bargain. As far as we are concerned, we have paid the five thousand pounds in full and someone has it. In the meantime, we have this." I took the wallet from my pocket and threw it on the table.

"His wallet! Have you looked in it yet?"

"Yes."

"May I?"

"Of course."

Alec picked up the long wallet and opened it. He took out £3 in bank notes, an underground ticket from Tower Hill, a couple of penny postage stamps and a cinema ticket. He looked in the wallet again and shook his head. "Nothing of use here. Nice wallet though."

"I thought the same but look in the lining."

He flicked through the different compartments, shaking his head but then he saw the label. "Ah, it's the name of the shop where it was bought."

"Exactly. Of course, he may have bought it second-hand or been given it or even stolen it, but there's a chance. I found something else too." I produced my notebook and showed him the notes I had copied out. "I didn't take the original in case he got wind that we are on his tail."

Alec smiled. "Good thinking. But it just seems to be a lunch appointment. The numbers could mean anything. A telephone number? What do you make of it?"

"The same as you. I don't suppose it's much use. Does anyone have the name 'Trixie'?"

"I think there was an American singer, Trixie something, but it's certainly an unusual name. I think the wallet is our best bet."

Alec offered to investigate further but I had the bit between my teeth and, leaving early that evening, I took the tube to Bond Street Station and walked down New Bond Street to the grand leather goods shop, Finnigan's. It stood on a corner plot, an attractive building of stone and glass. I walked in past a display of luggage and was directed by a commissionaire to the appropriate department for wallets.

As I approached the counter, I was noticed by one of the sales staff, a young man dressed in a black jacket and pinstripe trousers, with curly blond hair partially tamed by a substantial application of Brylcreem.

"Can I be of assistance, sir?" he asked.

"I found this wallet in St James's Park the other day and I was hoping to return it to its owner. Unfortunately, there is nothing to identify the person and I thought you might be able to help."

He picked up the wallet. "Ah, yes. I know this type. We have stocked it for several years." He looked inside at the label. "As long as we have the serial number – yes, there it is." He showed me a little tag attached to the main label and put the wallet down while he fetched the sales ledger. Flipping through several pages, he ran his finger down a column and finally stopped at the correct match.

"Here we are." He lay his index finger on the serial number. "Most kind of you to wish to return the wallet to its rightful owner, sir: it's a very good item. If you like we could send it off to him on your behalf, rewrapped of course."

"Well, that's rather generous of you," I said, looking at the name and address and memorising it as best I could.

The young man took a pad. "Not at all, sir. May I enclose a brief note on your behalf?"

"Just say that it was found in St James's Park, near The Mall. No need to give a name."

"Thank you, sir. I'll see it is sent off tomorrow, Mr?"

"John Flanders," I said, already prepared for that question. "Thank you and good day."

"Good day to you, Mr Flanders."

As I walked back down New Bond Street, I pondered the likelihood of the wallet buyer being our man. *Do people buy themselves wallets? Would he have given a real name or a real address? Was he the first owner? But what other leads do we have?*

Once on the tube I wrote 'James Burgoyne' and his address in Belgravia into my notebook, though I knew I would never forget it. I also realised this business was taking over my life: I was constantly leaving the office to attend to it, having meetings purely to discuss it and going to the club in the evening for briefings and debriefings.

The next morning, I telephoned Alec with the news of Mr Burgoyne and he said that he had received another letter. He invited me to a further meeting at lunchtime, to which I could only agree.

We had lunch together in his office, the door locked. "I don't think he has worked it out, but he's hedging his bets in any case," said Alec. He passed me the letter.

> *"Lord Keynes,*
>
> *Yesterday did not go well. Someone intercepted the holdall before I got to it. I do not know if you were involved in what happened but the fact remains, I did not receive my money. I expect you to telephone me again Wednesday at 11am on the first number I gave you to discuss payment arrangements. The price is still £5,000.*
>
> *Gaius Praetor"*

"Hmm, he's acting as if we did steal the money," I said. "We should refuse to pay on the basis that we did what he asked. What happened afterwards is his problem. Any sign that we will pay the money without complaining would confirm any suspicion he has that we arranged the robbery."

"I intend to deal with him before he gets any money," said Alec. "It's a pity Tommy didn't kill him: accidentally, of course."

I knew I felt the same, at least in the abstract, but changed the subject. "Before you go any further, we have to make sure that Burgoyne is the man we saw in St James's Park, after all good quality wallets are often bought as presents for someone else."

"Yes, of course. I wish we had more time: I could find out more about him, perhaps even locate a photograph."

"I will go to see him. He might remember me but that won't matter as I was there when his wallet disappeared."

"But won't he think it odd that Finnigan's gave you his address? That might make him suspicious."

"Yes. You're right, I shall have to find another excuse to call. I only need to see him briefly."

"You don't mind doing this job?"

"No. Best to keep you out of the way until it's time to put your plan into action."

"It's going to be tight. We only have until the day after tomorrow before we have to telephone him and that call must take place for the plan to work."

"It will be fine."

The next day, still struggling to find a good reason for calling on Burgoyne, I wondered if I might get away with merely telephoning him. But I was not certain that I would know him simply by his voice so I decided to grab the bull by the horns and pay him a visit. I spent the morning thinking of complicated reasons why I might wish to visit Mr Burgoyne, all of which collapsed under closer examination. Eventually, I decided on a simple solution. I would deliver a parcel. I went to Fortnum and Mason's and had them put two good single malts in a gift box and wrapping paper. That evening, at about seven o'clock, I stood outside a large house in a cream-coloured terrace. The house had a columned portico with the number painted black on each pillar. By the front door was a list of the occupants of the three flats into which the house was divided: Flat B was occupied by J S L Burgoyne. The front door was not locked and I entered the hall and mounted the carpeted stairs to Flat B. With a trepidation which surprised me, I pressed the doorbell, noticing my hand was shaking a little.

After a minute or so, during which time it crossed my mind that Burgoyne might be out, the front door swung open and a man of about forty-five or so, with slightly receding light-brown hair and a matching moustache looked at me and smiled quizzically.

"Mr Burgoyne?" I asked, realising that a positive answer would dash my hopes.

"Yes."

"I have a delivery for you. You have won a prize in the Lord Mayor's charity lottery."

He looked at me blankly. "I don't recall buying any tickets in that."

"The charity goes under various names."

"I see. Well, perhaps my wife bought them. She handles that kind of thing. I'm surprised you take the trouble to deliver by hand."

"Just the better prizes, especially if they are fragile." I handed him the package and the bottles rattled inside.

"I understand. This is my second piece of good fortune today."

"Oh?"

"Yes. A wallet I had purchased some time ago for my brother and that I never expected to see again was returned to me by the shop where I bought it."

"Really? A pleasant surprise?" I felt a pang of excitement and expectation that Burgoyne's brother might be our man. But the flame of hope was immediately extinguished.

"Yes, my brother lost it when he was last over here on leave, couldn't remember where. He's serving in Germany at the moment. Finnigan's said it was found in St. James's Park, near The Mall. I can quite believe that. He went to the Army & Navy Club the day he lost it. It was returned with the money still in it, lost a couple of documents but they are replaceable. He will be very pleased when he comes home, especially as it is in such good condition."

I smiled to cover my bitter disappointment. "Very good news."

"Yes. Two strokes of luck in one day. They say these things happen in threes, let's hope so." He laughed. "Well, thanks very much for bringing the prize round, Mr?"

"Williams. I hope you enjoy the prize."

"I'm sure I will. Thank you. Goodbye." He closed the door behind me.

I walked down the stairs totally dispirited, the false, cheerful expression falling from my face. After all we had been through, we were no nearer identifying the blackmailer. In my mind the smiling features of Burgoyne were replaced by those of 'Praetor' or whatever his name was and I wanted to smash my fist into it.

I telephoned Alec and gave him the bad tidings. I thought he might be panicked by the news but if he was, he didn't show it in his voice. "I'm only sorry that you went to all that trouble and expense."

I smiled. "That's no matter. I got back most of the £200 we had put in the holdall. Burgoyne seemed like a pleasant, decent man so I don't begrudge buying him a few drinks."

We agreed there appeared to be no option but to carry out

the blackmailer's instructions and that I would try to get some delay in paying the blackmail money to give us more time to track him down.

The next morning, I made sure I was in the telephone box by ten to eleven, wondering why Praetor always chose this time. Perhaps he was a creature of habit, always using the same modus operandi in his criminal activities and the same sort of target. Now I was caught up in his shady dealings, carrying out the instructions of a young man less than half my age to protect a man who had done nothing to protect himself. I shrugged inwardly, thinking *we are where we are*. While I waited for eleven o'clock, I inserted four pence in the box and was irritated when someone knocked on the door. I politely waved the man away, picking up the receiver and making the call. I pressed button A when a female voice answered.

"Can I help you?" she asked politely.

"Maynard here," I replied. Caught off-guard by this relatively friendly response to my call, I completely forgot to use Maynard's voice.

"Please ring the following number," she said, first dictating the number and then repeating it in a polite, pleasant voice. Then she said, "Goodbye" and was gone, leaving me to mutter my thanks and respond to her farewell. I waited until I had a line and dialled the new number. It was not the one Praetor had used the previous time. I was vaguely aware of the man waiting to use the telephone staring at me pleadingly through the window.

"Hello."

I recognised the voice instantly.

"It's Maynard," I said, in the right voice this time. The man waiting outside had given up and was walking forlornly up the street.

"Do you have my money?" he asked.

"You have already been paid."

"It was taken before I could get to it."

"I only have your word for that and you can hardly expect me to trust your word."

"I assure you it was taken from the bin before I could get to it."

"I'm afraid that is nothing to do with me. The money was put in the bin at the time you requested, so anything that went wrong afterwards is purely your concern."

There was silence at the other end of the line for a few seconds before Praetor replied. "I have not received the money and the price is still the same. The consequences of refusal to pay are still the same," he insisted, speaking rather robotically and, I sensed, without great conviction.

I kept reminding myself that delay in payment was our main strength in dealing with this obnoxious man and there was no relaxation of my stonewalling. "You are being totally unreasonable. You made your quite outrageous demand and I arranged to leave the money; you cannot expect me to pay twice because somebody else came on the scene. I have paid once and I am not paying again."

There was another long silence.

"I must have something." There was a hint of desperation in his gravelly voice which made him sound all the more repulsive.

This time I said nothing.

"You could afford it," he said eventually.

"I can't afford to hand over another five thousand pounds."

"I'll accept four thousand."

"I can't afford it."

"Three thousand."

"No. I'll give you two thousand and I must have a way of ensuring that you do not ask for any more."

"Two thousand five hundred and I promise I will never trouble you again."

*Promises are cheap,* I thought. "How do I know you are not just saying that?" I asked.

"I will keep my word."

I ignored his protestation; the man was a scoundrel and I had nothing but loathing and contempt for him. I had no intention of keeping my word to him, unless I had no alternative. "I shall pay the money but I want a sign that you mean to behave straightforwardly. Send me two of the original letters tomorrow. We must also have a more fool-proof way of exchanging the money and the rest of the letters. We cannot have a repeat of what happened before." I waited while he thought about the proposal, aware of a slight tic under my left eye.

When he eventually answered, he sounded less sure of himself. "I will decide later today how the exchange will happen this time and I will send you my arrangements tonight, together with *one* of the incriminating letters."

Before I could respond, the line went dead. As the conversation raced through my now throbbing head, there was a rap on the door and I was jolted from my thoughts. I looked through the glass to see a middle-aged woman glaring at me. I opened the door and came out. "Haven't you the patience to wait for a minute?" I asked. "Is your call a matter of life and death?"

"Er, no," she replied.

"Mine was," I said, letting the door go, rather than holding it for her, and annoyed by my slight feeling of guilt about my act of ungallantry.

"Well!" she exclaimed, exaggeratedly pulling the heavy door open as if she were single-handedly attempting to open the Golden Gate of Constantinople.

# XV

# *SOLVING THE PUZZLE*

I MET ALEC FOR YET ANOTHER TACTICAL MEETING at lunchtime that day. We were both gloomy about the situation; having no idea who the blackmailer really was, and with the opportunities for delay shrinking with each day that passed, a surrender and agreement to the terms of the blackmailer were becoming ever more inevitable. We had chosen to meet in a crowded bar as the weather was closing in. I thought Alec looked quite desperate, rocking backward and forward slightly as he lamented our failed attempt to identify the 'enemy' as he referred to 'Gaius Praetor'. I preferred to use the name even if it were only a nom de plume.

"Perhaps his name is a clue," he said. "He may be one of those arrogant types who delights in being able to outwit the inferior people he's dealing with. I did try anagrams of his name: Porter, Gore, Rouse, Gates, Prout, probably others, but the letters left over never make much sense. I may be wrong, of course.

As I listened, I found myself searching for other names from 'Gaius Praetor' without any luck. Then I had a thought. "Saxe," I said.

Alec stared. "What?"

I smiled for the first time that day. "Saxon Sydney-Turner. You know him?"

"I know of him. Maynard has written to him occasionally but I have never met him."

"He has a great mind and enjoys solving problems. He might see something we can't."

"Can he be trusted?"

"As much as anyone I've ever known. He's also one of Maynard's oldest friends. I'll ring him now." Within a few minutes I had arranged a meeting with Saxe at half past five that afternoon.

"You *will* impress on him the urgency of the situation," said Alec as we walked out of the bar, the strain of it all evident in his voice.

I nodded. "If he can't figure it out, we shall have to find a way of trapping Praetor. We are not giving up without a fight."

Alec patted me on the back and we said goodbye.

I went back to the office and copied out all the various names that Alec had come up with out of 'Gaius Praetor'. Then I added 'Rogers', but I could think of no others. I went through my work neither with enthusiasm nor commitment, waiting for my appointment time, which seemed never to arrive.

I arrived early at Saxon's flat. He had worked a little past retirement age, for the war effort, but had been retired for a couple of years. I thought he had aged rather since I'd last seen him and both he and his residence were untidy. There were books stacked all over the place, including two racing form books on his desk, and several editions of the *Sporting Life* and the racing pages of other newspapers piled on an armchair.

We shook hands and he offered me a drink, which I was pleased to have before getting down to business.

"I haven't seen you for a while," he said, without reproach in his voice.

"No, I'm afraid I've been remiss with most of my friends lately. I'm retiring once the war is over and I've got forty years of paperwork to go through, as well as handing over the reins. It's keeping me busy."

"I'm sure."

"Mind you, I sometimes wonder if I were to burn the whole lot, how many of those documents would ever be required in the future."

"If you burn just one, that will be the one that people need to see."

I smiled, nodding in agreement. "I saw Maynard the other day."

"I haven't seen him since I left the Treasury. How is he?"

"He works very hard and I think this commuting between London and America is taking too much out of him and so much depends on him."

Saxe didn't answer and I thought it was time I turned to the purpose of my visit.

"It's good of you to see me at such short notice, Saxe," I said and we raised our glasses to each other.

"Always glad to see an old friend."

"I do need your help, on a rather serious matter."

He raised his eyebrows. "Solving a 'real-life puzzle', as I think you called it when you rang?"

"It is, but I'm afraid it's not an amusement, it's a deadly serious business. Maynard is being blackmailed."

"Good God; whatever for?"

"Events in his youth of a sexual nature."

"Before he was married?"

"Yes."

"So, I assume they are not to do with young single girls."

"No, nor old married girls or anything in between. Were you aware of his homosexuality?"

"Not in any great detail, but I was aware that his preference was for young men. Surely past conduct that long ago would not be grounds for blackmail now?"

"He had rather a lot of adventures and apparently bragged about them in letters as well as making self-incriminating lists. If they became public knowledge, his reputation, his stature, would inevitably be affected. Even if it did not derail the important work he is doing, it would be a distraction and at the very least affect his concentration and commitment. The consequences could be very serious. Sorry to sound melodramatic about it, Saxe, but it's as bad as that."

"I see. What has he done about it so far?"

"Nothing. You see, he doesn't know. Maynard's health is quite fragile and his assistant is worried that it might not hold up if Maynard has all this to deal with on top of everything else. His assistant, Alec Harborough, has asked me to help him track this fellow down and…"

Saxon frowned. "And do what, exactly?"

"I'm not sure. I believe he hopes that he could find where the man lives and then use that knowledge to persuade him to give up the letters or drop the idea of blackmail under threat of exposing him to the police."

"And how could I be of help in finding this man?"

"This is where the puzzle comes in. We don't know much about him but he signs his letters and there is no need for him to do that so we assume it's some kind of alias. It might be possible that out of arrogance or mischief he is giving us a clue to his real identity, confident that we would not be able to discover what that is. He doesn't know how good you are at puzzles."

Saxon fell into one of his famously long silences but I did not rush to fill the void; I could wait.

"I am not as confident as you are about that," said Saxon eventually. "Nor am I comfortable acting behind Maynard's back. But I do understand why his assistant is trying not to involve him."

"Here are Alec's details if you need to contact him," I said, handing over Alec's card. "As a matter of fact, Saxe, I didn't want to go behind Maynard's back myself, but he is quite poorly at the moment; Lydia won't even let me speak to him. I feel we have no alternative but to leave him out of this. You'll help?"

He took my empty glass and refilled it. Another lengthy pause followed. He just stared at his glass, gently rocking it in his hand so the drink swirled but did not spill. Then he raised the glass, drank it back in one gulp and looked at me.

"I assume there is no time for me to think it over?"

"Time is rather tight."

"Very well, I'll do my best, Lewis. But if I am able to help identify this person, I want your word that there will be no use of violence in your dealings with him, contemptible though his behaviour is."

"You have my word."

"What do you have so far?"

I gave him the first blackmail letter with its demand for money and quotation at the bottom. I also gave him the list of names we had found from anagrams of 'Gaius Praetor'.

"These are the only clues you have?"

"As to his identity, yes."

He frowned. "Just a name which can be turned into a jumble of letters that may or may not be a clue to his identity and a quotation. What is his writing like?"

"He writes his letters in capitals but there are no spelling mistakes. I have spoken to him on the telephone and he sounds quite educated."

"So, a quite educated man who has a knowledge of literature and uses the adopted name 'Gaius Praetor'? It's not much to go on."

"I know; I don't have any great expectations really but you are probably our best hope. If you think it's not worth trying, I'll understand."

He smiled. "No, no, I welcome the challenge and anything I can do to help. Let's explore what we have and search for ideas. 'Gaius' is a common name, as in Julius Gaius Caesar. Gaius was a very famous judge in Rome in the second half of the second century AD. He was possibly the greatest jurist of that era. Praetor was the title of a magistrate in Ancient Rome. His nom de plume is stressing the law and his right to carry it out. That fits in with the tone of his letter, which points to him being a moraliser of some sort. This quotation confirms that. I don't see that helps much in identifying the man. Even if we find a name, it may not help us identify him. Is that all you have?"

I took out my notebook. "We did arrange to pay a ransom at one point and tried to apprehend him at the time. There was a scuffle and he was knocked down. While he was dazed, I took his wallet and copied a note I found in his inside pocket. This is the copy: it appears to be an arrangement for lunch with various people. What the numbers signify, I have no idea." I passed him the notebook.

He looked at the note in silence for a few moments. "May I keep this note?"

"Yes. Just tear it out of the book."

He did so and looked at it again. "You must know what this man looks like?" he said, looking up.

"Yes. I was closer to him than I am to you."

"That makes it much easier to pick him out if we could be sure where he was going to be at a given time."

"Yes. Look, I don't want to rush you but..."

"I know, come round tomorrow evening and I will let you know what, if anything, I have discovered." He ushered me to the door, a spring in his step, and closed the door while I was still making my farewell.

The following day, Praetor's next letter had not yet arrived and Alec and I assumed he had missed the post. For this we were grateful as we had as yet no inkling as to our next step. Alec accompanied me to see Saxon at six o'clock.

When Saxon opened the door, I was struck by the difference in demeanour from the previous evening. He looked years younger and smiled broadly as he welcomed us both. After asking us to sit down and pouring three drinks, he walked to his desk and picked up his jotting pad.

"I tried various ways of using the letters in 'Gaius Praetor' to find something of use, without anything standing out. Names such as Porter, Rogers or Page would be of little help. Only a really unusual surname would do and then how would we spot it in this anagram? I'm afraid, as far as I can see, it is merely a nom de plume."

"Have we reached a dead-end?" I asked.

Saxon smiled. "Not at all. The note you gave me is very interesting. As you say, it appears to be an arrangement for lunch with the people named. The name which caught my eye is 'Trixie'. It is an unusual name, and I have never met or heard of anyone with it. However, the word is sometimes used as a term for a particular kind of bet in horseracing. The better chooses three horses, say A, B and C, then places four bets: three doubles, A+B, A+C, B+C and one treble, A+B+C. If only one horse wins, the better loses everything. If two horses win, one of the doubles will pay out. If all three win, then the better wins all four bets."

Alec appeared puzzled. "So each bet is a kind of piggyback; the winnings from one horse are automatically placed as the bet on another."

"That's exactly right. The names Anna, Charles and Jackson are abbreviations of the names of horses. The fact that you said the note was scribbled means it was written hurriedly, thus the horses' names were not written in full. The note mentions Saturday and I have looked at the lists of provisional runners at the five racecourses in Britain that have a meeting this Saturday. I found one meeting at which three horses can be found which match approximately the names in the note: Anna Karenina, Charles the Fair and Jackson's Folly. The meeting is at Newbury. Whether the reference to lunch relates to the race meeting, I'm not sure."

"Well done, Saxe," I said. "You must have spent a long time on this."

"Not really. I had the necessary research materials to hand."

"What do the numbers refer to?" asked Alec.

"They are the particular races which each runner is in and their number: race number 1, horse number 2: race number 3, horse number 8: race number 4, horse number 12. The numbers tie in with the horses' names."

Alec nodded. "Thanks very much, Saxon. We know our man has a lunch appointment and also has a chosen number of bets which he may choose to place. Both may take place on Saturday and possibly at Newbury races. There must be a hope this information could lead us nearer to finding him."

"We are going to the races!" I said. "If he isn't there we have lost nothing but there is a chance that the lunch meeting is at the races and that he will be there in person to follow his horses."

"It's a long shot," said Alec.

"It's all we have at the moment," I replied.

We spent the next half an hour or so planning our tactics for Saturday. Newbury racecourse is only about forty minutes' drive from my home and I have been there several times over the years, both during the National Hunt season and for racing on the flat. During the war, facilities were reduced in scale but the fine stands were in full operation and there was a restaurant available in the members' enclosure. The racecourse has its own adjacent railway station and we thought that would be the obvious way to travel. The first race on Saturday was at 1.30 so anybody wishing to have lunch before the first race would presumably aim to arrive around twelve. As it was a racing day there would be trains arriving every twenty minutes or so between 11.50 and 1.20. We decided to get to the course early and wait and watch as the crowds turned up. We would arrive on the 11.50.

"We need a plan of what to do if we find him," said Alec.

"Let's sleep on it and share our thoughts later because until we are actually at the course we won't know what our options are," I suggested and the others agreed.

I had assumed that Saxon would not wish to accompany us but he offered his services since, as he pointed out, the blackmailer might recognise me and he might be able to assist in some way if Alec needed help.

Alec left immediately to go back to his office. I, tired and more sceptical, sought relief in another drink and reminiscences with Saxe of happier times we had shared with Maynard. Then I went home.

As usual, I was late, much later than Lina had been used to throughout my career. She didn't comment but I could sense she was a little troubled by this sudden change of habit, especially when Alec telephoned at about ten o'clock.

"I've had a few ideas and I wanted to share them with you so you can mull them over."

"Fire away."

"I thought if we could be in the restaurant at the same time, one of us could spill something over him, apparently accidentally, and offer to send him a cheque for the cleaning."

"Yes, that might work."

"Another idea was that one of us might suggest we thought we knew him and get into conversation. The third was that we might get to know one of his lunch companions in some way."

"They're all good ideas. I haven't given it any thought yet but I think we might work on those as options. Let's discuss them tomorrow."

Alec wished me goodnight and put the phone down.

"Who was that?" asked Lina.

"Just Alec."

"Again! He's always calling you. He seems to command so much of your time."

"We are thinking of going to the races on Saturday."

She frowned. "Really? You have never mentioned Alec in connection with horseracing before."

"We are taking Saxe. The poor old boy needs a bit of a lift."

She nodded, seemingly unconvinced, and said she was going up to bed, abruptly bidding me goodnight. I poured myself a brandy and spent several minutes trying to find a workable plan of action from those Alec had suggested. We had so little time to think and tomorrow the next set of instructions from Praetor or whatever his name was would arrive and perhaps forestall our plan for Newbury.

As expected, Alec rang me at the office the next morning. "The next set of instructions for the money drop has just arrived. They are much the same as last time. I'll go through it with you later but there is some good news."

"Oh, what's that?"

"He doesn't want us to make the next drop until Tuesday. This means we have Saturday to find out what we can about him."

"That is good news! Tally-ho for Saturday."

# XVI

# *A DAY AT THE RACES*

SATURDAY MORNING ARRIVED AFTER WHAT SEEMED an interminable wait. On the Friday night, I had one of those awful dreams where you have to get to a particular place by a certain time and everything conspires to stop that happening. Of course, it was just a dream about anxiety and frustration and that was uppermost in my mind when I woke. As I lay there, looking at the clock which showed half-past five, I was sure our man would not go to the racecourse but would have a lunch elsewhere in the country, comfortable in the knowledge that his Trixie had been placed with his turf accountant.

In preparation for the day, I had spoken to a committee member of the course whom I knew quite well and he had kindly arranged for me to collect three pass tickets for the members' enclosure when we arrived. This was a precaution to make sure that there was no part of the course closed to us when we conducted our search.

We met at Paddington and took a first-class compartment on our train, hoping that we would have it to ourselves. Unfortunately, we were joined by another party of three, with whom we exchanged greetings and shared views on the racing for the day. Saxe proved more knowledgeable than either Alec or myself and even suggested one or two horses that he thought might do well. When Alec was asked what he fancied he, for want of anything to say, proposed Anna Karenina, to which one of our travelling companions replied that the character in the book had more chance of winning the race than the horse. We all laughed, we three conspirators, without much conviction, doing our best to be convivial though our minds were elsewhere.

As the train pulled into Newbury Racecourse Station we were already off our seats and alighted quickly. Walking briskly, we were almost at the front of the crowd going through the ticket barrier and none of the people who went through before us looked very much like our blackmailer, as far as I could tell. We took our position near the newsstand, hoping to catch sight of 'Praetor', though only too aware that both Alec and I had seen him only once and Saxe not at all. In fact, every man in a bowler hat, and that was more than half the total number, looked like 'Praetor' to me. The crowd of passengers coming towards us thinned, then became a trickle. I looked at Alec and he shook his head as the last passenger, a rotund man in a tweed overcoat and a brown trilby, accompanied by a much younger, much thinner woman, came along the platform, puffing and wheezing in tempo with the stationary engine. As those last two disappeared past us, we stood rather deflated.

"What now?" asked Saxe.

"The next train?" I replied and looked at Alec. He nodded.

We went into the buffet and had a cup of tea and a rock cake and waited for the next train. The buffet was decorated with railway posters of days away, including one of *Racing at Ascot* with smiling punters in morning suits and summer dresses before they had laid their wagers. It was not a cold day, in fact it was quite mild compared to the bitterness of January, so we were not reluctant to resume our position outside to wait for the next train. A few minutes later, the 12.10 train arrived and we went through the same process as before and, once again, scanned the crowds as they left the train, staring at possibles and dismissing impossibles and finally accepting defeat: Praetor had not arrived by train in time for lunch before the first race.

"Do we try one more?" asked Alec.

"He could manage a light lunch if he arrived on the next train," I said, more in hope than faith. "But if we spend the time here, we may miss him if he has come down by car."

"We don't have to be in the restaurant in time for lunch," said Saxe. "We just need to see if he is in there."

We nodded and had a coffee this time and a dry corned beef sandwich. We didn't discuss the situation. We had a plan and all was not lost if the blackmailer was not on the next train; and he wasn't. I didn't feel disappointed this time because none of us had expected him to be, we were just going through the motions. Our hopes were now concentrated on the racecourse.

We entered the main course area and collected our daily passes for the enclosure from the stewards' office. With our passes flapping on treasury tags from our lapels, we made our way into the first-class enclosure and sought out the bars and restaurant in the grandstand. The first bar was full but we didn't stop to look round: we were heading for the restaurant. From the door we could see some of the tables but it was not possible to see them all.

"Good afternoon, gentlemen. Do you have a reservation?"

"No," I answered, smiling.

He looked down his list and shook his head. "We have nothing at the moment. Perhaps at a quarter past one?"

I smiled and turned to the others. Alec shook his head and I noticed his eyes were pointed behind the head waiter. I looked in that direction and there he was, our man, seated at a table in the far corner with two other men, still eating what appeared to be the main course.

I turned back to the head waiter, his attentive expression unchanged. "I think we'll give it a miss today, thank you; don't want to miss the first race."

The head waiter smiled. "Very good, sir. Perhaps we'll see you on another occasion."

We retreated from the restaurant area and stood in the bustling entrance to the stand. "Well, he's here," said Alec. "Perhaps we missed him or he came by car. The possibility of spilling something on him is not on. We'll have to think of something else."

"I think we should hang around with them in our sights and wait for something to turn up," I said.

"You must be careful," said Alec. "He might recognise you. You go to the bar and wait there and I'll lounge by the restaurant."

We did what Alec suggested but it was all rather awkward. I bought the drinks while Saxe kept an eye on Alec who tried to appear unobtrusive. But when I returned with the drinks, I thought he looked rather suspicious. Nobody else seemed to pay much attention. I suppose we were waiting around for about twenty minutes, then Alec raised his hand and out came 'Praetor' and his companions.

"You'd better get your bet on, Esmond, mustn't miss out on your tip," said the elder of them to 'Praetor'.

"No," said Esmond, smiling. "I'll stroll over to the bookies. Are either of you placing a bet?"

"I've already been down the card," said the other, younger man.

"I'll come over with you," said the elder man. "See you in our seats," he said as they went over to the betting ring.

"I think we should lay the same bet as Esmond," said Alec, "and with the same bookie."

"Good idea," I replied.

We all three walked over at a distance from the other group but then changed our minds and went to the bookie next to Esmond's. We didn't want any coincidences which might rouse suspicion. Saxe placed the same Trixie as Esmond and I laid some different bets to keep things interesting. While we were placing our bets, Alec was within earshot of Esmond but, unfortunately, did not pick up any more useful information. He followed them back towards the stands, straining to hear their conversation, while we hurried to catch them up. By the time we caught up with Alec, he was standing, waiting for us: Esmond and the other man were going up to their seats to join their younger companion. We followed them. The seats were not numbered and we took our place about twenty yards away from the other three.

"I managed to pick up something of their conversation," said Alec, as we took our seats. "They are not friends, it seems. Esmond said to the other man, 'Thank you for inviting me, Arthur; I am really enjoying the day.' The other one replied, 'It was the least I could do, after all you have done.' That was all I could catch before they started upstairs."

We sat in our seats, half watching the horses as they emerged from the paddock and half watching Esmond and his friends. The third member of their party was much younger than Esmond and Arthur, who were both in their fifties. He noticed we were looking at him and he smiled at us, more specifically at Alec, who smiled back. Meanwhile the runners and riders were cantering to the start of the long course for a novices' hurdles, in which *Anna Karenina* was the second favourite by the time the race started. Temporarily, we were distracted by the race and we cheered as *Anna Karenina* came in third because Saxe had laid his bet each way. I saw Alec look round at Esmond and his companions and they were also cheering.

In the second race, which was over the jumps over a distance of two and a half miles, *Charles the Fair*, our horse, led for most of the race but fell at the last and that was the treble bet lost. Alec asked if we wished to go for a consolation drink but we declined and he went off to the nearby bar. Saxe and I discussed different tactics to find out more about Esmond without a clear plan and I did wonder with some irritation why Alec had decided to disappear at this time. He missed the third race but returned ten minutes later.

"Where have you been?" I asked, abruptly.

"I have some news," said Alec.

"Oh, really?" I said.

Alec smiled. "His name is Esmond Templing."

"Good grief, how did you find out?" I asked.

"When I went to the bar, I found myself standing near one of his companions, the young one, and we got into conversation. He works for the same organisation as the older man, Arthur. I didn't find out what, but some sort of medical research. I said I thought I knew Esmond vaguely but couldn't remember his surname. He told me without hesitation and that his colleague had taken Templing out on a day at the races as an appreciative gesture for a large donation Templing made to their work. He asked me if I'd like to join them but I declined for obvious reasons and told him I had an uncle and his friend to look after. But I think we ought to watch the remaining races from elsewhere on the course, in case Templing takes too much interest in us." He looked over and waved to the young man and then we made our way to the open terraces.

The fourth race featured *Jackson's Folly* and he won by two lengths. We collected Saxon's winnings on one each-way double; he actually came out down a pound. None of my selections produced a return but it was of no importance: we headed for home, a little poorer but feeling that we had hit the jackpot.

# XVII

# *THE PHILANTHROPIST*

When we arrived back in London, we dropped Saxe off, went back to Alec's flat and began the search for Esmond Templing. We found only three Templings in the London telephone directory and just one with the initial E.

"I'll check the electoral register tomorrow but I think we have found him. It was almost too easy at the end," said Alec.

I laughed. "We did all the hard work before we got to this point. Even if he'd had a more common name, we'd have found him eventually. Where does he live?"

"Holland Park."

I nodded. "We'll start to make plans tomorrow. I don't think we should wait until Monday, do you?"

"Of course not."

"I'll call you in the morning. Well done, Alec; you were brilliant."

I rang Alec early, not having slept well. He had not had much sleep either.

"I couldn't sleep; I was too wound up about everything. First things first, Templing's letter. He wants Maynard, in other words you, to phone him again and he will tell you what to do next. Same procedure as before: you make one call and then you will be directed to another for the instructions regarding the money. Then, I shall have the opportunity to carry out the plan I've been working on from the very beginning."

"Which is?"

"To break into his home while you keep him occupied and, hopefully, take away the incriminating evidence against Maynard."

"You are willing to do this? The risks are enormous."

"It's the only chance to stop all this coming out sooner or later."

"Well, if you're sure."

He nodded. "After going through the plan in my mind over and over, I eventually, at about half-past seven, took a trip to Holland Park, to the block of flats where Templing lives. There are four floors and I assume his flat is on the third floor, judging by the flat number, so breaking in would be extremely difficult. There is a porter at reception on the ground floor and I went in and asked him for directions to get a chance to look around. Behind his desk, the porter has keys to all the flats in a cabinet, which was open when I saw it. I think my best chance of getting into the flat is to hope the cabinet is open and to get hold of the key."

I smiled. "But how?"

"I know; it's easier said than done. Somehow, the porter has to be distracted but I haven't yet worked it out."

But Alec did work it out and phoned me later with his instructions for my part in the plan. Once again, I was to act as Maynard and try to keep Templing occupied on the telephone as long as possible. Meanwhile Alec would endeavour to get into Templing's flat and remove any incriminating letters or other papers connected to Maynard before making good his exit. Alec didn't tell me the exact details of how he would gain entry. However, we both thought it best that I should make the telephone call from near the flat so that I would be on hand if needed. Alec had already noted a telephone box about fifty yards from the block of flats, on the other side of the road. I was to make the phone call from there and wave a handkerchief or something equally visible from the door of the box as soon as I had Templing on the line so Alec would know it was safe to make his entry. For whatever reason, Templing had given us a few days' grace, enough time for Alec to get organised.

The next morning, I dropped Alec off in the service road behind the apartment block then drove to my station by the chosen telephone box. It was five minutes before the appointed time but I took up my position in the box to make sure nobody else could take my place. I picked up the receiver and waited. A man in an overcoat and cloth cap started waiting outside the box and I pretended, perhaps too theatrically, that I was talking until my watch showed 9.59. Then I dialled the number, leaving the man outside miffed to see what he thought was me making another call. Once again, a polite woman gave me a second number and I put in another fourpence and dialled again. This provoked a tap on the glass and a rude gesture from the man outside to which I indicated I would be only a few minutes. As I recognised Templing's voice answer, I opened the door, said I would be as quick as possible to the bemused man, and waved my handkerchief ferociously in the direction of Templing's apartment block, the waiting man staring at my extravagant gestures.

"Hello," Templing answered for a second time.

"I'm here. I've got some fool waiting for the telephone and he keeps opening the door."

"Why do you always ring from a public telephone?"

"The conversation is less likely to be overheard or thought suspicious from a public phone box. I would have thought you glad that I am being so careful in such matters. You use a public box too, don't..."

He interrupted my intended soliloquy on the merits of public phone boxes which I had prepared to keep him on the line as long as possible.

"That's enough. I don't like being kept waiting. Is the money ready?" he said irritably.

"It all depends on what you mean by ready. I have the money available but I do not have it on me."

He sighed frustratedly. "But you have the money. In order that there can be no slip-ups this time, I want you to take the Circle Line train eastbound at Mansion House; the first train after twelve noon. Enter the train by the first carriage, the door just behind the driver. A woman will be waiting on the train and you will pass the bag containing the money to her and she will give you a small envelope with the letter. You will not get off the train at Cannon Street to try to follow her. If she is apprehended in any way, copies of the letters will be sent to the newspapers. If all is well after I check the money, the copies will be destroyed."

"How will I know the woman?"

The line went dead. I cursed the fact that I had been unable to keep the call going, especially as I had no idea of the location of the telephone I had just called. Realising that Templing could arrive back at the apartment block at any moment, I burst out of the phone box, inadvertently knocking the man waiting to use the telephone out of the way, and ran the fifty yards or so to the apartment building. I had no idea what I would do if Templing appeared but I hoped to have enough time to think something up by the time he arrived back at the flat. I knew Alec must be in the flat as he said he would be waiting for me on the corner of the street if he had been unsuccessful in gaining entry to it. There was nobody to be seen. I was breathing heavily after my exertion and, after a few deep breaths, I walked slowly towards the swing doors at the entry of the apartment block. As I stood there, waiting for I knew not what, a lady came out of the building and I had a brief glimpse of the porter. He was leaning on his counter, reading something. All seemed quiet. I relaxed; surely Templing was unlikely to use a telephone box near his home. I walked over to my car and moved it a little way up the road, to wait for Alec.

I sat in my car, staring up the road towards the entrance to the apartment block, resisting the temptation to look away. After several minutes I saw Templing, well dressed as I had last seen him, in bowler hat and overcoat, walking leisurely from the direction of the tube station, a newspaper under his arm. He would not pass my car before he reached the apartment block so there was no way I could apprehend him in a casual conversation. I thought, *I must raise the alarm, but how?* I jumped out of the car and walked swiftly towards him, unsure what I could do without arousing his suspicion. With my eyes fixed on him and my mind elsewhere, I didn't see the elderly lady come out of a building and I collided with her, knocking her to the ground. By the time I had apologised, helped her to her feet and made sure she was all right, it was too late and Templing had disappeared into the foyer. After a second or two of prevarication I followed him. He was at the counter, chatting to the porter, who was checking the post for him.

"I thought it was you," I said. "How are you?" I made my tone of voice as different as I could from that of Maynard.

Templing stared at me blankly. Clearly, he didn't remember me.

"Aren't you the chap who got knocked down and robbed in The Mall last week?"

He nodded slowly. "Yes. I don't remember much about it. Did you see it?"

"I helped you up afterwards. You went off in a taxi. No lasting effects from your experience, I hope?"

"No, Mr?"

"Flanders."

"Thank you," he said.

"That was a very bad business, in broad daylight, too. Similar thing happened to my cousin a few weeks ago. Well, I hope the police catch him, whoever..."

"Yes. If you'll excuse me, I have some work to do." He turned to the lift and pressed the call button.

Time was running out. "I found your wallet, after you'd gone off in the taxi," I called out to him.

He was about to step into the open doors of the lift but stopped and turned to me.

"Oh, did you? Have you still got it?"

"No. I found the shop's name on the label and I asked them to return it to you."

He appeared uncomfortable and a little unsure of himself but, after a pause, regained his composure. "Thank you. I am sure it will be returned in due course," he said, turning back to the lift. He disappeared before I could answer.

I stood, dumbstruck, bereft of ideas short of a mad run up the stairs in the hope of stopping him before the inevitable clash occurred and all our scheming and planning came to nothing. I knew it was hopeless and was ready to accept defeat.

"Is there anything I can do for you, sir?" asked the porter.

"Er, no thank you."

I wandered out into the dull, winter's day and, after a minute or two of indecision, walked round the back of the building to where the fire escape was located. Alec had told me he would exit from the building that way to avoid being seen by the porter. It could not be long now: either he would have finished the job and managed to get out before he was apprehended or he would not come out at all. I decided to give him another two minutes before I assumed he was in trouble. Suddenly, a few moments later, there he was, climbing from a window and clambering down the metal steps making, it seemed to me at any rate, a hell of a din. To my surprise, he had nothing in his hands.

"Were you discovered?" I asked.

"Yes. I think he's dead."

My heart, already pounding, jumped into my mouth. "What? Are you sure?"

"No, but I think he is."

"We had better check. Come on!"

Alec shook his head. "I can't go back in there."

"Where are the letters?"

"I left them behind; I panicked. There were so many. Maynard was not the only one."

He had turned a deathly pale and I thought he might faint.

"Did you leave the door open?"

"I don't know. I just ran."

"We are going back up these stairs. You keep watch while I check him and try to retrieve the papers."

"I can't go back."

"Pull yourself together." I shook him. "We have to do this or it will all be for nothing and Maynard will be lost."

Gingerly, we climbed quietly up the three flights of fire escape and scrambled through the hall sash-window. I felt all of my sixty years and, not for the first time, wished I'd kept in better shape. The hall was quiet and we padded along it until we reached the third door on the right. I tried the door but it wouldn't open.

"The key," I whispered.

He felt his pockets. "I think I must have left it in there."

"For God's sake!" I closed my eyes in despair.

"No, here it is." He passed me the key with his shaking right hand.

"Wait by the banisters," I said. "Only knock on the door if you see the porter coming up the stairs or hear the lift coming."

I let myself into the flat and closed the door behind me. It had a small hall or lobby; a telephone stood on a table. There were three doors off; the central one was open and inside I could see papers scattered everywhere on the grey and green patterned carpet. Pushing the door open further, I saw Templing lying on the floor. A large kitchen knife lay by his right hand; there was some blood on the tip of it. Blood seeped from a wound on his forehead. His eyes were closed and he appeared at peace. A sculpture of a lion, reminiscent of Landseer's lions in Trafalgar Square, lay a few feet away. A writing bureau had been forced open, its inner drawers removed and its contents strewn all over the floor.

I knelt beside Templing, just as I had that time in The Mall, and searched for a pulse. I couldn't detect one. I put my ear to his heart: nothing. He was dead all right and I experienced horror and relief simultaneously. God only knew where this would all lead but I was relieved I did not have to try to save him and that he wouldn't trouble us again. I could feel neither pity nor regret. A bedroom led off this room and I went into it in search of a case of some kind. I was immediately distracted by the furnishing and decoration. As well as a three-quarter size bed, a couple of wardrobes and an ottoman, there was a table, not a dressing table, more a console table. It was about four feet long and two wide with candles, currently unlit, and a crucifix in the centre. Its appearance reminded me of an altar. On the plain wall, above the table, was a picture of a blindfolded woman in Roman dress. She was holding the scales of justice in one hand and a sword in the other, and I recognised her as depicting 'Justice'. Above this picture was a small purple banner with a gold fringe and the word 'Praetor' written on it in an ornate script, also in gold. After staring at it for a moment, I looked round and saw a suitcase, which was just what I wanted, on the top of a wardrobe. Opening it and finding it empty, I took it into the drawing room and filled it with all the papers and documents I picked up from the floor or could find left in the bureau. Hastily, I searched the rest of the flat and any other letters or documents I found also went into the suitcase. As I closed the catches, I heard a rap on the door. I opened it gingerly and a terrified-looking Alec whispered that the porter was coming up the stairs. Taking the suitcase and key, we ran to the window, climbed out, closing it behind us and, as quietly as we could, went down the fire escape. At the bottom I pulled Alec to the wall of the building to keep us out of sight and we edged our way along the wall until we reached the road and the front of the building.

I told Alec to take the case to my car and wait for me there, while I went into the front entrance of the apartment block. The porter hadn't yet returned from his errand and, lifting the counter flap, I was able to put the key back on its hook. I made good my escape just as I heard the lift arriving at the ground floor. If my heart was racing when we reached the bottom of the fire escape, it moved into overdrive as I stopped outside the apartment block to catch my breath. As nonchalantly as possible, I walked slowly back to my car.

I had left the car unlocked and Alec was sitting in the passenger seat, holding his arm. There was a small stain on the sleeve of his jacket I hadn't noticed before. "Are you all right?" I asked.

"He stabbed me. Just a flesh wound, but it's bleeding rather a lot. Let's get out of here."

I started the car and promptly stalled it. After a deep breath, I started the engine again and we eased out onto the road and away from what I had already decided would be my last ever visit to Holland Park.

"What happened exactly?" I asked, as we set off to Portman Square.

"Well, at first everything went like clockwork. This morning I had arranged to be driven to Holland Park by a friend of mine. She had agreed to distract the porter while I left what I told her was a surprise birthday present for a very close friend by getting the key to his flat. She has done a bit of acting in the past so she was happy to be part of the joke. So, when we arrived near the apartment building, she purposely flooded the carburettor and went into the apartment block to ask the porter if there was a garage nearby. She being very attractive and he being a man, we were sure he would offer to take a look at the car for her. Sure enough, a couple of minutes later I saw them come out of the building and walk towards her car. I was waiting with a nicely wrapped box a little way away and as soon as you waved, I went in, took the key and went up to the flat. I expect the porter had no difficulty getting her car started but it didn't matter as it couldn't have taken more than a few seconds for me to get the key and start up the stairs. I had broken into the bureau and begun sorting through the documents for those we wanted when Templing came back. I didn't hear him come in until it was too late. The first I saw of him was when I heard a noise and he was coming towards me. I tried to push past him but he went berserk, wielding a knife of some sort. I evaded the first lunge but then he stabbed me. I grabbed his arm but he was strong and I thought he was going to kill me. I hit him with the first thing that came to hand, the lion sculpture, meaning only to daze him. I didn't intend to kill him but I'm not sorry he's dead."

"What happened to the gift for your fake friend?"

"It was just an empty box wrapped in paper. I left it behind. It'll be a murder enquiry now; I suppose I'm done for."

"Not necessarily. The porter didn't see you and I managed to put the key back on the hook. They will assume he let the person in himself and perhaps knew him. You have no criminal record so there will be no fingerprint matches or anything else to link you to the man. There is the young woman but I doubt the porter noted her number plate and, in any case, he is unlikely to mention that he left his post. But can she be trusted not to say anything?"

"I hope she will assume it is just a coincidence. I suppose she might think it odd but what can I do?"

"Act as normal. Tell her that the surprise present trick went well and, as a passing thought, mention that your friend told you someone was murdered in the block of flats on the same day."

Alec nodded, not very convincingly, but before he could express his unease we had arrived at his home. I poured us both a stiff drink and took off his jacket to dress his cut arm. The cut was over two inches long and the knife had made a deep wound in part of it; the blood was still seeping out and his shirt sleeve was soaked.

"You should have this looked at, you know, it needs stitches. Can you use the arm all right?"

He moved the arm around, wincing. "No damage to the works. Too many questions if I see a doctor. I shall call it an 'old war wound' if I'm asked in the future."

"I'll have to do something to stop the bleeding." I looked at the first-aid box Alec had fetched when we had arrived back at his flat. Apart from a couple of bandages and some plasters and cotton wool there were few other materials to hand. "This is going to hurt," I said as I poured some Dettol on a gauze pad and laid it across the wound, the gauze pad instantly colouring. I repeated this process with another pad and then put some plasters over the wound, after which I bandaged it, finishing with more tape.

"If the bleeding doesn't stop, in a while, you shall have to go to hospital. I will come back in a couple of hours to check up on you, but now I have some unfinished business." I topped up our glasses; we both needed another drink, although for different reasons.

"What unfinished business?"

"I am supposed to get on a Circle Line train just after twelve and hand the money over to a woman who will be waiting for it. Of course, I don't have to go now but I want to know for my own peace of mind whether Templing worked on his own or had accomplices. The last thing we need is another letter turning up in a week's time with new demands for money and now with the added problem of a dead body."

He nodded. "You're right. You must find out what you can."

"You are sure I can leave you with that arm?"

"It will be perfectly all right."

I looked at my watch; it was a quarter past eleven. I telephoned my office and told my secretary the client I had gone to see was taking me out to lunch and I would be back later in the afternoon. I knocked back my drink and set off at once for Mansion House tube station, estimating a ten-minute walk to Bond Street Station, ten minutes on the Central Line to Saint Paul's and another ten-minute walk to Mansion House down New Change and Cannon Street. That would give me a comfortable few minutes' spare at the station before the train arrived. I guessed right and by the time

I had bought my ticket and stood on the platform, the clock showed nine minutes to twelve with a train due in five minutes and another at two minutes after the hour. The platform was quiet, perhaps twenty-five passengers waiting for a train. I wondered if any of these were accomplices of Templing: the businessmen with rolled umbrellas and bowler or Homburg hats, the four women, one with several bags of shopping, another with a small dog and the other two dressed as office workers or perhaps one looked like a barrister, the two youths, probably junior clerks. If any of them did not get the next train, why would that be? There is only one direction for the Circle Line: round and round. Only if the person was waiting for my particular train or the District Line would they not take this next one.

The train approached and all the waiting travellers shuffled towards the edge of the platform, all except one. A man in his early thirties, dressed in a dark overcoat and carrying a newspaper, leaned back against the tiled wall, his frame encased in the circular sign of the station bearing its name. I watched him, staring at the train as it rolled past him and came to a halt. The doors opened, the passengers streamed off and the man stood upright. As the passengers thinned out I saw a young woman standing still and then she and the watching man saw each other and waved. They walked quickly towards each other, embraced and kissed and then walked past me, arm in arm to the exit; they didn't notice me.

I looked up at the clock; two minutes to twelve. The next four minutes passed like an eternity until I heard again the clackity-clack sound as the train neared its approach from the tunnel, saw the lights reflecting off the dark walls and then felt the woosh of air as the train came into the station in its gleaming red livery. There were even fewer passengers waiting to board this train and I was the only person who alighted or boarded through the front doors of the first carriage. I gripped the bag containing the 'money' and came face to face with a young brunette, her medium length hair combed high off the forehead, clipped at the side and loose at the back. She was standing despite the carriage being almost empty and I surmised she must be the person sent for the money, especially as she had an envelope in her hand. Her brown eyes were fixed on the bag in my hand and her dark red lips parted without expression. I glanced around the carriage to see if anyone else was watching us but none were.

The woman came towards me a little and held out her hand. "Are you Maynard?" she asked, clearly unsure.

I nodded and let her take the bag. "Don't follow me," she said, passing me the envelope.

The journey time between Mansion House and Cannon Street is a minute and as she spoke the train began to slow for the station. I noticed a man rise from his seat and come to the doors by which we were standing as the train slowed. He was about thirty, a couple of inches shorter than me but stocky and with the facial features of someone who was no stranger to the boxing ring.

I stood back and waited to see what the man did. The train came to a sharp halt and all three of us were taken slightly off balance. The door opened and the young woman and the man got off and walked briskly towards the exit; I followed a few feet behind. The woman looked back and saw me. She spoke to the man and they walked more rapidly. On impulse I ran and came up behind them.

"There is no money in the bag. Templing is dead. Let's talk," I said, holding both their shoulders and bringing them to a halt. At that moment I knew I had control of the situation. I had planned what I would do on my journey to Mansion House but they were taken by surprise. The news that Templing was dead had come as a shock and I felt I had the upper hand.

Some of the other passengers looked slightly put out, having to walk round this three-person obstacle, but they gave merely a passing glance. The woman began to wriggle free from my grip but the man stayed her arm. We walked into the concourse at the foot of the escalators and stood out of the way.

"Who are you?" asked the woman.

"I'm acting on behalf of Maynard. Who are you?"

"None of your business," she said, her voice more strident now.

"What's your game?" asked the man. His voice was gruff, perhaps intentionally so.

"I'm here to give you the facts. Templing has been removed and his business with Maynard is at an end. Look in the bag." I spoke with authority and as my feeling of control of the situation grew, I sensed theirs fade.

The woman opened the bag and pulled out wads of neatly cut newspaper. After a further rummage round inside the bag, she threw it towards me. "How do we know you're speaking the truth?" she asked.

"If I'm not, Templing will get in touch with you to ask what happened to the money and you will be after Maynard again. You will know soon enough."

"We don't need Templing," said the man. "We can handle it." He was not convincing.

"So, what's your hold over Maynard?" I asked.

They looked at each other. "Blackmail," said the woman.

"I know that. What hold do you have over him?"

They were silent.

"If you are Templing's partners, you will know what the blackmail is for. Get in touch with us and tell us what you know and your terms but don't try to be too clever; remember Templing." I looked at them, forcing a slight smile.

"Look, mate," said the man. "I was just paid to protect this lady when she collected the money. I don't want any trouble."

"How much were you paid?" I asked.

"I was due £20 on delivery."

I took out my wallet and gave him £25 in fivers. "Here's a bit extra; let's call it quits."

"Thanks, guv."

"What about me?" asked the woman.

"I thought you were Templing's partner, so it's up to you."

"I was to be paid £25 to collect the money."

I smiled when I saw the man's head swing round and stare at her. "So, you are not Templing's partner?" I asked.

She shook her head.

"Here's twenty-five pounds," I said, repeating the offer to the man.

"You gave him more than he asked."

"He was honest with me. Do you want it or not?"

Without any further resistance, she accepted the proffered notes and they both turned towards the escalator. I watched them until they disappeared then opened the envelope. There was just a sheet of plain paper in it. So Templing had been bluffing too. I chuckled to myself and went to the westbound platform to begin retracing my steps back to Alec's apartment. As I stood waiting for the train, I was aware that sweat was running down my face and my hands were shaking. From the moment I had stepped off the train it was as if I had been playing a role and had felt supremely confident, now the reaction of relief set in. I wiped my forehead with a handkerchief and by the time the train pulled in I was feeling more at ease. By the end of my return leg, with its two relaxing walks, I was feeling quietly pleased with my successful expedition. For the moment I was able to forget what had gone before.

I was relieved to find Alec smiling and calm when he opened the door to his apartment.

"How are you?" I asked.

"The arm hurts but I can manage with it. I've been resting so I haven't looked at the papers in the case yet."

I inspected his arm. The bandage had a small patch of blood showing but it was not seeping out. I had popped into a chemist on the way back and had a fresh supply of bandages and plasters so I took off the old dressings and applied new ones. "I should get rid of these today. We don't want them to be seen by the cleaner."

"I'll put them in the incinerator after you leave. How did you get on?"

"There were two people on the train: a young woman who made the exchange and a man of thirty or so who was there to protect her. I followed them off the train and took them to one side where I told them Templing was dead. I am quite sure that these were people Templing used to do jobs for him. They appeared not to know the details of Templing's activities and were certainly not directly involved in the blackmail operation. I doubt very much we will hear from either of them again, especially as I told them we have dealt with Templing. We were not the only ones bluffing. The envelope from Templing contained a blank sheet of paper so we would have exchanged merely sheets of paper and had to go through the whole business all over again."

Alec laughed. "What madness life is. So, what's next?" he asked.

"I shall go back to work and it might be better if you did too, when you feel up to it, to acquire some sort of alibi in the unlikely event that you need one. Remember to keep your jacket on at all times when out until that bandage can be taken off. But the main thing is to carry on as normal. Such witnesses that exist will soon forget the exact details of who they saw and what they did on a particular day. Most people have enough on their minds to preoccupy them. I'll come round this evening and we'll go through the papers in the case and decide what to do with them."

Alec nodded and closed his eyes. He looked all in and I wondered if his nerve would hold but prayed it might.

He shook his head. "I wish I could get what happened to Templing out of my mind. If they find any link between him and Maynard, I am bound to be a suspect."

"Don't worry. We have done all we can to clean up behind us. Even if they find out Maynard was being blackmailed, the police won't suspect you. The time to start worrying is if and when you are interviewed." I could see Alec was jumpy and I decided not to tell him about my appearance in the foyer and my conversation with Templing. He was already on the edge.

# XVIII

# *LOOSE ENDS*

I RETURNED TO MY OFFICE, HAVING SUPPOSEDLY visited a client, and slumped into my chair with a whisky from my drinks cabinet. I felt absolutely drained: the adrenalin had completely worn off and exhaustion had set in, as had a thumping headache. I realised I hadn't eaten anything since breakfast but, though hungry, I couldn't face food at the moment. I told my secretary I was not to be disturbed as I had some serious research work to do and I just sat there, going over the morning's events, looking for potential difficulties and threats to Alec and me. I had not been shocked by Templing's death; I had seen plenty of better men than him shot to pieces or die a lingering death in the two world wars and, as far as I was concerned, this man deserved neither sympathy nor retribution.

I have always thought blackmail the most heinous of crimes, even worse than murder in many cases. There is something about the extortionate control over the life of another, who has usually done no harm to the blackmailer, which is both so sordid in its premise and relentless in its execution, that I can find no extenuating circumstance whatever for it. When the victim is a criminal, the blackmailer betrays the whole of society because it is the individual against whom the crime was committed and society to whom the criminal should pay for the crime, not the blackmailer. But worse, when the blackmailer's victim has committed no serious crime but is guilty of behaviour which might threaten his or her private life or career, the blackmailer is guilty of both extortion and hypocrisy in the way he exploits the frailty of others, often as a judgement on them while choosing to ignore his own culpability. This view was reinforced when that evening I called to see Alec. On the way, I had finally relented to the demands of my body and popped into a café for a cup of tea and a sandwich, which refreshed me more than I expected.

I found Alec reinvigorated too. Colour had returned to his face and he seemed more at ease. The wound in his arm had stopped bleeding and the pain had given way to a steady ache, which he had bombarded with codeine. After letting me in, he showed me the floor, covered by an array of letters and documents, some of them tinged with age. He had placed them in seven or eight piles and there were odd ones which he had arranged in the form of a fan. There was also a mauve account book. It was lying open and I could see it contained one name per page and underneath each name a list of payments, most in hundreds of pounds but a few in thousands.

"You've been very busy," I said and clapped him on the back.

"Templing was quite an expert," he said, gesturing to the paraphernalia in front of us. "He had at least eight current clients, for want of a better word, and there are others he appears to have dropped. Presumably he had taken all they had or perhaps they refused to pay any more and he did his worst, or just gave up on them."

I had picked up the mauve book and was looking at some of the names where Templing had drawn a line under the payments. "Or they chose a different way out," I replied. "I knew this man and was never sure why he had chosen to take his own life."

"There's something else I have to tell you."

"Oh?" I looked away from the ledger.

"Either I didn't find most of the documents relating to Maynard or Templing had only one. I think he was bluffing all along." He picked up a two-page letter lying on the sofa and passed it to me.

I didn't particularly want to look through the letter. I wasn't sure what I would find and worried that it might influence my opinion of or sympathy for Maynard. But I had to know that what Alec and I had done was worth it and that we had protected Maynard's reputation and his standing in society. What if it were trivial, ambiguous tittle-tattle that would have been dismissed as such by the police and society at large? Then, everything we had done would have been for nothing. I had no choice but to read it.

The letter was apparently from Maynard to a man whose name I didn't recognise. It stated how much Maynard had enjoyed a night spent with the man the previous week, giving two explicit intimate details. It also recounted several brief interludes Maynard had enjoyed with conquests he'd made on the London streets. From this letter and from what Alec had told me, in his youth he was clearly someone who relished and lauded the expansiveness of his sexual activities to an extraordinary degree. In fact, though I believed myself to be a man of the world and past the age when I was easily shocked by whatever people got up to, I thought the whole business rather distasteful. Though trying to maintain an open mind, I found Maynard's behaviour at this time rather sordid and beyond what I thought would be acceptable in society. It struck me as too much at odds with his moralistic pronouncements on what constituted a 'good life' with its emphasis on ethics, beauty, friendship and loving relationships. I also detected a hint of that arrogance which often pervades the attitude of the elites of all kinds that the rules which apply to ordinary people do not apply to them. They often forget that those ordinary people don't see the matter in quite the same way and Templing would have been able to exploit him because of it. Maynard's arrogance had resulted in recklessness through his failure to protect himself from the risk of the very situation which had led us all here. But he was still my friend.

"It's explicit enough to be troublesome," I said, "but perhaps not as bad as we originally thought."

"One letter like this is enough. If Maynard is exposed as a homosexual that will be all that matters. It will no longer be Maynard Keynes, the world's leading economist, the creator of a new world financial system, a philanthropist and major supporter of the arts, and incidentally a homosexual. It will be Maynard Keynes, the homosexual, etcetera. It will be as if that is the single most important fact about him, by which he is recognised, and of course it happens to be a crime. Nobody refers to a person who is heterosexual as if that is the most important quality about them; we talk about their achievements and the good they have done."

I smiled. It was all so much humbug: Maynard's superior aestheticism and the moralistic prurience of those who would bring him down. When in doubt, I found those who enjoyed judging others the more repellent. "You are right, of course. Our efforts were not in vain," I said.

I opened the mauve book again. Of the many people listed in the book, there were a few I knew by name or had heard of, as well as the one I had known personally. "I think more people than we could have imagined will soon sleep better in their beds," I added.

Alec shook his head as he looked down at the mass of papers around him. "It's the scale of the operation that I find extraordinary. I haven't looked at all of these letters but I am amazed that Templing managed to get so much incriminating evidence on people he didn't know personally."

"Presumably there is a market for matters of this kind, as there is for everything else, and he was probably a key player in it. Once he was known as a dealer, people would have sought him out to offer the letters for a quick payment. Not everyone can be bothered with the mechanics of blackmail: I'm sure I couldn't."

"The letters didn't take much sorting as he was a neat archivist." Alec waved some of the letters from one pile. "This man, a Harley Street doctor, has been having an affair with a patient for years and somehow Templing has got hold of his letters to the woman. Or this judge: a member of some sort of club for illicit sex. Most of them are about sexual misdemeanours of one sort or another but there are a couple of people involved in financial irregularity plus a swindler and a politician who it could be proved lied to Parliament."

I handed Maynard's letter back to Alec. "I imagine this letter came into the hands of one of the less scrupulous, casual sexual partners who went to the recipient's home. Maynard has been a bloody fool."

Alec shrugged. "He is entitled to do what he wishes in his own home."

I remembered my friend Lyndon's criticism of Maynard's behaviour and found myself agreeing with him. "Yes, but he didn't have to write it all down, for God's sake. Anyone who commits their private life to paper risks it becoming public and is asking for trouble."

We both fell silent, me feeling anger and frustration as I reflected on the capacity of a genius like Maynard to combine pearls of wisdom with crass stupidity, Alec nursing his aching arm.

"What do you have in mind to do with all these papers?" I asked when I had calmed down a little.

"I thought we might burn them."

"I agree. Shall we do it now?"

"It could be tricky. I would have to use the stove in the basement and might be observed. I thought you might be able to have a bonfire."

"Are you mad, what if some of the papers were caught up in a wind and blew God knows where? There is also the question of my wife, who is bound to be curious. Haven't you a fireplace with a grate?"

"No."

"Look here, the fewer times this lot is moved the better. It'll only take a few minutes. I'll burn it and you keep watch." I knew I sounded tetchy and I felt it. I just wanted this whole appalling escapade over and done with.

Reluctantly, Alec helped me gather up the papers and put them in the suitcase. Then we took the lift to the basement. The boiler was run off coal and the large stove was blazing brightly to meet the needs of many households on a winter evening. Alec said he would do the necessary and opened the small, side door. But as he pushed in the first batch of papers he winced and I took over to protect his arm. I couldn't see why he had been so reluctant to use the incinerator: the papers were only seen for a second before they disappeared into the stove and were gone almost as soon as they started to brown.

The last handful contained Maynard's letter. Alec held back my hand for a moment. "That letter from Maynard, perhaps we should give it to him?"

At that moment, we heard footsteps on the stairs. "He should have taken more care when he wrote it," I said and threw the whole batch in, slamming the door shut as the maintenance man appeared.

A pleasant looking man of about fifty, dressed in dark green overalls over a collar and tie, nodded to us. "Evening, gentlemen. Can I be of assistance?"

"Good evening, Hammond," said Alec. "No thank you, just getting rid of some superfluous notes to a document I have been preparing. All done now."

Hammond looked through the inspection window. "Yes, we don't want too much paper going on in one go. It can leave too much ash." He nodded as if in approval.

"Well goodnight, Hammond," said Alec and we turned to take the stairs.

"Goodnight, sir," said Hammond, taking a shovel and walking over to the coal cupboard.

We returned to Alec's apartment and had a drink. "I think I've had enough excitement for one day. You'll get rid of the suitcase?" I asked.

"Yes, there's nothing to indicate who owns it. I'll sell it to a junk shop, somewhere far from London."

"What about that?" I asked, pointing to the mauve account book.

"I thought I might keep it."

"Why?"

"In case there are repercussions for what we've done. I would have evidence regarding the sort of man Templing was. I shall keep it somewhere safe."

"All right. Arm still holding up?"

"Throbbing a bit. I'll keep an eye on it but there's no sign of infection."

"Good. I suggest that if you get any problems, you have a good story to tell the doctor."

He nodded. "I'll think of something."

We were wrapping things up and I had an overwhelming desire to be done with it. After a few pleasantries and mutual congratulations at the end of the expedition, I took my leave.

"Thanks, Lewis. I couldn't have done this without your help. Though he'll never know it, Maynard is greatly indebted to you." He shook my hand.

"You are the hero of the piece. You saved his bacon, not me. I'd rather we never mention the matter again."

"Of course. I hope the next time we meet it will be under more relaxed circumstances."

"Yes, indeed."

I drove home that evening, vaguely aware that the Templing business was over but unable to work through the events of the day in my mind. So much had happened and yet none of it seemed real. Was Templing really dead? Had we left any clues to who we were? Had we seen the last of the couple on the Circle Line? As to emotions such as triumph, relief, guilt, none of them were present, just a sense of unease, of disquiet, of fear of the future. My discomfort was not alleviated when I arrived home. Lina was quiet and monosyllabic in her conversation and seemed distracted over dinner.

As we drank our coffee, I could resist asking no longer. "What's the matter? You seem very subdued."

She looked up quizzically. "That's a strange question from one who has hardly spoken since you came home. You look ill, no, not ill, more as if you have had a terrible shock about which you cannot speak. What is going on?"

What could I say? I couldn't face the reality of the day in my own mind, let alone try to explain it to someone else, even the woman I loved. "Nothing," I said.

"Are you having an affair of some kind?"

I laughed. "Whatever makes you say that?"

"It's not meant to be funny. Suddenly, without telling me why, you have begun working late most nights, spend a lot of time out of the office and often have a bath before dinner, which you rarely did in the past. If it's not a bath, you spend your time pacing round the garden. Even the children have commented on *that*."

"I have had to see Alec several times."

"But you have never before met Alec outside working hours."

"It's been about Maynard's work abroad and such matters." I hated telling her lies, especially feeble ones like this, but I was stumped for an alternative that I could at this moment articulate.

She looked at me, her expression a mixture of scepticism and irritation. "Why on earth would you be involved in Maynard's work abroad and, if you were, why would you be meeting Alec instead of Maynard?"

"Just a few issues that we need not bother Maynard with; he's under a lot of pressure at the moment," I said, grateful for an answer which was the truth, if not the whole truth.

"And early evening baths in late October?"

"Like the walks in the garden, I find them relaxing after a hard day, especially when I am hot and bothered." This was also true but I was beginning to find the inquisition irritating and forcing me into a corner. "Look, can we drop the subject, all these questions? It's becoming rather tiresome."

She snorted. "If there is something serious going on at work or to do with Maynard that is involving so much of your time, I think you should tell me."

"It's nothing to do with my work and it will have no impact on us."

She stood up and poured herself a brandy, something she rarely did after dinner. She waved the decanter at me but I declined. She sat down and drank rather more than a sip of her drink. Then she took a deep breath. "Is there something going on between you and Alec?"

"Going on? How do you mean?"

"Well, have you formed a close relationship in some way? After all, you are spending rather a lot of time at his apartment."

"What are you implying?"

"I'm not implying anything. I have only met Alec twice, both times to do with the re-opening of the Royal Opera House. He's very good-looking and is obviously attracted to men."

"How do you know?"

"Women usually do."

"What are you trying to say, exactly?"

"Well, one can be inclined that way without it ever leading to anything unless the right person comes along, but lots of Maynard's set are, you know, and the thought suddenly crossed my mind."

"That I am too?"

"I would try to understand, if that's what you want. Obviously, I can't compete on the same terms."

I went over to her, sat down and put my arm round her. "Of course not. I love you and you are the only one. I have no interest in anybody else, certainly not Alec nor any other man, nor any other woman for that matter."

"Then why?"

"Will you trust me if I promise to tell you the truth, as much as I feel able to?"

"Yes." She looked at me, apprehensively, and took my hand.

"I am sworn to confidentiality as to the details but let me just say that Maynard has been in a serious spot of bother which could have had untold consequences for his career and his reputation. Alec asked me to help him sort it out to avoid any difficulties for Maynard, as he is not very well and has so much else going on in his life. Naturally, I agreed and I am pleased to say that it is all settled now. Please don't ask me to give you any more details because it would put you on the spot if you were questioned about it. I can assure you it's all over now and our lives will be back to normal."

"I won't ask you anything about it, if you promise me it's all finished."

"It is."

She kissed me. "You must think me a complete fool."

"Not in the least. You had every reason to wonder why I was behaving differently. I should have told you something of it but everything happened so fast and I was completely tied up in it. I'm sorry."

She patted my hand and, true to her word, she never raised the subject again. At the time, I was just so relieved that I didn't have to tell her the whole truth and demand of her the trust and understanding I had been willing to give Alec. Later, it crossed my mind many times that she may have decided to accept my flimsy explanation whatever the truth behind it and that it was enough to know it was over. I took her act of love in the same good grace with which it was given.

But of course, it wasn't all over for me, not quite. The next day I invited Saxe out to lunch as I knew he would want to know if we had tracked down Esmond Templing. We met at Simpson's and had roast beef; the usual wartime shortages were still at play and we had the last of the rib. I wasn't very hungry but if anything could revive my appetite the beef would and duly did. When we met, Saxe's expression was one of anticipation and after the exchange of a few pleasantries, I answered his unasked question.

"We found Templing. It wasn't too difficult."

Saxe's face opened up into a broad smile. "Really? That's excellent news. Our trip to the races was a success."

"Very much," I said, opening my napkin and tucking the corner in my collar.

"Have you had dealings with him, or should I not ask?"

"You have a right to know, but not here," I whispered.

We talked instead about the day at Newbury and about the racing rather than the purpose of our visit.

"I think we might have had a more successful day if we had been able to concentrate on the sport rather than looking out for the man," I said.

"I'm sure you are right," said Saxon. "We didn't get a chance to watch the horses parade, to look for good and bad signs: nerves, irritability, friskiness, sweating, that sort of thing."

"You're right. That's why I'm surprised you don't go to the races more often."

He smiled. "Idleness and ennui, all too often my fatal flaws."

We discussed racing and gambling in general terms over our dessert of sweet suet pudding and custard but I could see Saxon was itching to hear more about Templing and I called for the bill as soon as we had finished.

After lunch we strolled the mile and a half or so back to his flat, talking about the apparent fading away of the Bloomsbury Group he had been such a part of.

"Do you see many of them now?" I asked.

He shook his head. "Some of those I was closest to have died."

"Lytton Strachey, I suppose, for one."

"Yes, we knew each other from the beginning. The poor man had a terrible death and they could never give an accurate diagnosis."

"You often stayed with him, didn't you?"

"Yes, at The Mill House in Tidmarsh: happy days."

"I suppose you knew Carrington quite well too?"

He didn't answer for a few moments, lost in reverie. "Yes, she was there and Ralph Partridge, her husband. When dear Lytton died so young it was all too much for Carrington. She couldn't live without him, poor girl. Such a loss, talented but diffident about her ability. I have one of her paintings."

"Roger Fry's dead too, and Virginia."

"Yes, Virginia, poor tortured soul. We had an empathy, I felt. She liked me to play the piano for her while she read; she found it soothing. Her wedding to Leonard was a small affair but she invited me; that was kind." His voice cracked a little and he broke off, changing the subject.

"What happened regarding Mr Templing?" he asked, as he opened the door to his flat.

"He was dealt with."

"That sounds rather ominous," he said, walking into the living room and throwing off his coat.

"I'm afraid it is. Alec broke into his apartment to recover the incriminating evidence about Maynard, there was a struggle and Templing was killed."

"My God," said Saxe. "You said there would be no violence."

"It was self-defence. Templing went for Alec with a knife and Alec hit him with the first thing that came to hand. He did not intend to kill him, I assure you. Don't shed any tears over Templing, Saxe, he was a nasty piece of work. We found letters that showed he was blackmailing for money dozens of people at one time or another. He was a human leech."

Saxe nodded. "I think we need a drink. What a terrible business," he said as he went over to his drinks table. "So this man Templing was a highly organised criminal and had been blackmailing people for some time."

"Yes. From the documents we found, he had put lots of

people through the mill. I think he was also a very peculiar person: I got the impression he believed there was some virtue in what he did."

"Oh, why do you say that?"

"You remember he used the alias of Gaius Praetor? In his apartment bedroom he had a purple banner with the word 'Praetor' on it on the wall and a picture of Justice by it. They were over a kind of altar with candles and a crucifix."

Saxe frowned. "That is interesting. As we discussed before, Gaius was a Roman jurist and Praetor was a magistrate in Rome so he perhaps saw himself as an agent, an enforcer of the law or of morals. His surname, Templing, with its origin in the temple or the Knights Templar, may have added to this sense of being destined to uphold moral codes or practices. A person who believes he is morally justified in his crimes will be less likely to experience remorse and pity for his victims. I suppose he may be unable to."

"Rather like a psychopath?"

"Not quite. Surely a psychopath is driven purely by self-interest whereas Templing may have believed he was acting for the greater good, that he could do no wrong because he was on the side of justice. He was still hopelessly deluded, of course."

"Not to mention, dangerous," I added.

Saxe nodded. "Is it all over now? Templing was not part of a larger gang?" he asked, as he refilled our brandy glasses.

"Not as far as we can tell. He worked alone, it appears, and used various accomplices to run errands for him. I don't think we'll hear from them again, in fact I'm sure of it. He had arranged for the payment to be exchanged on the tube and I met his accomplices, a young woman and a protector, and when I told them Templing was dead, they took fright. I don't think they had any of the information Templing was using; they were his stooges."

"That's great news. Alec and you have made the world a better place, I feel. If there is another accomplice hiding in the woodwork and I can be of further assistance, you will let me know, won't you?" asked Saxe, just before I left.

I assured him I would, though I was confident that it was all over and the terrible memory of Templing's crimes and his subsequent comeuppance would, like most unpleasant experiences, soon lose its edge, blunted by time. Of course, I knew there would be repercussions from time to time when further news came to light about Templing or his activities, so I was prepared when Templing's death appeared in the newspapers, the morning after my lunchtime meeting with Saxe.

As I was eating breakfast, the newspapers thumped through the letterbox and I walked out to the hall to pick them up. I passed the *News Chronicle* to Lina and looked at the front page of the *Daily Telegraph*. The map of the European theatre showed further shrinking of the territory held by the forces of the Third Reich. The western allies were through Holland and into Germany in the west and the Russians had advanced into Germany on the approach to Berlin. Having read the article with some satisfaction, I turned the page and saw the headline on page three, *Murder of Reclusive Philanthropist*. Accompanied by a picture of a smiling Esmond Templing was an account of an apparent burglary which had been interrupted by the return of Templing from a walk and had resulted in the intruder killing him and making good his escape. Nothing of importance had been stolen, according to the police, other than the presumed contents of his desk drawers. The police were seeking witnesses, particularly a Mr Flanders who had spoken to Mr Templing in the foyer of his apartment block, and a young lady who had parked her car in front of the building while she spoke to the porter. Most of the article, however, was concerned with the upright character of Templing and his several acts of considerable generosity to charities over recent years, most of which he insisted be recorded as anonymous while he was alive. One or two quotes of sadness and sympathy from beneficiaries of Templing's munificence were recorded. I checked the obituary page at the back of the newspaper but he had not qualified for an entry there.

"Some bad news?" asked Lina. "You look as if you have seen a ghost."

"Someone I met once has suffered a violent death after a burglary."

"Oh, Mr Templing. He's in here too. How did you know him?"

"I didn't really know him. I exchanged a few words with him once or twice on a commercial matter."

"A dreadful business," she said. "Poor man, so kind and generous but murdered for nothing, it would appear."

I grunted non-committedly and, in the absence of elaboration, Lina returned to her newspaper.

# PART THREE
# *CONSTANCY*

# XIX

# *PATIENCE*

In the days and weeks afterwards, life went back to normal, that is, to a new normal. Alec and I did not make contact: I, and I think he, wanted to put our brief excursion into the world of crime behind us. I certainly had no wish to bring the events of that day in Holland Park to mind. Initially, I enjoyed a period of semi-amnesia when the whole episode was just a blur and my conscience was so anaesthetised that the death of Templing was no more than a matter of fact. Later, the fog cleared and I began to be able to review the break-in and the killing of Templing quite calmly. I was pleasantly surprised that I still felt not a twinge, not a jot, of guilt. I was glad Templing was gone and, as he would probably never have faced the noose, it seemed that through his death he had inadvertently but truly met his just deserts and paid appropriately for the misery he had inflicted on others. I settled back into my old routines and waited for the memory of Templing's death to fade in both clarity and importance. But it didn't happen.

Despite my best efforts to put them behind me, the events in Templing's apartment gradually returned to haunt me without any sign of diminishing. Not in a Dostoevskian way; as I have said, there was no guilt for what we had done nor remorse for the fate that had befallen Templing. It was simply a vague fear that, somehow, we would be found out. The young woman who distracted the porter might put two and two together, the porter had clearly remembered my approach to Templing in the apartment block, even remembering the name I'd used, the taxi driver who saw Templing knocked down might remember me too or Tommy Felstead, my old boxer friend, might recognise the case if it were in the newspapers and have an attack of conscience or perhaps fear for his own safety. This sense of disquiet was magnified when the story of Templing's murder and plaudits of his life continued to appear in the newspapers. Naturally, I did not contact the police, despite the invitation to 'Mr Flanders' to do so. Sometimes at night I would wake and find myself checking for clues that could betray us but finding none, without ever being sure there were none.

Slowly, as the weeks went on, the death of Templing at last began to recede into the past, the fear of discovery relented and the dreadful memories became blunted, just as I had expected they would. Eventually, I noticed one day that I hadn't given the matter any thought for some time and there was a part of me which wanted to believe that it had all been a bad dream, though I could never quite give my mind a free rein on that particular illusion. Then, out of the blue, I answered my telephone at home and it was Alec.

"Hello, Alec, how are you?" I asked, with just a touch of apprehension.

"Hello, Lewis. I have to talk to you. The police have made an arrest."

"Good God. How could they have? Who?"

"I'll explain all when I see you."

I put the telephone down slowly. The same old Alec: telephoning me with half a story and leaving me hanging, with no choice other than to follow his instructions as I had to know the rest of the tale.

With Maynard still in America, we met at his office the following lunchtime. Alec had arranged sandwiches but I wasn't in the least hungry and had had a restless night. I hadn't seen anything in my newspaper but it was mentioned in the *Daily Mail*.

"Do you know what happened?" I asked, biting into a beef sandwich without much relish, either on the meat or from my appetite.

"Yes, I have a few contacts in the Met, as you know. Apparently, the man arrested was being blackmailed by Templing too."

"I thought we'd found all his blackmail material."

"Yes, so did I. I must have missed something. It may have been elsewhere in the flat or he could have had it on him. I didn't search him." He shuddered at the thought of rummaging through the clothes of a dead man.

"Who is this man?"

"He's a senior director of a city bank, apparently, Bellington & Thorpe. Maynard knows him."

"What's the name?"

"Danvers Troughton."

"I know him too. A good man, so far as I know." Inside, I shivered a little; the waves of the scandal were creeping back a little closer to our shore. "But this man is innocent. They won't have any evidence to convict him."

"Well, as he was being blackmailed for some indiscretion with a customer of the bank and an unauthorised loan of some sort, he won't be seen as 'innocent'. Presumably, he hasn't provided a satisfactory alibi so far. His personal life and position will already be compromised: I can't let him go to trial. I shall have to go to the police. I'm sorry if it drags you into it too, Lewis."

I bridled at Alec taking the decision without discussing it with me; it was a matter of my self-preservation as much as anything else. I put my hand up. "Now hang on, old chap, let's not do anything hasty. I agree we can't let him take the blame for this but let's at least wait until he is sent for trial. Then we will find a way to help him, you have my word."

Alec agreed to my call for patience, without much resistance; perhaps he was glad to delay his heroism in case there was another way. Unfortunately, the other way didn't present itself. We watched, helplessly, as the police did what they often do so well and began to assemble a case against the wrong man, based on circumstantial evidence and the notorious hunch.

In the meantime, Templing was laid to rest, after some delay while post-mortems and other inquiries were carried out and an inquest conducted. His funeral was held at a packed church near his home and was reported in most of the daily papers. As well as a brother and two cousins and their families, the congregation included representatives of several charities and the eulogy, delivered by his brother, extolled the great benevolence of a man who was uninterested in wealth or personal luxury but who devoted most of his income to those in need. He said that the words of his late brother's favourite hymn, which was included in the service, were an inspiration for how he lived his life and he read the first verse of *To Be a Pilgrim.*

*He who would valiant be*
*'gainst all disaster,*
*let him in constancy*
*follow the Master.*

*There's no discouragement*
*shall make him once relent*
*his first avowed intent*
*to be a pilgrim.*

After the service, representatives of the charities who had enjoyed Templing's generosity were interviewed by reporters. There seemed to be some confusion as to the source of Templing's wealth but this was overlooked in the prevailing narrative of a good man struck down by an intruder. Fortunately, the participants in the interviews were spared any blushes from difficult questions as the precise nature of Danvers Troughton's supposed motive for wishing to kill Templing had not yet been divulged to the press.

# XX

# *KINDNESS*

FINALLY, LATE IN MARCH, MAYNARD WAS ABLE TO fit lunch with me into his very busy schedule. He invited me to Quaglino's along with Alec, whom he wished to thank for all his devoted work over the past few months, not that he knew the half of it. The restaurant had been renamed 'Meurice' since 1940 after the Italian Quaglino brothers fled the country to avoid internment, but everyone still referred to it as Quaglino's. The restaurant had retained its popularity, however, rather as the Royal House of Saxe-Coburg and Gotha had kept its popularity by responding to anti-German feeling in the Great War by changing its name to 'Windsor'.

I was rather shocked by Maynard's appearance. It seemed that every time I saw him, he looked worse than the last time. Of course, I knew his health had been precarious for years while his devotion to duty and the causes he espoused left him with little time for recuperation, but he looked really quite ill, especially as he had lost weight and his colour was not at all good. I could not prevent myself from commenting on the fact but he dismissed my concern that he might have been overdoing it with a casual referral to a job "needing to be done".

When I asked Maynard how progress was going on the talks with the US, he spoke of his frustration and difficulties with his opposite numbers in the American administration. He didn't go into much detail but, in a nutshell, I gathered that the Americans thought the British were acting rather off-handedly, as if they were somehow superior, when they had no grounds to believe as much, given their parlous economic and financial situation. The British resented that, having borne the brunt of the financial cost of the war, they were receiving little sympathy from their most important ally. When I pressed him a little, he thought the Americans resented his better grasp of the world economic situation and were being bloody-minded because of it.

Maynard was keen to change the subject and, when we moved onto lighter matters, he was his old sparkling, entertaining self and his colour improved. Eventually, he asked Alec about the murder of Templing and the arrest of Danvers Troughton.

"Any news on the Danvers Troughton case, Alec?"

"Not yet," said Alec, colouring slightly.

Maynard didn't appear to notice and called for some more drinks. "I find it impossible to believe that Troughton is capable of murder," he said. "I have known him for nearly thirty years and never seen him lose his temper, let alone become violent."

"One never knows what one is capable of in extreme circumstances," I said, attempting to maintain the fiction that Alec and I had no idea of what had actually taken place.

Alec nodded. "I am sure he is innocent," he said with complete conviction. "The case won't get as far as the Criminal Court," he added, with less conviction.

Maynard leaned back in his chair. "He was being blackmailed by his supposed victim; I think you told me? Dreadful business. One has to be very careful not to let information about one's private life get into the wrong hands or this sort of fate could well befall anyone."

I dare not look at Alec and neither of us replied.

"Wonder how Templing got hold of all that information," mused Maynard, glancing over at Alec. "I suppose it will all come out at the trial but at the moment Mr Templing is still being portrayed as a saintly victim."

Alec looked a little uncomfortable and presumably felt bound to answer. "I gather there's a market in this sort of thing. This chap may well have had other people he was blackmailing."

"Yet, the police alighted on Troughton." Maynard shook his head.

"Perhaps he hasn't got an alibi," I said.

"That's a surprise, too," said Maynard, stroking his moustache. "Unless, of course, he can't say where he was without getting himself into more hot water." He raised his eyebrows, a conspiratorial smile flickering on his lips.

"Apparently, the police have evidence that Troughton threatened to kill Templing if he didn't let him off the hook. Obviously, they believe that's enough to tie him in as the murderer," said Alec.

This was news to me and, inwardly, I gasped at this revelation. I hoped that Alec would say no more. The danger that he would let something slip that gave away our involvement was always present while he continued talking. A sense of foreboding was also rising in me as once again the disastrous possibility of the wrong man being sent for trial was becoming more likely. Any hope that such an event would not materialise was seeping away and with it my hope that Alec and I would not have to step forward.

The drinks arrived and Maynard changed the subject, though I have no idea what he said.

Unfortunately, the worst fears harboured by Alec and myself were realised a week later. Danvers Troughton appeared at the Magistrate's Court and was committed for trial for murder at the Old Bailey. I remember staring at the small item in the newspaper and wishing like a child that I could turn the clock back before that fateful day when I walked into Maynard's office just as Alec received the second blackmail note. Alec was quick to telephone me and, in a voice filled with resignation and defeat, expressed his intention of going to the police. Of course, I was full of solicitude for his position but I was very conscious too of the repercussions for both of us if Alec carried out his plan. I had already given some thought to this potential turn of events and, when Alec told me what he was thinking, immediately came up with a counter proposal.

"If you go to the police, you could end up on the gallows. Why don't we write an anonymous letter, telling the police they have the wrong man and spelling out the details of what happened in a way that probably only the killer could know. As no evidence has been presented yet, that would be sure to raise some doubts for the prosecution."

Alec was quiet for a moment or two. "That might work," he said. "I think we should send a copy of it to Troughton's solicitor too."

"Excellent idea."

We sat down that evening in Alec's flat and typed a letter to the Commissioner of the Metropolitan Police with a copy to Troughton's solicitor, whose details Alec had soon found. We wrote from the position of the killer and set out everything we could remember: the exact time when Alec entered Templing's flat, his being interrupted at some time after eleven o'clock while searching through the documents, being attacked with a knife and stabbed, hitting Templing with the statue in fear of his life and inadvertently killing him, the empty box wrapped in blue crepe paper that was left behind and the damage done to the bureau to open the drawers, the dozens of documents related to past and present blackmail victims, all removed except for the one he missed. Finally, at the insistence of Alec and much to my alarm, he affixed his fingerprints to the bottom of the two letters. As he pointed out, the police were bound to have his fingerprints already and this would be conclusive evidence that the writer of the letter had been in the flat. We posted both copies of the letter in a pillar box in Holborn.

Predictably, though unfortunately, Alec's contact in the Metropolitan Police was not involved in the case and we were totally in the dark as to the impact of the confession letter until a couple of weeks later. Then it was announced that the case against Troughton had been dropped. Alec's friend in the police told him that a confession letter had been received and it would remain on file, but it was not relevant to Troughton's release. Any friend or acquaintance of Troughton would have been able to have written the letter, using information from Troughton himself. Instead, Troughton had produced an alibi, confirmed by a senior member of the civil service, name unknown, who was a fellow member of the private club where Troughton had taken a Turkish bath and received an exhaustive, lengthy massage.

"Why didn't we see how useless a confession like that would be?" said Alec, when we met.

"I'm sorry," I said. "How could we check its worth without giving the game away?"

"They've got my fingerprints too, now."

I refrained from pointing out that I had urged him not to add that evidence to the letter. "Still, at least Troughton is off the hook and there is no traceable evidence pointing to you as a suspect."

# XXI

# *ENDURANCE*

THE POLICE, HAVING LOST THEIR FIRST PRIME suspect, were in search of another and would presumably revisit such evidence as they had. Every day, I would find myself scouring the newspapers, both at home and in the office, for news of any developments in the murder investigation. Alec had thought it best not to use his contact in the police for news as he was supposed to have been taking an interest on behalf of Maynard, someone who knew Troughton well. Consequently, we knew no more than anyone else what was going on. Then, a week or so after Troughton was cleared, I saw a small item in the *Evening News*, saying that, in connection with the murder of Templing, the police were asking a Mr Flanders and a young woman, thought to be driving a light blue sports car, possibly an MG, to contact Scotland Yard or their nearest police station. The newspaper revealed that both of these people were known to have entered the apartment block where Templing lived, not long before he was last seen alive. As I read it, I couldn't help but smile, a humourless smile. Luckily, there was no description of Flanders so no link with me, not that I intended to do anything.

I was not the only one to spot the newspaper item. The following day, Alec telephoned to say that his actress friend had called and wished to see him and his friend, 'Mr Flanders'.

"God, Lewis, this is quite alarming news. It looks like a trap of some kind."

"I thought you said you could trust this woman," I said, containing my anger.

"I do, I think I do. I'm just perplexed as to why she wants to see you. But at least she hasn't gone to the police," he added, searching for a silver lining in this latest cloud.

"As far as we know."

"Yes, I'm sorry, Lewis, but will you come over to the flat this evening?"

I was tempted to refuse and try to remain at arm's length from this latest threat but I was aware that Alec's nerve could fail him and I wanted to keep what control I could over the situation. Reluctantly, I agreed.

I arrived early in the hope that we might agree on our story and perhaps decide tactics. Alec was looking very worried, his natural good looks drawn and pale. He poured me a drink and topped up his own glass.

"How well do you really know this woman?" I asked.

"I have met her a few times. I've known her for about six months."

"Is that all? I assumed she was someone you knew quite well and could trust if the situation became difficult."

"She seemed the type that doesn't ask questions and would be willing to take part in a practical joke."

"Doesn't ask questions? Well, we shall see. Whatever happens, don't let her divide us. Don't commit to anything without me having the chance to express my view."

"Of course."

At that moment the doorbell rang and Alec, pushing back his hair, went to the door. "Jacqueline, how are you? Come in," he said in a touch too cheerful voice.

"This is…"

"Flanders, John Flanders," I interrupted, "how do you do?"

"How do you do, Mr Flanders? I am Jacqueline Peters."

She was extremely attractive, mid to late twenties, in a fur coat which she took off to reveal a navy-blue dress, cut just above the knee. She removed gloves and then her hat to reveal her blonde hair. I thought she reminded me of another actress: the full lips, large eyes and engaging smile were reminiscent of the late Carole Lombard. She sat down on an armchair, her legs elegantly displayed, and took a cigarette case from her bag. Cigarette inserted in a holder, she waited for Alec to light it.

"Drink?" he asked.

"Have you a gin and Dubonnet?"

Alec raised his eyebrows. "That's quite a combination."

"The Queen's favourite, I believe." She laughed.

Alec looked through the bottles on a drinks tray, produced a bottle of Booth's and another of Dubonnet and poured a drink of half and half. She thanked him, examined the glass briefly and took a sip. "A little too much gin, darling, but it will do."

"Well, you asked to see us both," I said.

"Yes." She ignored me and turned to Alec. "Tell me, Alec, what was the name of that friend you played the birthday surprise trick on when I acted as your decoy?"

"Er," replied Alec, scrambling unsuccessfully for a name.

"There wasn't one, was there?"

He didn't reply and I could hardly intercede on his behalf.

"I knew there was something fishy almost at once. After the dear funny little porter proudly started the car for me, I drove round the block and parked about thirty feet further away from the apartment entrance than before. I thought I'd wait for you and I looked forward to sharing with you the story of the practical joke over a drink or something. I expected you to take only a few minutes but when you didn't appear I supposed that perhaps you had been very quick and I'd missed you. I was about to drive off and then I saw Mr Flanders here run along the road and follow a plump man wearing a bowler into the apartment building. I was intrigued; once you get into it, watching people's behaviour is quite an interesting pastime. A couple of minutes later, Mr Flanders came out of the building and he appeared flustered and uncertain what to do. Then he walked round the back of the building and I wondered what he was up to. I waited for a minute or two but, when nothing happened, I decided to move on. I was bored with hanging around. As I passed the little road down the side of the apartment block, I saw you and Mr Flanders talking near the fire escape and I supposed he'd been in on the joke and you had completed it together. I didn't give it another thought. Then you rang a few days later and told me the joke had gone well but you didn't give any details. Instead, you alluded to the fact that Templing had been murdered. I commented about it being a coincidence and that was it. I thought it a rather strange conversation but nothing more."

She puffed on her cigarette and took another sip of her drink while we waited for what was to come.

"When that chap Danvers Troughton was arrested, I dismissed my vague concerns that you might have been up to something odd and accepted your story at face value. But when the police showed an interest in both me *and* Mr Flanders, I didn't need to be Dr Gideon Fell or Monsieur Hercules Poirot to work things out. There was something going on between you and Templing. What *was* your business with him, Alec? Or did you intend to kill him? Or *did* you kill him?" She turned to look at me, a slight smile crossing her face.

"That's ridiculous," I said.

"I don't think you're in a position to get cocky with me," she replied, her expression hardening, her accent less refined.

She turned back to Alec; her previously dulcet tone had become harsh and threatening as she continued in the same vein. "I don't like being treated like a dupe, especially by a so-called friend and your middle-aged chum, particularly if I end up being charged as an accomplice. I don't know what your relationship was with Templing and I don't care, but you deceived me and now the police want to talk to me, as well as you, Mr Flanders. What do you think I should do?"

"I'm sorry, Jackie," said Alec. "I was being blackmailed and I just wanted to get the incriminating evidence to take the pressure off. He came back earlier than I expected and attacked me with a knife. I hit him to defend myself; I didn't mean to kill him."

"Shut up, you bloody fool!" I shouted at him, too late. I was flabbergasted by his sudden admission. In his loyalty to Maynard, whatever the cost, he had put himself in the hands of someone I doubted could be relied upon to protect him.

She smiled like an indulgent aunt. "Honestly, Alec, I can guess what you were blackmailed for. You really must be more careful where you put your little stick of Blackpool rock. I suppose I'd be wasting my time with you as well?" She looked over at me.

I thought it best not to disabuse her view of me and smiled weakly.

"Is this the truth, Alec; is that what really happened?" Her voice had resumed its sweeter tone.

"Yes."

"And you were trying to help him?" she asked, looking over at me.

I nodded.

"Or were you being blackmailed too?"

"No," said Alec. "He was not involved in the break-in or Templing's death, he has just been a good friend to me."

She inhaled deeply on her cigarette and put it out as she exhaled with a deep sigh. "I suppose this could have happened to half my male friends," she said. "He'll be no loss: the vile swine, living off the fears and sadness of others. If I go to the police and it comes out that I have been involved in a crime, my career will probably be ruined, even if I don't get accused of anything myself. So what do you suggest?" For the first time when asking a question, she looked to me for an answer.

I was cheered by the realisation she had no more wish to go to the police than we did. "If you don't go to the police, it looks suspicious," I said. "I managed to replace the key on the porter's rack so there is no clue as to who, if anyone, took the key. Nor is there any evidence that you were the accomplice in a scheme to obtain the key. You just need a good reason to have been parked on that street.

"Which I don't have, as I didn't think I'd need one, so that..." she paused. "Hang on; when Alec left the car, I popped into that newsagent's to buy some cigarettes and a magazine."

"But that wouldn't explain why you were in Holland Park," said Alec.

"I live in Little Venice and I went shopping in Notting Hill then drove through Holland Park on my way to South Ken to go to Derry & Toms and I realised I had no cigarettes. I stopped, went to the shop and then, when I got back to the car, it wouldn't start."

"That sounds all right. You might even get some good publicity from it," said Alec, also encouraged by the turn of events.

She smiled. "Perhaps. I suppose you can't afford to step forward, John?"

"No, it might be difficult."

"Thought so. Well, I won't say anything about either of you but, as you used me rather, I think I deserve some reward. I'm thinking of something more substantial than dinner at the Ritz."

"I think we've been here before," said Alec.

Jacqueline laughed. "Not blackmail, I wouldn't think of it. Let us say a small compensation for the misuse of my time and for causing me mental anguish."

"What did you have in mind?" I asked.

"Nothing as sordid as money. I love my flat but a little cottage in the country would be nice for when I want to get away or enjoy a quiet weekend. Somewhere in Sussex or Kent, I think, perhaps near the South Downs." She looked at Alec at first but he stared at me and now she did too.

I smiled. "Choose what you want, within reason, and I'll sort it out for you," I said, after a pause.

She smiled. "That's very gracious of you, John. I think I misjudged you at first, thinking you were just another person whose private life had become messy, but actually you are a good man. Alec is lucky to have you as a friend. No rush about the cottage, there's still a war on. When the V2s are finished I'll be in touch with Alec; I won't be greedy, I promise."

She finished her drink and rose to leave. As Alec helped her on with her coat she said, "Don't worry, gentlemen, your secret is safe with me and I shall put on my best acting to deal with the police." Then she was gone. She had never had any interest in me and I got the impression that she no longer wanted much to do with Alec. True to her word, she would later visit the police and recite the story she had prepared without involving us in any way. She would keep her part of the bargain.

"It's very good of you to agree to buy her a cottage, just like that," said Alec.

"Cheap at the price. Don't forget, at one time I was considering paying Templing £5,000. I always thought there would come a day when I would have to put my hand in my pocket. She'll be able to get something to suit for under a thousand."

"Good of you, nonetheless. I couldn't have raised it, at least not without facing some awkward questions."

Perhaps it was the addendum to the thanks, the making of yet another excuse as to why I should have to take responsibility, or just the accumulation of everything and this the last straw, but my equanimity finally snapped.

"Look, Alec, to be frank, I'm just sick to the teeth of everything to do with blackmail, and Jacqueline and you and Maynard, for that matter. I just hope this will save us from any further trouble, if this is in fact the end. Goodnight."

I took my coat and hat and left without looking back at him. I was glad to have got my true feelings off my chest and earnestly hoped I would never hear from Alec again, other than to tie up the loose end of Jacqueline's cottage.

The following summer Jacqueline selected a cottage near Rye and I arranged the payment through Alec. We conducted the details by telephone and letter and, so far as I was concerned, that was the end of it, though in a way, it never could be the end. When there is a supposed murder, the police always keep the file open and there are always energetic, ambitious officers seeking to revisit an unsolved crime, journalists looking for a scoop or another angle to make a name for themselves and ordinary people who have no connection with the case but who like to bring some excitement into their inconsequential lives by becoming the expert of something about which most people don't give a damn. But even if none of these things happen in reality, their possibility lingers in your mind, so they may as well be real.

Perhaps it was the continual flare up of the case from time to time or an obsessive compulsion on my part but whatever it was, some strange sense of foreboding took root in me after the incident with Jacqueline. I couldn't seem to forget about the killing of Templing and all the loose ends left dangling, even though I had no contact with either Alec or Maynard. At first, it was every day, a look through the newspapers, a moment of suspense when the telephone rang, the occasional sense of fear when there was a knock at the door; all giving moments of dread. Later, the uncomfortable moments occurred only once or twice a week but always, when it struck me, the dread was just the same. At night, it was worse. I would wake in a sweat, worrying about my fingerprints on the apartment key, the thought of being recognised in the street by the porter, Jacqueline changing her mind and telling the police everything, Alec confessing, a confederate of Templing having copies of the blackmail letters. Sometimes these thoughts would be transposed in dreams and I would awake certain that we had been discovered. Although I was spared the guilt which would have pulled me down further, I sometimes gave into superstition and the thought I might be punished in some way as a form of retribution, perhaps through the loss of one dear to me. I was relieved when the war ended and my son came home, safe and sound, and the sense of impending disaster waned a little. Whether Alec was beset by a fear of retribution I never knew, but I thought not, as he had saved someone he loved, his idol.

# XXII

# *CHARITY*

I NEVER FELT QUITE THE SAME ABOUT MAYNARD again. It wasn't his fault; he was the potential victim, not the one responsible for what followed after the blackmailer obtained his letter. Nevertheless, whenever I met him, I was reminded of the terrible events Alec and I had been party to on his behalf and I resented the fact he could behave as if it meant nothing, because of course, to him, ignorant of the facts, it did mean nothing.

Through 1945, as well as his work towards the peacetime economic settlement, Maynard worked tirelessly as Chairman of the Arts Council and Lina was often engaged in the charity events leading up to the re-opening of the Royal Opera House. I kept a low profile and avoided getting involved and I think it was for Lina, rather than for me, that we were invited as his guests to the re-opening in February 1946. It was a gala performance of the *Sleeping Princess,* the ballet in which Maynard had first seen Lydia dance. He looked tired and worn out, but through his lacklustre image I could see his excitement and happiness about the evening shining brightly. I found myself warming to him again and congratulated him on his triumph, for which he refused any of the credit, attributing it to the many volunteers who had made it possible.

"It's not just the Arts Council. I was thinking of your tireless work for the new international monetary system and for the economic debt settlement."

He grinned. "If you have read the debate, you will have seen that the House of Lords wasn't too impressed. They think I sold the country down the river, whereas of course we were in a fire sale. I think my usefulness is coming to an end. But let's not worry about that now, just enjoy the show."

It was a marvellous evening and all was going well until Maynard whispered to me that he was feeling unwell. He didn't want to make a fuss and fortunately, as we were in a box, I was able to help him to a quiet room without attracting too much attention, Lydia bustling along behind us. He sat in a chair and I loosened his collar and bow tie. Lydia, who had dealt with this situation several times before, whispered to me that he was having a heart attack and she took charge, knowing what to do until medical help came. A doctor soon arrived and after a while Maynard began to feel much better. He agreed to go to the hospital, just as a precaution, and within a few days he was back to his parlous version of his old self. He promised Lydia he would soon step down from his excessive workload; whether he did so, I do not know. In any event, a couple of months later, while breakfasting in bed, he cried out and his wife and his mother rushed to his side and were with him when this last heart attack took him.

The funeral was not a national event but was attended by family and close friends. Maynard had wanted to be laid to rest in the crypt of his beloved King's College Cambridge but his brother Geoffrey did not apparently know his wishes so he was cremated and his ashes scattered over the South Downs.

Like everybody else, even great people are unable to control events after their death.

There followed a memorial service at Westminster Abbey. I attended it, along with the great and the good and those who always attend such events because they would see him as one of their own and hope perhaps some of his greatness would reflect on them. King's College was well-represented, as was the Treasury and the great financial institutions. Among them I saw Foxy Falk, Maynard's old stockbroker friend and member of the Tuesday Club, who had collaborated with Maynard both as an economist and an investor. Many from the political classes were present too. The Prime Minister, Clement Attlee, whose Labour government had implemented many of Maynard's proposed reforms to government management of the economy, was there, as were other prominent members of both government and opposition. Leading members of the once great Liberal Party, for which Maynard had worked tirelessly but ultimately futilely during the interwar years, turned out in force. It was a great tribute by a grateful nation to a dedicated and outstanding public servant. Yet I believe that those whose attendance Maynard would have been most delighted to see at the service were the depleted ranks of the Bloomsbury Group. As one would expect at such a time, much praise was heaped upon Maynard and his many great achievements, qualities and virtues. This was not a time for an assessment of Maynard in the round, that would be a matter for historians and biographers in the future.

Alec was at the memorial service and I sought him out to thank him for ensuring that I had received an invitation.

He smiled. "It was the least I could do after all you did for him, and Lydia wanted you to come too."

"One can't help but feel that all that we did was eventually for nothing," I said.

"We prevented a scandal and made sure he could complete his work," he answered.

"Possibly, but he was so important that if he'd taken the matter to the authorities, they might have dealt with Templing and covered it all up. That's what powerful people can do, especially for each other."

Alec smiled thinly, "We will never know. I am glad we spared him the possibility of humiliation and ruin."

I shrugged. "Well, in his lifetime anyway. Eventually the biographers and those who feel they have the right to judge will rake over the corpse and dig up all the dirt; they always do."

"We did the right thing by him; what else is a friend for?"

"You're right. I am being churlish. We can't control the future, or the past for that matter. I have heard several people say something to the effect that 'If only he hadn't worked so hard, he might have enjoyed many more years.'"

Alec shook his head. "They misunderstood what made Maynard tick. He loved work and lived for it and, the committed atheist that he was, he believed that anything of worth had to be done now, in the only time he had. And like all of us he knew that devoting our attention to work and other distractions help to keep us away from confronting our own mortality and the void to come."

"What will you do now?"

"Lydia asked me to carry on for a while to help deal with all his papers and so on. After that, I suppose my connections will come in useful. I have no responsibilities to worry about and I'm not interested in making a lot of money so I shall be fine, whatever happens."

"I received an invitation from Lydia to drinks at Gordon Square. Will you be going?"

"No. I have other matters to attend to." He shook my hand and, as he walked off, I wondered if I would ever see him again.

I went on to the reception at 46 Gordon Square, which had been Maynard's London home for the past thirty years. Most of the Bloomsbury Group I knew and who were still alive were there together with their acolytes and outer circle, among them Maynard's brother, Geoffrey, David Garnett and the younger Bells, including Angelica whom I had met at Charleston when she was a young girl. The district of Bloomsbury had been much damaged in the war and I thought its shabby decline matched that of the set that had taken its name. Like me, the older members were well into their sixties or nearer seventy, and collectively their name no longer represented a radical new movement in art, literature, morals, society or anything else. Their emphasis on individual morality, the supremacy of aestheticism in civilisation and the triumph of reason seemed merely deluded by the outbreak of the Second World War. Maynard himself had lamented as much when he wrote, "We completely misunderstood human nature, including our own." But even if events had not called into question the philosophical pronouncements of the Bloomsbury Group, time would have done; new movements in art and thought, like fashions in clothes, belong to the young, not the middle-aged.

Lydia was charming and everybody was full of happy reminiscences of Maynard, who had died at the zenith of his career, while for many of the rest of us, the peak had come much earlier. I was pleased to see that Lydia had invited friends from other areas of Maynard's life, among them Foxy Falk. When he saw me, he came over.

"A day for happy memories, as well as sad thoughts," he said.

"Yes, especially for you. I remember how much you enjoyed working with Maynard."

He smiled. "Yes, we were fairly young and full of ideas for our 'new economics' but it was Maynard that made something of it. I just chipped in from time to time."

"I seem to remember you worked together on some sort of investment model."

He laughed. "We thought we could find a fool-proof system for predicting share movements, the holy grail and all that, but we soon realised there is none. There is no shortcut to expertise and understanding of share price movements."

I smiled. "Maynard certainly had a flair for the market and tremendous self-belief."

"Yes, everyone makes mistakes but Maynard never lost his nerve and always came back stronger. He lost two fortunes but not the third," said Foxy, a smile of reminiscence crossing his face.

"I always thought that he was by nature a gambler. He never flinched at taking a risk."

"You're so right. When he related a successful call in the market, he was every bit as pleased as when he made a breakthrough in economic theory."

Foxy wandered off to talk to an economist friend and I was left with my memories of Maynard. Now that the dreadful business of Templing was fading, the true essence of Maynard, as I knew him, was reasserting itself in my thoughts about him. I had known academic economists, investors, speculators, businessmen and government officials over the years but Maynard was, almost uniquely, all of these. His economic theories were informed by all the realities of the complex economy with its market imperfections and political interference and the irrationalities of the herd instinct and subjective belief masquerading as objective judgement. I suppose he was for me a heroic figure, an economist who was also a participant in the real economy through government fiscal management, playing the markets and operating in the world of business. He had become the world's dominant economist for a generation and I was glad that I had known him and been a friend to him.

I was stirred from my thoughts by the voice of Saxe. "Lewis, lovely to see you."

I smiled to see my old friend who was in the company of Leonard Woolf. I thought both of them looked more morose than I remembered. But then I hadn't seen Leonard since Virginia's death and caring for her during her long periods of fragile mental health must have taken its toll. Not knowing him very well, I avoided mention of the tragedy of Virginia's death but asked about his professional life.

"Oh, I keep busy, you know," he replied, and I didn't press the matter.

Saxe was equally vague about how he spent his time and I felt he had lost the spark of interest in life almost entirely. Perhaps I expected too much. For all I knew they were silently making the same observation about me. I briefly chatted with Duncan Grant and Vanessa Bell and one or two other people whom I knew in passing before I had the opportunity to speak to Lydia. We revisited happy memories of the ballet and the reopening of the Royal Opera House and she was sure that, as much as anything, would be Maynard's lasting testament. She asked after Lina and invited us down to her Sussex home, Tilton farmhouse, which I had never visited. I agreed to go and made my farewells to those I knew before I quietly slipped away.

It was the last time I met members of the Bloomsbury Group in their natural surroundings. Lina and I went down to Tilton a few weeks later. For me it was a kind of pilgrimage in honour of Maynard to the place where he had lived and died and to which he was devoted; he had made that clear by taking the title Baron Keynes of Tilton for his peerage. The white farmhouse was situated on the northern edge of the South Downs and had the most magnificent views over the Sussex countryside, on which Maynard's ashes had been scattered. Lydia pointed out a few items of interest and then she showed us into the house. It had originally been quite small but Maynard had enlarged it to accommodate his library and collection of, mostly French, artworks, notably those by Delacroix, and Cezanne. We laughed as we viewed the pictures, recalling again the story of how Maynard had represented the British government at an important auction of French artists during the Great War. The artillery of the advancing Germans could be heard clearly in the auction room and frightened off several of the bidders. Maynard, whose nerve was rather more resilient, had stayed until the end and obtained a Cezanne as a bargain for himself, as well as those he had bought for the government.

We enjoyed a leisurely lunch and Lydia was a perfect hostess, attentive, witty, charming and a good raconteur. I tentatively broached the subject of her future plans but it was too early for that. She had spent nearly ten years caring for Maynard while his health had declined and it had left her little time to think about herself. It was evident that, without her dedicated nursing, Maynard would not have been able to work as long and as effectively as he had.

On the drive down to Tilton I had told Lina that I intended to raise a sensitive subject with Lydia concerning Maynard's private life as I felt she had the right to know. Lina nodded and asked if I wanted her to disappear while we talked. I shook my head, saying that she would know sooner or later anyway.

Now, as we strolled in the garden after lunch, I turned to Lydia and asked, "May I raise a very personal issue with you concerning Maynard?"

She stopped walking and looked up at me. "As you were his friend, I assume you mean no harm to his memory?"

"No, of course not. It is something that you may become aware of in the future and I should rather you heard it from me than from another source."

She smiled timidly. "Tell me."

"Do you know anything about Maynard's intimate private life before he met you?"

Her smile broadened into a grin and then she laughed. "You mean about his taste for young men?"

"Yes," I said, rather sheepishly.

"Of course, I knew, though probably not everything. Duncan, Arthur Hobhouse, Lytton and his brother and others too numerous to name, all were his lovers. By the time I knew him he was more interested in a younger generation. Do you remember Sebastian Sprott?"

"I remember him," said Lina. "Wasn't he one of the young men who came to Charleston that day we went with Saxe?"

"Yes, I seem to remember he told a story about him and Maynard on holiday in North Africa," I said.

"Well, Sebastian was Maynard's last male lover, at least as far as I know. They were still intimate with each other when Maynard and I fell in love. Maynard was very happy with that arrangement." She half-smiled, her eyebrows raised. "I wasn't."

"I can imagine," said Lina.

"They planned to go on holiday together again at Easter in 1923 and I gave Maynard an ultimatum. That was the end of Mr Sprott as far as Maynard was concerned and I made sure he didn't regret it." She smiled, her eyes moistening a little. "We were very happy together, despite his friends at Charleston."

"How do you mean?" I asked.

"It's not that they tried to come between us but they didn't attempt to hide their feeling of superiority over me, especially the sisters. Vanessa thought I was stupid and as much as said so and Virginia was patronising, 'damning with faint praise', I think the phrase is. I never fitted in. I tried but I just didn't."

"Well, I am sorry, Lydia. I'm sure you found it most upsetting. To feel they are so superior and exclude even the wives of their own set, they must be the most dreadful snobs," said Lina.

"I'm surprised Maynard put up with it," I said.

Lydia gave a look of resignation. "He would never allow anything to come between him and them; he loved them too much. They gave him something I couldn't: intellectual stimulation, artistic appreciation, call it what you like."

I attempted to cheer Lydia up. "I'm sure there was no intention to offend by the Bloomsbury types and Maynard, especially Maynard. People tend to gravitate towards others like themselves and sometimes the sense of camaraderie and collective well-being extends to excluding others by omission rather than by intention. The longer the group persists, the more likely that is to happen. I've seen it happen at school, at university, in the army; it's everywhere. The Bloomsbury Set have been close for thirty years, beginning when many of them were quite young so it's only to be expected that they became a tightly knit group, bound together through their love of the arts and a certain philosophy. Perhaps they don't mean to be rude; they probably get carried away and don't notice that not everyone feels part of it. You were an unintended victim of that sort of behaviour."

"I would like to think you are right, although Clive Bell did once apologise for the off-hand way they had sometimes spoken to me."

There was a long pause, then Lina changed the subject and we continued our walk round the garden. Soon after our visit, Lydia sold the house in Gordon Square and lived permanently at Tilton, where she retired from public life. I thought this a shame as she had experienced some success as a broadcaster during the 1930s. Perhaps things had moved on and she was no longer in demand or perhaps it was her own choice. We kept in touch and I act as one of her financial advisers on an ad hoc basis. Lina and I visit her occasionally, when we are in Sussex.

I also kept up my friendship with Saxe but didn't realise that his life had taken a turn for the worse until some years after the war when he wrote to say that he was moving from Great Ormond Street to a smaller apartment. Another of Saxe's friends told me that he had lost most of his once substantial capital through his gambling habit and was now finding it difficult to make ends meet. I was pleased to contribute to a little fund to keep him afloat but I was saddened to witness Saxe's decline, which none of us seemed able to reverse.

# XXIII

# *FORTITUDE*

My life now resumed the pattern I had anticipated for my retirement. The interests I had pursued in my youth returned to the centre of my life and I now had the time to consider whether I might apply some of my energies to other ventures.

Now a member of the MCC, I spent many summer days in the pavilion at Lord's, meeting old friends and watching sumptuous days of cricket, sometimes from the Long Room or in front of the pavilion and other times from the top tier, or even that little balcony which looks out from the bar at the top of one of the towers. I also umpired for my local cricket club, occasionally even being drafted in to bat when they were one short, and I played a decent game of golf from time to time. I embraced the whole summer sporting season; Ascot, Wimbledon and Henley, which was only a few miles down the river. I frequently entertained those of my friends and family who shared my sporting interests. My family grew with the arrival of grandchildren and I enjoyed playing the role of the active and indulgent grandfather. I continued to manage my own investments, still enjoying the thrill of beating the markets. Lina and I travelled a great deal in Europe, especially in Italy which had always been my first love outside England. As well as reinvigorating old friendships I expanded my circle of friends as Lina and I found time to explore my new freedom from work. I looked forward to an enjoyable old age until such time when slowing down became inevitable and some, as yet unknown, malady equally inevitably sent me to the knackers' yard. But I thought too far ahead too soon.

As the years passed, I would sometimes reflect that the day would surely come when Maynard's past came to light and his reputation was affected to a greater or lesser extent. I comforted myself with the thought that at least Alec and I had avoided that day in his lifetime and if his atheism was correct, it would never concern him. In 1951, an official biography of Keynes by Roy Harrod was published and, true to the style of the time, Harrod omitted any mention of Maynard's personal weaknesses, ignoring completely his sexual life. I read the book with relief that Maynard's secrets were safe.

Then, in the summer of 1952, out of the blue, I learned that Alec had been arrested. I well remember that fateful day. I had been at Lord's watching the end of the second test between England and India. Over lunch I had enjoyed the company of two old Cambridge friends, Neville Plaice and Lyndon Ashley. Neville was much the same as ever, the David Niven moustache now grey and the hair rather sparse but otherwise his energetic, agile self. Lyndon's health, however, had declined over the last few years: not because of just one thing, more a combination of conditions which had sapped his constitution. He rarely came up to London these days, so I was delighted he was able to make the trip from his home in Bedfordshire. We spent a pleasant time, recounting to each other amusing tales of the old days, correcting others' memories as necessary and updating news on mutual acquaintances. Ashley's brother, Bertie, whom I'd not seen since our Cambridge days, was now a Bishop in Kenya and his seriousness had moderated somewhat as his pastoral responsibilities had increased. He had been trying to get Lyndon and his wife to join him out there, in the White Highlands, where the climate would be good for him, but Lyndon was reluctant to abandon his roots.

On my return home, after a very enjoyable day of watching cricket in the company of old friends, I sat in the riverfront garden with a chilled glass of Chablis and read the newspaper, which I had merely glanced at in the morning. I read the odd item, pausing to reflect on the day at Lord's and making a mental note to see more of Lyndon in case his health declined further or he emigrated to Kenya. I was also distracted by events on the river, looking up from time to time to watch the boats negotiate Hurley lock. After waving to a couple of children on a passing motor cruiser, I turned back to the newspaper and an item caught my eye. It was a short report that an arrest had been made regarding the murder of Esmond Templing, which had taken place more than seven years before: Alec was named as the accused. I sat stunned for a few minutes, the seeming impossibility of Alec's arrest after all these years refusing to sink in. I rose from my seat and went into the house. When, finally, I was able come to terms with the situation, I experienced a tremendous surge of sympathy towards Alec. He was about to pay the price for his loyal support and courage in saving Maynard. The fact that I had not been contacted by the police indicated that Alec had not mentioned an accomplice, and certainly not me. I was determined then to help him in any way I could and I told Lina as much immediately.

"Gosh, I didn't notice that," she said. "There must be some other explanation; I can't imagine Alec killing a fly." She read the item I pointed out to her. "Esmond Templing, I remember that name, so unusual. I think you knew him."

"Vaguely. I am sure Alec's innocent," I replied. "I will give him whatever assistance I can."

"You must," she said, touching my arm.

In that moment of empathy, I knew now was the time to tell Lina at least something of what had happened when Alec became embroiled with Templing, even if not the whole truth, for all our sakes.

"There is something I have to tell you," I said, guiding her to an armchair in the morning room. "You remember that business towards the end of the war when Alec and I were involved in helping Maynard with a project and I told you I had promised not to tell anyone, even you, about it?"

She smiled. "And I thought you were having an affair."

"This man Templing was a blackmailer and he was attempting to blackmail Maynard over his past sexual life."

"My God, and Alec became involved?"

"Alec intercepted the blackmail demands because he thought, quite rightly, that it would be too much for Maynard's health, which was declining rapidly. Alec had this mad idea of tracking the blackmailer down, breaking into his apartment, and stealing the incriminating documents. I tried to talk him out of it but he was determined. Unfortunately, Templing returned to his apartment while Alec was still there and there was a fight and Templing was killed, accidentally."

"Were you involved in some way?"

"I helped to find out who the blackmailer was and helped Alec afterwards but I did not take part in the break-in nor was I there when Templing was killed."

Lina's face was white. "Thank God. But, how did you let yourself be caught up in this?"

I shrugged. "Alec was trying to save Maynard and he asked

for my help. I didn't want to help at first but eventually I felt I couldn't refuse. Saxe helped too. We found a cryptic note and Saxe was able to make sense of it, eventually leading to us finding the blackmailer."

"So, you have lived with this for seven years, you poor thing." She squeezed my hand and I was grateful she wasn't choosing this moment to chastise me, even if it might come later after she'd had time to think it over.

"How did the police catch Alec after all this time?" she asked, as the colour began to return to her face and she patted her forehead with a handkerchief.

"I don't know."

"Did he murder Templing?"

"No. Templing stabbed him and he acted purely in self-defence. Don't worry, when Templing is shown to have been an evil man rather than the paragon of virtue he posed as, Alec will get off."

"I hope so. But will you be dragged into the trial?"

"I doubt it, I shouldn't be too concerned." I wasn't as confident as I sounded.

I had not seen Alec since the day of Maynard's memorial service and had largely forgotten about him, only recalling him in the context of Templing's murder, which inevitably cast a shadow in my life from time to time. As the story unfolded through the newspapers, it appeared that Alec had been arrested initially in connection with a matter of gross indecency and it was subsequent police investigations that found a connection between Alec and the killing of Templing. I was surprised by the news but not totally so. In the early 1950s, under the direction of the then Home Secretary, the police adopted a more active crackdown on homosexuality. Charges were more commonly made and undercover policemen engaged in the entrapment of homosexuals in known meeting places. I have no idea why there was this change in attitudes. But whereas after the Great War, there was a loosening of the moral strictures of society, after the Second World War there developed a mood to find a more ordered social environment again. This change in attitude manifested itself in people being put, and expected to remain, more firmly in their place. Perhaps in one last effort to maintain the rigidity of the class system, the public were required to exhibit an oppressive conformity of behaviour and manners. Whatever the reason, the campaign against homosexuality smacked of prejudice disguised as a moral crusade.

I visited Alec the following week in Brixton prison, where he was being held. His tie had been taken away but, as he was on remand, he was still dressed in his own clothes. It had been six years since I had last seen him and he was little changed except for signs of being tired and under strain. He smiled and said how happy he was to see me. "Thank you so much for coming, Lewis. I have a good solicitor but you are the only person who understands my plight," he said softly.

After asking how he was, my next question was, inevitably, "What happened?"

He lit a cigarette and recounted to me the events at the police station following his arrest.

Initially, Alec was charged with procuring another (an undercover policeman as it happened) to commit a homosexual act, a charge which Alec vigorously denied. His fingerprints were taken and he was asked if he had ever been charged with an offence or had his fingerprints taken before, to which he answered that he had not. He did not ask for his solicitor at this time as he was sure that this was a trumped-up charge and would soon be dropped, at worst with a caution. After all, he was a man with an impeccable personal and professional record. By this time Alec was a lecturer in economics at a redbrick university, where he was feted for his close association with the great man, John Maynard Keynes. He had recounted their relationship in a written memoir, which obviously omitted the episode of Templing's attempt to blackmail Maynard.

After his arrest, Alec went through the events of the evening several times to a jovial-looking, uniformed police sergeant, explaining and reiterating that he had not gone to the lavatory to pick up anyone, as that was not his way, but that the undercover policeman had engaged him in conversation, making some suggestions to which he had not responded but to which another person present had.

"So, this is a case of mistaken identity, are you saying, Mr Harborough?" asked the interrogating officer who, by the frequency with which he looked at the clock, was nearing the end of his shift.

"Or a misunderstanding, at the very least," replied Alec.

"Well, I'm not inclined to take this matter further," said the police sergeant, sitting back in his chair and glancing once more at the clock.

At that point there was a knock on the door and another policeman came in and whispered to his colleague. The sergeant nodded then turned to Alec. "I hope we shan't keep you waiting too much longer but my senior officer would like a word. It could be some while as he has to get over from another office. Would you like a cup of tea?"

Alec nodded, unconcerned. The sergeant left a constable on duty and disappeared. There was a delay before the tea arrived and another delay until the senior officer arrived. At first Alec was merely bored and tired of looking round the green and cream painted office with a desk similar to many he had seen at the Treasury. But then he experienced just a scintilla of concern that there was such a long hold-up after the sergeant had announced there would be no further action. Eventually, a plain clothes policeman entered the interrogation room, carrying a file and a couple of sheets of paper. He was a tall man of about forty, dressed in a well-cut dark-blue double-breasted suit and carrying a trilby hat. Alec's first reaction was that this was a man who was fastidious about his appearance. He had no time to make a further judgement.

"Good evening, Mr Harborough. I am Detective Chief Inspector Matthews." His expression was not unfriendly but he was not smiling. He pulled up a chair and sat next to his colleague. Then he took a sheet of paper from the file and held it up for Alec to see. "Have you seen this letter before, Mr Harborough?

Alec could feel the colour drain from his face as he stared at the piece of paper. He recognised it immediately as his letter of confession to the accidental killing of Templing. Shocked, he was rendered speechless.

Without waiting for an answer, the chief inspector continued. "The fingerprints you very kindly appended to the letter match the fingerprints taken at the station this evening so I don't think you can deny it, do you?"

Alec shook his head.

"They also match some of the fingerprints taken at Mr Templing's flat, including those on the small statue of a lion. What do you have to say to that?"

"Nothing, at the present time."

"Please stand and take off your jacket and roll up your shirt sleeves, as close as possible to your shoulders."

Alec did as he was told and the prominent, rather ugly, scar on his left arm was revealed.

The chief inspector's demeanour immediately became more formal and he charged Alec with the murder of Esmond Templing. After being cautioned, he was taken into custody and placed on remand at Brixton prison.

"There you have it, Lewis," Alec said, after he had told the whole story of his arrest. "I'm afraid I put the noose round my own neck," he added stoically.

Inwardly, I cursed the fact that he'd insisted on putting his fingerprints on the letter but now was not the time to reproach him on the matter. "Have you appointed legal representation yet?" I asked.

"My family solicitors will investigate the possibilities regarding a barrister."

"Tell them to get the best."

"I'm not sure."

"I'll pay," I said and gave him the names of a couple of QCs whom I knew. "Of course, there will be others. Just choose whom you want and I will deal with the financial side."

"I can't expect you to pay for my defence."

"Nonsense. I have the easy part," I smiled and added, quietly to avoid being overheard by the nearest prison officer, "after all, I am an accessory before and after."

"That's very good of you. Don't worry, I promise I will not mention you to the police or in the trial. There is something else I would like you to do for me."

"Anything."

"Do you remember the mauve book?"

I did indeed remember the book; the one containing the names and payments of Templing's victims. I nodded.

"I keep it in safe custody with my bank. I want you to retrieve it for me and hang onto it in case I need it for my defence."

"Perhaps I should give it to your defence counsel?"

"No. I don't want the names of any of those listed to come out into the open unless I have no choice. It could ruin them still."

"But your solicitor would protect them, surely."

"You know what it's like: once it's in the public domain, anything could happen. I have left the key with my solicitor and he will give you my letter of authority to enable you to have access to my safe deposit box."

"If that's what you want, of course."

A couple of days later I visited Alec's solicitor in Weybridge, at the peculiarly named Messrs. Finney, Tolley and Memory. The offices were extremely old-fashioned, the outer one almost Dickensian, and I was escorted by an elderly clerk with half-moon glasses into the office of Mr ARH Tolley. This gentleman was slightly younger than his clerk and I guessed his age as older than mine, though not by much. He was wearing a sombre suit and a wing-collar, a collar I had worn once but not since the outbreak of war. His dress, like his demeanour, added to a sense of gravitas and reliability about his person. I was suitably reassured.

"Mr Durrington, how do you do? Please take a seat," he said in a business-like manner, pointing me to a leather chair which had seen better days and had acquired a not uncomfortable dent in the seat, presumably the result of the gravitational impact of many hundreds of clients.

I shook his hand and sat down, taking in my surroundings. The office was similar to the outer, but more elegantly furnished with a grand mahogany partners' desk and Georgian bookcases. A couple of faded armchairs stood against one wall, a wooden filing cabinet against another and occasional tables, chairs and standard lamps gave a pleasant background to the whole. On the walls hung certificates of professional achievement and recognition in black frames under glass. The overriding image was of a firm of solicitors who knew their business, had operated successfully for many years, and did not overcharge their clients to such an extent that they could lavish their income on ostentatious furnishings or decoration. I glanced at the rows of neatly stacked volumes of books on all aspects of the law, property, taxation, company and so forth, and spotted several with the publisher, Tolley, and the subject 'tax law', on the spine.

"Any relation, Mr Tolley?" I asked, pointing to the relevant volumes.

He smiled. "A distant and more successful cousin."

"I believe you have a safe custody key and a letter of authority for me," I asked, getting straight to the point.

"Indeed, I have." He passed me an envelope which lay on his desk and, having satisfied myself it contained the two, I put the envelope in my inside pocket.

"I advised Mr Harborough to engage the best so far as counsel is concerned," I said.

"Yes, that is very generous of you. I have a few in mind, based on experience of the type of case, sympathy with the client's plight, that sort of thing. I'm sure we shall have no difficulty in selecting the right person."

"Perhaps you'll let me know in due course."

"Naturally."

"This is a bad business," I said.

"An extremely unfortunate series of events. Mr Harborough confessed to a crime to help another, but was then arrested for a crime he didn't commit, which led to his exposure for a crime long forgotten."

"If only the police were not so zealous in their prosecution of the laws against homosexuality these days. Why is that do you think?"

"The winds change in the matter of crime, just as much as in anything else. The force behind the wind may be the powers that be, the government, the law, the church and so on, or it may be public opinion, though it is when both move in the same direction that the wind shifts 180 degrees."

He sat back in his chair and interlaced his fingers, settling them on his midriff and I realised this was a subject to which he had given much thought.

"Let us take a simple example from history. In 1530, everyone, apart from a few heretics, considered themselves a Catholic and would not doubt it when prayers were offered for the Pope at mass. Thirty years later to be a Catholic in England was to be a criminal, liable to loss of civil rights for certain and quite possibly to execution. Many of the people at public executions were calling for people to be burned or hanged or drawn and quartered simply for believing what they themselves had believed when they were young. The law had changed and most people changed with it, without barely a hesitation. Few people challenge the existing law when it is in force or wish to bring it back once it has gone. It was after the Reformation that the laws against homosexuality were codified and from 1560 the punishment was execution. Now, this position was so absurd that cases were rarely brought as none in the law would wish to punish the crime so severely. The consequence was that it was a law which was not enforced and most people were content with that."

"When did things change?" I asked, taking an offered cigarette.

Tolley lit our cigarettes and continued. "In 1861 there was a desire by the Victorians to modernise the law on sexual matters, principally to protect young women and girls, particularly serving girls from their employers demanding their *droit de seigneur*. The age of consent was raised from twelve to thirteen and, as an afterthought, buggery was retained as a crime with a prison sentence. This was rarely enforced as there had to be an eyewitness to the buggery and no other intimate behaviour between men was considered by the act, so the legislation was treated with a light touch. Unfortunately, the desire to clamp down on male brothels led to the 1885 act which made any sexual relations or intimacy between men, even in private, a criminal offence. This was the law which led to Oscar Wilde's downfall: 'posing as a sodomite' as the Marquess of Queensberry carefully worded his accusation."

"But why the increase in prosecutions now?"

Tolley shrugged. "Since the war we may be going through one of our periods when people like a crackdown on crimes they don't participate in themselves. As Macaulay put it, 'We know no spectacle so ridiculous as the British public in one of its periodical fits of morality.'"

"But surely the law won't be enforced just because the people desire it. There must be active encouragement on the part of those who matter in government to enforce the law."

"Of course. There is a whiff of puritanism around at the moment, in elements of the government, the church, the media and so on."

I shook my head. "But why the pursuit of a crime which usually has little or no impact on anybody else?"

"Ah, the Puritan mind. I must quote Lord Macaulay again, a man whose wisdom I greatly admire and respect. He said, 'The Puritan hated bear-baiting, not because it gave pain to the bear, but because it gave pleasure to the spectators.' I think the analogy is apposite."

"With attitudes as they are, there could not be a worse time for Alec to face a prosecution," I said, pessimistically.

"It is a difficult case because of the confession; his homosexuality is a red herring but of course some jurors may take an antagonistic attitude from the beginning. A good barrister will soon deal with that, and thanks to you he will have a good barrister."

The next day I went to the bank, obtained the mauve book and took it home. It brought back too many ghastly memories for me to dwell on the contents for long and, after a brief look through the book, I locked it away in the small safe in my study. I also wrote to Tolley, offering to appear as a character witness for Alec. Although I had told Lina I wouldn't get involved in the trial, I thought it was the least I could do as Alec had promised to leave me out of it.

# XXIV

# *UNDERSTANDING*

I went to see Alec a few more times while he was on remand and, with regular visits from family and friends, I thought he seemed in good spirits, though this may have been an act for those who cared about him. After several weeks had passed, Alec appeared in the dock at the Old Bailey, where he pleaded 'Not Guilty' to the charge of murder. He was represented by Sir Grafton Stanyer QC, one of the most prominent criminal barristers in England and one of those I had suggested. The prosecution was led by another distinguished silk, Sir William Trenton QC. The judge was Mr Justice Witherendon, whom I neither knew nor knew of, though I thought the name was familiar.

I attended the court every day to lend my moral support if nothing else. Alec's parents were also regular attenders and I got to know them both quite well. They were in their late sixties. The father was a retired, slightly blustering, colonial civil servant who was clearly torn between shame over his son's reckless behaviour and subsequent appearance in court and admiration for Alec's bravery in not kowtowing to blackmail. The mother was a calm, restrained woman who told me she was determined to hold herself together so that her son need only worry about himself. Neither expressed any comment on their son's private life. Lina, relieved when I was not approached by the police as either a witness or a co-defendant, took a keen interest in the trial but chose not to attend it.

I had been in a courtroom twice before, once on jury service and the other time as a witness in a dispute over a debt owed to my firm, neither case at the Old Bailey. For the first time I had the opportunity to follow the proceedings closely and once the novelty had worn off, I saw the courtroom for what it was: a theatre. The presiding judge, high above the rest of the action, in his bright costume a sharp contrast to the black panelling surrounding him and seeming not an ordinary human being but a species all of his own. His was the role of a sage observer as in a Greek tragedy. Similarly, the barristers and the clerk wore costume and wigs like those of the late eighteenth century. However, there was no attempt to make the wig cover their real hair entirely, so it confirmed the sense of a charade rather than the dress of an earlier period. The language of the drama was formal, often euphemistic in choice of dialogue and replete with antiquated courtesies and compliments between the principal characters, judge, counsels and clerk. The judge, despite presiding, sat to the right of the central chair on the bench which was always left empty should the Lord Mayor of London wish to attend the trial. The atmosphere was intense but fortunately July that year was not particularly hot and was consequently quite cool on the days the trial took place.

The most important players in the final act of the drama would be the jurors, a mainly silent chorus, who could ask questions but rarely did. Observing while the others played their parts, they would give the one- or two-word answer which decided the fate of the man or woman in the dock. As the judge instructed them as to their duties at the beginning of the trial, I looked at the jury of ten men and two women. From their faces, staring impassively at the judge, I could detect nothing of their feelings about the case nor their prejudices. But I knew Alec started at a disadvantage. Templing was seen, not only as the victim of a brutal killing, but also as an upright citizen and philanthropist. Nothing had yet come to light in the newspapers about his blackmailing activities and he was therefore regarded as unquestionably a good person. Alec, on the other hand, once the trial opened, would be depicted as somebody of questionable morality: how else would he be liable to blackmail? I wondered how many of these jurors were inclined against homosexuality, either seeing it as an immoral act or because it was a crime. It was impossible to know their individual opinions and how these would affect their judgement. Nor could I make an assessment of the judge, his robes, half-rim glasses and wig having the desired effect of rendering him inscrutable and enigmatic.

Sir Grafton Stanyer was a member of my club and when I saw him from time to time in the library or at the dining table, he was an amusing and affable man, neither pretentious nor condescending. Yet at court, in wig and gown, he metamorphosed into the epitome of the great advocate and a man whose evident integrity and depth of knowledge gave him command of the court. His stature appeared to grow to reflect his importance, his baritone voice deepened and resonated, his facial expressions and gestures took on thespian proportions, his hands, when not clasping his gown in statesman-like mode, used to emphasise the wisdom of his observations and the gravity of his questioning. With his eloquence and grandeur matched by his energy and strength, he seemed both older and younger at the same time. Here was a man who would demolish the lies and establish the truth of the case.

The counsel for the prosecution, Sir William Trenton, had a very different persona. His demeanour was less serious, even rakish. His stance was casual, one hand often in his pocket and his default expression was that of a smile: of encouragement for a prosecution witness, of scepticism for a defence witness, of amused incredulity when listening to his opposing counsel and of patient deference when spoken to by the judge. He was the man who had seen it all before, a man of the people who would guide the jury through the vagaries of the legal system to come to the right decision.

In his opening statement, Sir William explained, in his matter-of-fact way, that there could be no doubt as to the actual events of the fateful day. A killing had taken place and it was for the court to determine whether it was murder as charged. His opening remarks were routine but what he said next filled me with a sense that for Alec, all was lost.

"The case for the prosecution is straightforward and indisputable. The defendant killed the deceased in his own home, after being disturbed during a break-in to obtain some documents, itself a felony. Killing a person during the commission of a felony is, according to the law, murder." He paused and his expression lost his slight smile as he stared at the jury. "There can be no exception to this rule."

The case for the prosecution was based largely on the statement of Alec himself in his letter to the police. It was supplemented by the evidence of forensic experts and police witnesses. They confirmed that Templing had died as the result of a heavy blow with a stone object to the left temple. Death was caused by damaged arteries bleeding into the head. In Templing's flat, letters had been found which pointed to the licentious behaviour of at least one person but neither that person nor anyone else had admitted they had been blackmailed by the dead man, except for the defendant.

However, he claimed to have destroyed all the evidence of his own misdemeanours and apparently some incriminating documents related to other supposed victims of the deceased. In the circumstances, the only confirmed evidence is that the defendant had broken into Templing's flat either to steal material concerning himself or for other nefarious reasons unknown. It was a straightforward open and shut case.

Having heard the case set forth by Sir William Trenton, I doubted Sir Grafton Stanyer could mount much of a convincing defence. But then I am not a barrister.

In his opening address, he disparaged the 'parody' of the characters of the two people involved and announced his intention to show that the maligned defendant was in fact the innocent and peaceful victim of the mountebank and blackmailer, Templing.

The defence case concentrated on the characters of Alec and Templing and, in his introductory statement, Sir Grafton described Templing as an evil man. He explained that Templing was a sophisticated blackmailer who had used his connections to build up a portfolio of the weaknesses and failings of others, criminal or not, which he would use for extortion. He had used the profits of his blackmail to finance his image as an altruist and philanthropist who used his wealth in the generous support of many charities. Stanyer called a forensic witness who confirmed that Alec's scar on his arm was likely to have been caused by a knife several years before. He agreed that the effect of the blow to Templing's head would have been unpredictable, in that death had by no means been inevitable or even likely had the injury been elsewhere on the head or merely a glancing blow.

A principal witness for the defence was Danvers Troughton, the man previously charged with Templing's murder. He said that he had been blackmailed by Templing and had more than once made payments to him. He knew of at least one, possibly two, other people who had been blackmailed by Templing, as Templing had hinted as much to him and he fully believed that Alec was correct in stating that Templing had blackmailed many people. When asked how he thought Templing was able to build up such a great deal of material about his clients, Troughton said he believed that Templing had links with a variety of sources such as private detectives, people with information to sell and probably police officers. Stanyer also called witnesses from two charities who were major beneficiaries of Templing's largesse. Both always received the donations from him in cash and had no idea as to the source of his wealth. A witness from Templing's bank confirmed that his account, though often with a very healthy balance, gave no indication as to the source of his income, though Templing had hinted that he had overseas interests, particularly in South America.

Sir Grafton called Alec to the witness box and began with Alec's letter of confession to the police. "Mr Harborough, you are on trial purely because you wrote a letter to the Metropolitan Police admitting your involvement in the death of Mr Templing. Why did you write this letter, putting yourself in a position of risk?"

"Because I could not let an innocent man be tried for murder."

Sir Grafton nodded admiringly. "An act of considerable compassion and integrity. Why did you break into Mr Templing's flat?"

"I was being blackmailed because I am a homosexual."

"Being a homosexual is not, of itself, a crime."

"He claimed to have letters relating to my private life which could jeopardise my career if they became public knowledge."

"So you were not overly concerned by the risk of prosecution, more that your career might be compromised?"

"Yes."

"What did you hope to achieve by your break-in at Mr Templing's flat?"

"To recover the letters."

"That was all? There was no intention to rob Mr Templing of anything else, nor to harm him in any way?"

"Absolutely not."

"How did you break in to Mr Templing's apartment?"

"I had been in the apartment before when Mr Templing first told me of his intention to seek 'financial assistance', as he referred to it. I noticed that he had a spare key to the flat on the mantelpiece and I stole it while Templing went to get us both a drink. On the day of the break-in, I waited for Templing to go out and then let myself in to the apartment."

"Did you have any accomplices or any other assistance from anyone else?"

"None."

"What happened when you entered Mr Templing's apartment?"

"I broke into the desk and found many letters and other incriminating evidence about several people, including myself. I gathered them all together and was about to make my escape when Mr Templing returned. I didn't hear him come in and he burst into the room with a knife in his hand."

"What were your thoughts when you saw Mr Templing coming towards you?"

"That he intended to kill me. He stabbed me in the arm and I grabbed his wrist with my left hand but I was sure he would stab me again if he could get free and my arm was getting weaker."

"So, you were in fear for your life. What did you do then?"

"I reached behind me to a table which had something hard on it and I picked it up and hit him on the head. He dropped the knife and fell to the floor. I realised then I had hit him with a stone lion and assumed he was knocked out. I finished putting the documents in a case and made good my escape through the hall window and down the fire escape."

"You didn't check to see if Mr Templing was all right?"

"I was afraid he might come round and I was scared. Also, my arm was bleeding a lot and I thought I might faint before I got out of the apartment."

"What was your intention when you hit Mr Templing?"

"To save my life."

"You did not intend to kill him?"

"Not at all. I would rather he hadn't come into the room. I intended him no harm."

"Thank you, Mr Harborough." Sir Grafton nodded and sat down.

For a few moments I was reassured by Alec's evidence and I hoped the jury would be as impressed as I was by his clarity and sincerity. Of course, much of what Alec had said was untrue but only in regard to the detail, in order to protect others, notably Jacqueline and myself and the memory of Maynard. Then Sir William began his cross-examination.

"Mr Harborough, you have given an account of your activities which led to the death of Mr Templing and we have to take your word for what is a description of events that is uncorroborated by another. Let that pass for a moment. What you haven't told the court is why you chose to embark on an expedition which involved taking the law into your own hands and led to the death of another human being without choosing to go to the police, since blackmail is a serious crime carrying severe penalties for those convicted."

"If a person blackmails you on the basis of your own alleged crime, it is difficult to go to the police as you face the possibility of your private life being investigated, a prospect I found uncomfortable."

"So, you are a criminal?"

"I don't believe I am but the wording of the law allows an interpretation which makes any homosexual liable to be accused of an illegal act."

"I am obliged to the defendant for his explanation of the law," said Sir William sardonically. "But come come, Mr Harborough: you are a criminal because you gained false entry to effect your burglary. You stated that you had no accomplices in your break-in but is that true? The Mr Flanders who appeared in the apartment block and delayed Mr Templing's return to his apartment and was then seen later in the vicinity of the building has failed to come forward as a witness and proved to be untraceable. Was he your accomplice?"

"No. Nobody else was involved."

"I put it to you that the reason you are in the dock is because you have placed yourself outside and above the law. You have pre-empted the role of the police and the law courts to bring a criminal to justice, you have destroyed evidence that might have enabled a conviction and proved that element of your story alluding to Mr Templing's blackmailing activities, if indeed these documents actually existed, and you acted as judge, jury and executioner in dealing with Mr Templing."

"Objection, M'Lud," intervened Sir Grafton, "pure conjecture."

"Sustained," said the judge.

"As Your Lordship pleases," said Sir William. "Mr Harborough, you have stated that the death of Mr Templing was accidental; that you were merely trying to protect yourself from the knife which he was wielding. But isn't it the case that when you picked up the stone lion you were perfectly aware that such a heavy implement struck on the head could kill a person and in your anger and resentment towards Mr

Templing you struck him harder than was necessary to save yourself?"

"I didn't have time to think. I was afraid and instinct took over. I didn't mean to kill him."

"No further questions."

As the trial neared its end, the prosecution and the defence gave their final summaries. The prosecution's summary was to the point. Whatever the initial cause of Alec's actions, the simple truth remained: he had broken into the home of Templing to commit a theft of papers, thereby committing a felony. In an attempt to escape the homeowner's legitimate action to apprehend him, he had, intentionally or unintentionally, killed Templing. Under the common law rule of felony murder, as defined by later interpretations, when an offender kills, regardless of whether or not there was an intent to kill, during the commission of a felony, that person is guilty of murder. This long-established principle holds because, when a person embarks on a felony, there will always be the risk that quarrels, resistance and violence may occur and such violence and its consequences are entirely due to the commission of the felony by the perpetrator.

There it was, in black and white, with no extenuating circumstance, no mitigation, no right to plead self-defence. The perpetrator of a crime which involves the death of the victim of the crime is a murderer.

Sir Grafton Stanyer did his best to persuade the jury to see Alec, not Templing, as the victim and to override the cruel certainty of the felony murder rule with recognition that Alec was only in this position because he had nobly confessed to the crime to save another. It was a tour de force of a plea for mercy comparable to that of Portia in *The Merchant of Venice* and I prayed it would win the hearts and minds of the jury, as it had mine. But there was still the judge to come and his reminder of the need to concentrate purely on the evidence could make all Stanyer's brilliant oratory count for nothing.

At the end of the closing statements, the judge adjourned the trial for the day, leaving his own summing up for the morning. While I watched the judge speak, I found myself again trying to remember where I had seen his name before; such an uncommon name, yet I couldn't place it. I realised that, at sixty-eight, my memory wasn't as sharp as it used to be but it was still bothering me when I returned home at the end of the day.

"How did it go?" asked Lina, who had each day grown more concerned as I reported how tenuous Alec's situation was, especially in view of the felony murder law.

I shook my head. "I'm not very hopeful. Nothing has changed. I keep wondering where I have seen the judge's name before. I am sure I have come across it."

"How will that help?"

"I don't know."

I went to my copy of Who's Who and there was one person with the name 'Witherendon' and it was Mr Justice Witherendon. He had been at Winchester and Oxford so I didn't know him from my youth. There was nothing in his brief biography to suggest our paths had crossed. I checked my address book and list of telephone numbers to no avail. I was about to give up when I thought of Templing's mauve book, still in my safe, which I had flicked through not so long ago. I opened the safe, took out the book and turned the pages until I saw the name: 'A C Witherendon'. A quick double check of Who's Who showed the entry as 'Witherendon, Arthur Carstairs'. According to the ledger, he had paid Templing three payments of £200, at six monthly intervals, the last six weeks before Templing died.

I thought back over the trial and how the judge had

not once shown a flicker of variation to his calm, constant demeanour in his conduct of the case. Perhaps this signified total detachment, as it should, but a small part of me clung to a hope that he might use his unique position to aid Alec in some way through a lesser sentence, if that were possible. I didn't tell anyone, not even his parents. I had resigned myself to the conviction of Alec and didn't want to give them false hope. I did consider getting a note to Alec to inform him of my discovery but dared not raise his expectations either.

The next morning, I arrived early and chatted with Alec's waiting parents, reassuring them as well as I could, given my own doubts. As I sat in the courtroom I looked in vain for any sign of optimism from Sir Grafton Stanyer as he sat still in his chair, his hands folded on his brief. Alec was brought up and the judge took his seat, bowing to the standing throng.

The judge glanced down at his notes then removed his spectacles and looked paternally at the jury.

"Ladies and gentlemen of the jury, you are required to fulfil a solemn duty which involves determining the guilt or innocence of a man who is charged with the most serious of crimes and one for which the penalty is death. We know that the defendant has confessed in writing to killing Mr Templing and has further admitted the fact in his own evidence before the court. Now, you may feel, having heard all the evidence, that Mr Templing was, while the victim, a criminal in his own right, a blackmailer of the defendant, Mr Danvers Troughton and probably others. You may consider his behaviour despicable and his character reprehensible and that he is as much to blame for the events of that fateful day as the defendant. However, you are not here to judge the moral integrity of Mr Templing. He may well have been a criminal and a hypocrite but in this case he was not acting criminally when his home was invaded and so he is not on trial. Nor are you to take into account the character of the defendant, who might well be considered by some a noble figure. Here was a man who had escaped detection for his crime for seven years and doubtless would have remained undetected had it not been for his act of generosity, purely to prevent the conviction of an innocent man, Mr Danvers Troughton. By his sending that detailed confession, including his own fingerprints, to the Commissioner of the Metropolitan Police, the defendant placed his future and his fate in the hands of others and that has led directly to his being on trial, but that is irrelevant to this case. Nor are you required to discern the defendant's reason for killing Mr Templing, whether it be intentional murder or intent to injure or merely self-defence since the reason does not alter the case.

"You are to consider only the evidence and nothing but the evidence. If the defendant was instrumental in the death of Mr Templing while committing a felony he is, according to the law, guilty of murder and the sentence to be imposed, terrible though it may be, is not your concern. In the absence of any reasonable doubt, it is your duty to find the defendant guilty. Please now consider your verdict, taking as much time as you need. Yours is a solemn duty."

I looked again at the jury as the usher led them to their room. They all appeared thoughtful and I guessed they were already considering the heavy burden placed upon them. It was nearly two hours before they returned.

The foreman was asked to rise. As he did so he gave a note to the usher for the attention of the judge. The judge looked at the note and lay it to one side.

"Ladies and gentlemen of the jury, are you agreed upon your verdict?" asked the clerk.

"We are."

"How do you find the defendant: guilty or not guilty?"

"Not guilty of murder but guilty of manslaughter."

"And that is the verdict of you all?"

"It is."

I breathed a deep sigh of relief and sensed it was echoed throughout the court.

After the jury had been thanked, Alec was asked to rise and in response to the question, "Have you anything to say why sentence should not be passed upon you?" he said simply, "No."

The judge looked at him impassively. Under my breath I thanked God that Alec had been spared the dread moment when the black cap was placed on the judge's head. There would be no sentence of death.

"Alexander Harborough, the jury has taken the decision to find you not guilty of murder but guilty of the lesser crime of manslaughter. This verdict, proscribing leniency by the jury, is one which I am obliged to respect. In sentencing you I will be mindful of your past good conduct and exemplary character. I sentence you to prison for two years, to run from your first being placed on remand."

Alec nodded and thanked the judge. As he turned to go down, he looked over and smiled at me and as I returned the smile, I thought that greatness in a man comes in many forms.

The judge bowed to the court and took his leave, a slight smile playing at the corners of his mouth. The members of the jury went their separate ways, quietly wishing well to each other, all signs of tension gone. The defence and prosecution counsels shook hands, smiling and exchanging humorous comments, neither appearing unhappy with the result. I sat back in my seat for a few moments, in no hurry to leave the arena where the law had been applied but something closer to justice had prevailed. This feeling was reinforced little more than a year later when Alec was released from prison and was able to return to university life. We remain friends, joined by our loyalty to Maynard and bound together by our quest to maintain his reputation until the time might come when he will be judged by his public deeds, not his private life.

# *ACKNOWLEDGEMENTS*

There have been many fine biographies of John Maynard Keynes but I am particularly indebted to *The Return of the Master* by Robert Skidelsky (Lord Skidelsky) and *Universal Man: The Seven Lives of John Maynard Keynes* by Richard Davenport-Hines for their incisive depictions of his character and personality.

I am also grateful to my wife, Carolyn, for her helpful comments during the writing of this book.